Brizzolara, John

Wire cutter.

WIRECUTTER

John

WIRE

DOUBLEDAY & COMPANY, INC.

Brizzolara

CUTTER

GARDEN CITY, NEW YORK   1987

Library of Congress Cataloging-in-Publication Data
Brizzolara, John.
Wirecutter.
I. Title.
PS3552.R535W57   1987   813'.54   86-19757

ISBN 0-385-23437-6

To *Diane* for all the years
and all the faith
And for *Geoffrey* . . . for always

Acknowledgments

I would like to thank . . .

Deputy Chief Gene Smithberg of the U.S. Border Patrol Brown's Field Sector, who was extremely helpful, courteous and nothing like his fictional counterpart depicted in these pages.

John Bellardo, the public information officer in San Pedro.

Agent Steve Garcia, who drove me up and down the border one night I'll never forget.

Danny "Tokes" Lopez, who showed me how it was done from the other side of the wire.

Jeff "The Boss" Mariotte at Hunter's Books in La Jolla.

Sharon Jarvis and Shaye Areheart for taking a chance.

WIRECUTTER

1

IT WAS ALWAYS night in the Hillcrest Club, one of those Southern California cocktail lounges with the red vinyl booths, artificial plants, Formica bar and no windows. Anyone coming in off the street, no matter what time of day or night, had to stand in the doorway blinking either fierce sunlight or blinding neon out of his eyes for a good thirty seconds before they adjusted to the greasy lighting inside. If you didn't like who you saw coming in, you had enough time to duck out the exit by the rest rooms before he could spot you. The door led to the parking lot by the entrance ramp to Route 163. It locked automatically from the inside so that you couldn't come in that way—you had to walk around the side of the building along a narrow concrete path. This arrangement made it a long shot that your car would be recognized by a wife, secretary or neighbor if you needed a few fast shots before 8 A.M. It also made the place perfect to soak in when you didn't want to run into creditors without notice.

It was late afternoon and I didn't think I was avoiding anyone in particular. I owed the phone company eighty dollars and my landlady twice that, but I wasn't worried about them sending anyone around to collect. I was working on forgetting the dead man I had left behind me that morning and the mess I had made over the weekend while trying to trace one Herman Villez in Tijuana. I wasn't expecting any more excitement when the front door of the Hillcrest Club swung open and two figures were silhouetted against the feral brightness of University Avenue.

One of them must have weighed in at 250 or so and was tall enough to have to duck the door frame. They both wore nice suits. People with nice suits don't often drink at the Hillcrest. They had followed me from T.J., but I didn't know that. That's probably because I'm not really as bright as I like to think I am. All that business with the cops had distracted me on the ride back up.

I kept drinking my beer and resumed my conversation with Bananas—a sixty-seven-year-old, shell-shocked Anzio vet and a pleasant drunk—a great guy to talk to when you didn't have anything in particular to say and felt like saying it.

"Why is it," I asked him, "that every joint like this one in San Diego County has plastic ferns? I mean *anything* will grow in this part of the country, even in the dark, choked by alcohol and tobacco fumes. Why phony plants? You tell me that."

The old man smiled a gummy smile and said the only thing I'd ever heard him say in the three years I'd known him, the only thing anyone had heard him say—as far as I know—since Anzio. "God bless America," he intoned, "nickel and dime."

That was Bananas' act. His entire act except for holding out his thumb and forefinger horizontally when he wanted another shot of Kessler. More often than not he made as much sense as anyone else in that place.

As I was agreeing with Bananas, I noticed the two guys who had just come in sidle down the bar toward me. A San Diego Gas and Electric worker on the barstool next to mine decided it was time to take a leak. The taller guy, sleek black razor-cut hair, Wayne Newton mustache and knife scar at the edge of one eye, occupied the vacated seat. He turned and spoke to me in quiet Spanish, smiling like we were old friends. He looked vaguely familiar, but

we weren't old friends. I had a nagging suspicion we weren't
going to be new friends either.

"You are a very nosy *cabron*," he said. The smile he wore was
like a cellophane bag that was making it hard for him to breathe.

I didn't say anything, no gems came to mind.

"Very nosy, much *huevos*, eh? You must be tough, such a curious
little cat. You are tough, eh?"

"Just who in hell are you"—a reasonable question I thought—
"or would that be telling?" Actually, I now recognized both him
and his partner as the pimps I had seen around Coahuila. I
noticed his friend had maneuvered himself toward the rear door
and was pretending to study the jukebox.

"I asked you if you were a tough guy." His smile was history
now. I was quickly trying to figure why a Tijuana pimp who
looked like Conan the Barbarian in a Pierre Cardin suit and his
sidekick would follow me across the border and pick a fight in a
San Diego bar, but nothing added up. Okay, they weren't pimps.

"Sure," I told him in English, glancing around the room to see
who might step into this on my side. It didn't look good: Bananas,
Eddy Nunzio, the bookie who was older than Bananas, his girlfriend who turned heads in Vegas as a showgirl when you could
still count the neon signs, Carl, the squirrel behind the bar who
was given to fits of deafness and blindness at the sight of Abra-
ham Lincoln's portrait, and Stevie McLain, the delivery kid from
Mayfair Market who, on a good day, might whip his weight in
week-old celery. "Tough, that's me. See this beer? That's just a
chaser. A minute ago I was drinking straight shots of molten
copper."

He frowned as if he were considering ordering one himself.
"You were in Tijuana asking a lot of stupid questions. Why are
you looking for Nabor? What do you want from him?"

"I'm not looking for any Nabor. I'm looking for Herman Villez."

"This Villez I don't care about. The other man you were
describing is a friend of mine. With the holes in his face."

Pockmarks. So now I had a name for the *pollero* or *coyote* and
someone who might lead me to him. I brought out the photograph that Juana Villez had given me. I showed it to Conan. He
looked at the family portrait, the dapper-looking gent in the

broad-striped suit and mustache, the heavy woman dressed in black who peered at the camera as if it were a drunken mariachi who wanted to marry her daughter, Juana Villez at age nineteen, whose awesome beauty survived the crude photography, and holding her hand, Herman Villez in his midtwenties, grinning negligently from beneath a thin mustache and shoulder-length hair.

I tapped the photo indicating the boy in the Western shirt, his thumbs hooked into his Levi's. "This is who I'm looking for. His sister lives here now. She sent money to him to pay a *pollero* to bring him across. She told him to see a man with pockmarks somewhere in Coahuila. Said his name was Morelos, but of course everyone's name is Morelos, no? I didn't know his name was Nabor." I smiled at him. "Anyway, this Herman Villez paid somebody. He was supposed to meet his sister in San Ysidro. He never showed. She hasn't heard from him and she's worried. She doesn't know that many people up here and her English isn't all that great. I told her I'd ask around and take a look, that's all."

He nodded gravely and took my elbow in a grip that would have cracked open a live lobster. "Let's have a talk, just you and I." His smile was back and he had me on my feet looking up at a set of perfectly white teeth the size of dice. He ushered me quickly toward the men's room. His companion, who looked like a mongoose in a serge suit, nodded at him and turned his attention back to the jukebox. He looked up every few seconds to make sure no one tried to give me a hand. No one did. My escort lifted me off the floor and pushed open the door to the men's room with the back of my head. Inside, the meter reader or whatever he was, was combing his hair. When the door struck him in the back, he yelled, "Hey!" and spun around.

With one hand, Conan yanked him out the door. He fell to his knees behind my dancing partner. I couldn't resist. I pushed off from the sink and butted him in the chest with my head and one shoulder. He was supposed to topple over, tripping backward over the guy behind him on his hands and knees. The old gag. It didn't work. He just looked at me as if I had disappointed him terribly. Then he sent his fist into the bridge of my nose.

After the light show had died down and the roaring in my ears had quieted to the sound of distant surf, I could make out what he was saying: ". . . things that are none of your concern. It can be very hazardous. I don't know your Herman Villez. No one does. You will never find him. It's too bad for his sister, but maybe he will show up soon. Who knows? A thousand things might have happened. Maybe he was arrested by *Inmigración.* You must not come to Coahuila and ask questions anymore. If you do, you will be killed."

That was the second time that day that I had been told that.

"You understand now, don't you?" He seemed genuinely concerned, apologetic, as if he were telling his favorite kid about matches. There was blood all over my hands, the sink, the floor and my shirt. He offered me his handkerchief. I waved it away, and as we walked out of the men's room, I pretended to search the pockets of my jeans for my own. He paused to replace the cloth in his breast pocket while standing between me and the exit to the parking lot.

My fingers closed over the keys in my pocket. I splayed four of them between my fingers and made a fist. I could sense his partner behind me, but not close enough to worry me. I brought my hand out of my pocket, began to turn and then spun toward the steroid nightmare from *Gentlemen's Quarterly,* bringing my arm around like a whip. My fist full of keys connected with his left eye and he staggered backward, bringing both hands up to his face. I kicked him in the groin and he went lurching out the rear door, which closed and locked neatly after him.

I turned and the mongoose was already on me. He swung at me and I ducked. I hit him twice, quickly and hard in the stomach. He bent over looking toward the rear door, waiting for the big guy to reemerge with a war axe or something. I grabbed his right collar with my left hand, his left collar with my right. With my wrists crossed just beneath his Adam's apple, I began digging my knuckles into his windpipe. As I stood there doing that for a while, I heard what sounded like a wrecking ball being sent up against the back door. Then it got quiet. The guy I was holding turned a bad color and stopped fighting me. I dropped him and ran for the front door. On my way out I noticed that there was no one left in the place except Bananas.

On the street I was nearly as blind as the guy who came bounding around the corner of the Hillcrest, still clutching his eye with

one hand. I wasn't unhappy to see blood running from between
his fingers onto his suit. If I'd had a handkerchief, I wouldn't have
been able to resist offering it to him, all apologetic and letting
bygones be bygones, landing myself in traction. As it was, I did
the smart thing and ran into five lanes of University Avenue rush-
hour traffic, dodging and weaving like a linebacker. I didn't look
back for three blocks.

I congratulated myself that I had lost him and decided to cele-
brate. The only place I could get served looking the way I did, I
figured, was my apartment.

2

ONCE INSIDE my two-room bungalow on Robinson and Third, I decided against a drink. I was too busy shaking and throwing up. Conan had broken my nose, my right eye was swelling closed and I couldn't breathe. I lay down on my Salvation Army couch and tried not to pass out. The way to do this seemed to be to stare at the ceiling around the corners of a washrag filled with ice cubes. If I closed my eyes, the blackness was too inviting. I had to be careful not to look at all the blood too. The sight of blood makes me sick. Like I told the man, tough, that's me.

After a while I put on a record by Mink Deville, took two Tylenol with codeine and practiced breathing through my mouth while I tried to think of what to do next.

So I was wrong about their being pimps. At least they weren't *just* pimps. It was a safe assumption that they were in the smuggling business. Maybe the girls were a sideline or maybe I was wrong about that altogether. I didn't know. I did know that the big guy hadn't recognized Herman Villez or his name. That wasn't surprising. Even if they had moved him across the border, there was no reason they should remember his face. I also knew that if I went back down to T.J. and stuck close to Conan, there was a good chance I'd eventually run into Nabor or Morelos or whatever his name was.

I wasn't too crazy about the idea.

Nabor/Morelos was a sensitive subject down there. That meant he was not just a garden-variety smuggler. Juana had said his fee was unusually high, but that he guaranteed safety. Detective Bevilaqua of the Tijuana police had done a take on my description of him. It all pointed to his being well connected.

I felt my broken nose and thought about the dead man. I decided that T.J. was out of the question, at least for a while.

I could hang out at the Casa del Sol in Chula Vista, where the illegals rendezvous, exchange information about work and connect with "Mules" to drive them to L.A., but that would probably get me nowhere. If they didn't talk to Juana, they wouldn't talk to me, and if Herman Villez showed up there, he would get in touch.

That left the man who had hired Juana Villez and brought her to the United States to dance in his club. The man who recommended Morelos. My boss, whom I'd never met. Mr. E. Walters.

I wasn't too crazy about that idea either, but it was the only one I had that, as far as I could tell, didn't involve my getting killed.

Juana would want to know what I had found, but she was working tonight and I didn't have anything positive to tell her. I listened to the rest of the album, felt the pain pills kick in and watched the shadows crawl across the piles of clothes, overflowing ashtrays and dirty dishes in my apartment.

I put Little Feat on the stereo and poured some Ancient Age into a clean coffee cup I found. After a while I had another one.

When it was fully dark and I was feeling just wonderful enough to think about it, I decided to go in to work on my night off and see her. Thinking about Juana made my face and the back of my neck burn like a schoolboy berserk with new hormones.

In the bathroom mirror I could see that I looked battered enough to hope that she would want to kiss it and make it better. I thought about that while I took a shower.

* * *

When I walked out of my apartment, my hair was blown dry, there were two more pain pills under my belt and I was wearing my best chocolate suede sports jacket and Hawaiian shirt. The Canary Island palm in front of the next bungalow was silhouetted against the nearly full moon. A hint of Santa Ana winds gave the night a velvet feel. I cooed back at the pigeons in the palm tree and waved at my neighbor Wayne. Wayne ignored me, the pigeons cooed back. Whistling the guitar hook from a Tom Petty song on my way to my usual parking space, I felt ready for anything.

I don't think I stared at the vacant curb for more than a few minutes before I remembered I had left my Maverick in the parking lot at the Hillcrest Club.

Would they be waiting for me? Did Wayne Newton the Barbarian rip my car apart with his bare hands?

I walked back up the sidewalk and let myself in again to the mock Moorish little house. I phoned the Hillcrest and got Gordon, the night man.

"York, you okay?"

"Yeah, how's my car?"

"All right, I guess. I heard about what happened. What was that all about?"

"Later. What about the two guys?"

"They split just before the cops got here."

"Are you sure?"

"Yeah, I'm sure."

"Thanks."

I walked back to the Hillcrest through my neighborhood—the only area in San Diego, aside from the Barrio in Logan Heights, that you could really call a neighborhood. A lot of the old residents were complaining about the number of gays coming in opening boutiques featuring unicorns and X-rated greeting cards. It didn't bother me except that it was hard to find a place to drink without a guy in a mustache and work boots singing Streisand songs or some overweight girl in a flannel shirt calling you "Jocko." When the area wasn't being called "Homo Hill" it was called "Little Saigon." The Vietnamese opened restaurants, barber shops, delicatessens, flower shops and produce stands. Unicorn boutiques and hair salons came and went, but the immigrant businesses did a solid trade.

Sometimes during the rainy season I would stand outside the Phuong Nam and listen to the waiters or the old men who gathered at the Number One Barber Shop and I would close my eyes to find myself in another time, another life. I didn't do it too often.

Gordon looked upset when I asked if I could borrow his car for a few hours just in case they were still in the area and watching mine. I told him not to worry about the car or the money he owed me on last week's Padres game and took the keys.

The TransAm smelled like a dumpster behind a McDonalds. There were Big Mac boxes and empty milkshake cups all over the floor. Still, the 427 engine pulled me from 0 to 60 in about seven seconds as I headed north on 163. It was just the car to be in if I was followed. A loop north, nearly all the way to Miramar Naval Air Station, proved no one was following me. I turned around and headed back toward San Diego. I listened to Steely Dan on Gordon's cassette.

The Low Down's thirty-foot neon dancer that flooded Pacific Coast Drive with garish colors for nearly a block either way was doing a stuttering bump-and-grind with her left hand missing. Maynard was getting the sign fixed. He had told me himself when he hired me as a security guard three months earlier.

Dick Holster was working the door that shift. He swore it was his real name. I even saw his driver's license once under the little flashlight they issued to us that brings out the watermark on California licenses—it also shows up any cute X-acto knife work on the date of birth, which is mostly what we look for on the IDs of the Navy kids who come to the Low Down.

Dick was a quiet, competent man. He worked for the San Diego Police Department for a year and then quit. He never told me why. He was cool and fair with a dry sense of humor and I would want him on my side of any trouble. I knew he subscribed to *The National Centurion,* some gun magazines and *The Survivalist,* owned some property in the mountains and had once applied for a PI license but didn't get it. He didn't have the kind of authority complex I expected to go along with this package, he didn't need to feel bigger than he was or push anyone around. He was a little hard to figure. Anyone who wanted to be a private detective was probably immature. My ambition was to sing like Ray Charles.

"Nathaniel York?" he read. "I thought York was your first name." Dick was paying me back for all my cracks about his name and my insistence on seeing his license that time. He handed back the card with the miniature photo of me that a girl I once dated said made me look like "a dissipated Dondi."

"I don't mind Nathaniel, but no one ever uses it. People always insist on Nat or Nate or Nathan. None of which are my name. So it's York."

"What happened to you?" He shined his flashlight in my eyes.

"Plastic surgery. I've decided to turn Japanese."

For a Monday night, it wasn't a bad crowd. Two dozen sailors in Levi's, windbreakers and haircuts from an old yearbook were seated around the horseshoe stage watching Liz do toe touches, running her hands over the insides and backs of her thighs.

I could watch Liz dance all night, she was good at it. She had fine suntanned legs that were nicely muscled but not too muscled, a perfectly hemispherical ass that moved more ways than one and high breasts, no more than a handful but enough to draw the eyes upward. She worked hard at dancing and it showed. She was also naturally sexy in the way that some women are no matter what kind of shape they're in; it comes through in the eyes, in the smile and in the air around them.

The sailors might as well have been watching a training film— "This, men, is a woman's backside"—for all the life they showed. From the bouncer's point of view, that was just fine. If you seemed to be enjoying the show a little too much, you were asked to leave.

On the floor next to Dick were all the checked motorcycle helmets, briefcases and bags. We started checking briefcases and bags about the time the idea of whipping out dildos at the girls became all the rage. The helmets we checked because we didn't like the idea of getting hit with them.

I wondered who the briefcases belonged to and I scanned the room. They weren't hard to find. Off in the corner where the timid guys sit they laughed a little too loudly with each other and pretended they were too well laid to really care about Liz's charms. Their ties were loosened at identical angles to their collars. They probably operated computers across the street at Major Turbines and had names like Harvey and Norm.

They should get together with the sailors and go to a movie.

I chose a barstool next to the waitress station and said hello to Suzy Lee. Maynard had the DJ bill Suzy as "The Red-Hot Yellow Peril." Smiling prettily at me from beneath jet bangs, she said, "Can't get enough of the place, eh? What is it?" Her face twisted in mock puzzlement. "The atmosphere?" She was wearing a blue silk kimono she didn't bother to close. I admired the way she tugged at the top of one black stocking that gleamed wickedly in the low light of the bar and adjusted a garter belt. "My magnetic personality?" Her wink used both eyes, all of her face and her shoulders.

I ordered a Coke and said, "You know, you're the most scrutable Oriental I've ever met."

Her laugh sounded the way a puppy does when you step on its tail. "I'll tell Juana you're here."

3

IT HAD BEEN on a slow night like this one that I had first seen Juana. They might have been the same fresh-faced sailors around the horseshoe and I remember a handful of old-timers, machinists from the plant down the road who peered up at the stage with lifeless, secretive eyes from over the tops of their beers. I had been watching the girls make the rounds in their G-strings to see if anybody needed refills. The drill was to scan the girls as they leaned toward the customers; if anybody touched them where they shouldn't, they were out the door.

Juana was carrying a tray and following Suzy Lee to see how it was done. Trailing they called it. She was waiting her turn to go onstage and dance and she looked scared to death. She must have been twenty-one—they're very conscientious about that kind of thing in topless bars because most of them are run by very sensitive interests—but she looked seventeen. She was wearing a tight blue skirt that was about as long as a mayfly's memory, sandals and what looked like a man's white shirt tied up in front like a halter and rolled at the sleeves. I guessed her to be five feet tall. She looked so good with her clothes on I didn't want her to take them off. Her face, in the bruised lighting, looked like a Mayan carving of some regal, delicate bird. Her eyes were and are huge and dark—soft, but with a kind of wariness that isn't quite disillusionment. Her hair was long then, all the way to her waist, black and rich like a jungle night. All the girls at the Low Down were beautiful—they had to be—but Juana, all flashing eyes, sculpted cheekbones and velvet sienna skin, could have made Helen of Troy look like a transvestite with a hangover.

She would look up at the stage, trailing the dancer—I forget who it was—the way she trailed Suzy Lee; trying to drink in the movements and memorize them, knowing she was about to go on. You could tell she was about as familiar with the atmosphere as she was with the moon's.

When she approached the bar, she would let Suzy Lee order first and then repeat after her as the bartender set up the drinks, "Meelair Lite" or "Jean and Towneek." Then she would smile up at the bartender—it was Clifford that night—for confirmation on her English. Cliff only scowled at her. Nothing personal, that was just Cliff. In a place where the dancers collected tips from the men in the horseshoe of barstools at the lip of the stage and then collected tips as waitresses when they weren't dancing, there wasn't much left over for a twenty-five-year-old bartender that looked like Karl Malden. I sympathized with him up to a point, but suspected that he wasn't quite human. Anyone who didn't melt when Juana smiled couldn't be quite human. I smiled at her for both of us and lied to her in Spanish that her pronunciation was very good. Her cheekbones seemed to lift even higher as her smile broadened in my direction.

Suzy pressed herself against me and wrapped her arms around my waist. She introduced us. "York is the big strong hunk who protects us from the bad horny men. Stay away from him, he's mine." She narrowed her eyes at Juana and then laughed, letting me go. "I wish."

In Spanish I made sure Juana knew it was just Suzy's sense of humor, adding that it wasn't going to be easy being the most beautiful dancer in the place. I wasn't just saying it.

It got me another smile. "You are *Mexicano?*"

I shook my head. "No, I—"

"*Cubano. Si?*"

I told her I was a lot of things, none of them Hispanic unless you counted the Corsican.

"Where did you learn to speak Spanish so well?"

I could listen to her voice all night and for the first time since taking the job I thought about doing just that. I made it a rule not to sleep where I ate, or however the old saw goes, partly because it was a good idea no matter where you worked and partly because most of the girls at the Low Down were either gay, into more dope than even I felt comfortable around, had whacko boyfriends with guns or interesting combinations of all of the above.

"I learned Spanish in high school, but not very well. I picked up more from some Puerto Rican people in my neighborhood in New York. Again, not very well."

She assured me that King Carlos never spoke better. She was probably right. I was being modest and King Carlos probably lisped.

The dancer onstage finished up and Larry, the disc jockey, started gabbling about fine foxes and funky stuff and flash dancin' mamas.

"I have to go." She looked toward the stage as if it were the gallows. "My first time, you know? I'm nervous."

"I know. Don't worry about it. You'll be fine."

Her smile had collapsed. A ghost of one flickered that was more of a facial tic and then she headed for the backstage curtain. The previous dancer emerged and began circulating, taking drink orders from the sailors and the old men.

We all listened to Bob Seeger sing "Fire Down Below." It sounded like he was in the room.

Larry interrupted the record and introduced her. ". . . straight from Mexico City, hotter than a jalapeño, welcome our newcomer, Juana! . . . *Do you wanna?*" Larry played with the delay on his console and his words echoed around the dance floor. He mixed the volume up on Pat Benatar's "Shadows of the

Night" and Juana appeared blinking into the spotlights. She wore a black, silklike pair of pants that I recognized as belonging to one of the other girls. The pants could be untied on either side of the ankles, calves, knees, thighs and waist and would come away in a few deft movements if you had enough practice. She wore a Harry Belafonte–style balloon-sleeved shirt that revealed enough cleavage to explain her getting the job without any experience—if it needed any explaining. On her head, covering part of her hair that was tied up in the classic Spanish style, she wore the kind of hat that Zorro wears. In her hand was a bullwhip. She tottered a little inexpertly on high heels and blinked into the footlights.

The getup must have been Maynard's idea. I looked toward the rear of the room and saw him leaning against a pool table with his arms folded and a happy grin on his face. He looked like somebody's idiot son.

It took her only a few moments to adjust to the lighting and the spike-heeled shoes and then Juana began to move with the kind of grace you associate with expensive and exotic cats. She took it slow and trailed the whip around her neck like a snake, playing with the grip end without quite touching it, holding it out as if it had a mind of its own and were trying to touch her everywhere. She kept her eyes on the whip as if it were hypnotizing her or she it. By the end of the first song she had thrown her head back and allowed it to touch her throat and slide downward while she sank to her knees, her eyes still closed. She made the thing look alive and I envied it. So did the rest of the lads. The sailors and the old men got to their feet and applauded and shouted. They waved money in the air and laid it out on the edge of the stage. She moved leisurely around the horseshoe, smiling and bending to pick up the money with her legs tightly together. I don't know where she got that routine, but it was a big hit. Not as athletic as most of the acts you see at the Low Down maybe, but she didn't need to execute flying splits or yoga positions.

She still hadn't taken off anything but her hat.

On the sound system, the Rolling Stones started up "Beast of Burden." She tossed the hat full of money to the side and the whip on top of it, moving with the same languid tension and bridled sensuality. The routine was that the second number was the cue for the dancer to earn her money topless. Usually this was worked up to with a gradual tease, but Juana simply stared into the spotlights, unbuttoned her shirt and let it drop unceremoniously to the floor. She looked in the general direction of where I was standing and then met my eyes. Her breasts were full and pearlike and smooth, only slightly lighter than the rest of her skin, the stuff dreams are made of: lonely dreams full of frustration and ache, the kind that leave the pillow full of sweat and the sheets a tangled mess. She danced for the next two songs looking at me every few moments and smiling.

If anyone tore up the bar or raped the waitresses, I missed it. I was lost somewhere in a pair of eyes.

I never had a chance.

Since she was the new kid, she had worked the last show. At closing time she had said goodnight to me and started walking down Pacific Coast Drive along the shoulder of the road. When I had killed the switch on the big neon sign, she disappeared into the night. I locked up as quickly as I could and called out after her in Spanish to wait.

I saw her stop and turn, silhouetted against a pair of oncoming headlights. I ran to catch up. "You're not walking far at two in the morning I hope."

"No, not far. I live there." She gestured up Laurel to an Edwardian-looking house that had long since become low-income rental units specializing in transient clientele.

"You live with Liz?" I knew that Liz had a one-bedroom place she shared half the time with her coke dealer boyfriend, an incorrigible little scamp I had to eighty-six one time for pulling a buck knife on some Navy chief. Juana nodded.

"How about a late dinner or an early breakfast? Hungry?"

"No. Maybe some coffee." She smiled. "I never went out with a policeman. I'll feel very safe."

I looked down at my uniform. "I'm just a rent-a-cop. Consider me rented."

We walked back up the street to my car and drove to the Silver Gate Diner. She drank coffee and so did I. I ordered an omelette and played with it while I babbled on about the Low Down and Maynard, past jobs, New York, San Diego, the Padres; all of them seemed to be the wrong things to talk about while trying to impress a woman with a face that would bring a statue to life. She didn't say much, just nodded and smiled and stirred her coffee long after it was cold. She showed me her first night's tips, about sixty dollars, which was almost impossible on a Monday night at the Low Down unless you happened to look like Juana. I congratulated her and told her not to wave cash around in the Silver Gate Diner at 2 A.M. "Tell me about yourself," I said, "anything at all. I'm getting tired of my voice. How did you get the job dancing? Just walk in?"

"No, the owners have a hotel in Ensenada where I was working as a maid. They offered me the job and said they could arrange the papers. They said I would make a lot of money. It seems to be true." Instead of looking happy at this, she seemed to be puzzled, as if it were the only thing they told her that *was* true. Maybe it was just the expression someone might wear if they were bone tired from dancing and waiting tables for eight hours. "I have my green card," she said brightly, and then, as quickly, her expression darkened again. Hurriedly, as if to cover something, she went on. "Anyway, I want to take lessons to dance and to act."

"You should give them."

I had heard that Wolf Enterprises, the company that owned the Low Down, had interests in Mexico. That jibed and it didn't tax my imagination to think they could buy a green card for her like they might buy a new pool table. I didn't know how much juice that would take, but they might well have it. Still, with all the juice in the world, an army of tame, well-connected lawyers and some key friends at the Bureau of Immigration and Naturalization, it would take a couple of months to get a residency permit, what they called the green card though it wasn't green. Sometimes it could take up to a year and even then it could fall through.

Something had been bothering her. She was leaving a lot out. In a strange country after her first day at a pretty strange job, sitting across the table from a stranger in a mock cop's uniform, it wasn't likely she'd give me an epic and detailed life history; but I got the feeling it wasn't me or the job or geography that made her seem sad and afraid.

No doubt they had told her that they would make her a star in the United States, that if she just took off her shirt and danced in their club, Hollywood would be beating the door down in no time. I wasn't going to tell her otherwise. Things happened around the kind of beauty Juana had.

I drove her back to Liz's apartment and took myself home. She had agreed to meet me for dinner the next night before our shifts began.

We had seafood at Anthony's and watched the tourists yell at their kids and take pictures in front of the Star of India and the tuna boats. She wasn't any more eager to talk about herself, and I held up both ends of the conversation by making up names for all the people that walked by. I became more convinced that there was something on her mind but I was going to wait for her to spill it, if she ever decided to.

When the conversation turned to movies, she brightened up. She knew more about American movies and movie stars than Rona Barrett. I was left in the dust, but neither of us minded. She recounted plots from movies I'd never heard of and delighted in describing what everyone was wearing in what scene. I was happy just listening to her voice; it sounded the way cool silk feels against hot skin.

". . . You would look like him a little if you had a mustache." She squinted at me.

"Who?"

"Burt Reynolds. You're not listening. I am boring you."

"You could read me the phone book without boring me. You like Burt, eh?"

"I told you, he is my absolute favorite. If I could become a movie star, I would make all of my movies with him."

"I'll grow a mustache."

For the next two weeks I took her to every matinee in San Diego County that didn't have a title like *Wet Housewives* or *Lavender Truckers*. She held my arm once while Burt Reynolds kissed Goldie Hawn. I made a mental note to buy Burt a drink if I ever met him.

On her nights off, she told me, she was going to school to learn English, but she didn't say where. When she offered to make me a dinner of *carne asada* and seviche in my apartment, I didn't turn her down. I bought a bottle of Frascati, a bottle of Beaujolais and a bottle of El Presidente brandy. Over the finished dinner—which was better than any I'd ever had in the too many mediocre Mexican restaurants in town—we drank brandy and she told me that my mustache was funny-looking. I pretended her English was bad and that I thought she had said that it smelled funny. When she leaned closer to place her nose near my upper lip, I kissed her and she kissed me back. Long and hard. The world dissolved into soft lights, a velvet tongue and the scent of her hair like sweet earth and night-blooming jasmine. I held her for a long time, her head against my chest, until I felt a dampness on my shirt and her shoulders shake in my arms. I lifted her face and saw the tears and streaked makeup.

"Okay. Tell me about it," I said as gently as I could.

She shook her head and used a Kleenex. She had drunk far more than she was used to and she started to pour another. I took the snifter from her.

"This won't help, but maybe I can."

"I'll make some coffee," she said.

She got up and walked a little unsteadily to the kitchen. I followed her. She leaned against the sink and lowered her head. She started to sob again. I held her and after a while she started to tell me about Herman Villez.

"When I left Mexico I promised my brother I would arrange for him to join me here as soon as I could. The man who brought me here, Mr. Walters, would not help me except to give me the name of a man in Tijuana who would smuggle him across for three hundred dollars. It is more than the usual amount, but I was told he guaranteed safety. The man's name is Morelos and he, Mr. Walters, said he could be found in the bars in a district called Coahuila. He was described to me as a man with holes from some disease on his face. I wrote to Herman and I sent him the money. I received a letter from him two weeks ago saying that he had arrived in Tijuana and had met the man. He said everything was arranged, that he was to leave in a few nights. He told me to wait for him at the Casa del Sol in Chula Vista until he arrived. I waited there for three nights when I was not working and then another three nights the next week. I took the trolley. That's where I have been. I lied to you about the English lessons. I showed his picture to the *alambristas* there, but no one had seen him. Or if they had, they said nothing. They are all very frightened and always lie, even to their own people. They trust no one. I must find this man Morelos and ask him what became of my brother. These *coyotes* are dangerous men and I am afraid. My brother and I are very close, he has always taken care of me and now I must take care of him. I've failed. Something terrible has happened to Herman. He may have been arrested or killed. You always hear of the terrible things that happen to the *alambristas*."

The word meant, literally, "wirecutters." It was the term Mexican illegals used instead of *mojados*, or wetbacks, along this part of the border because you didn't have to cross a river to get here, just a fence. She lied to me about the English classes all right, and I sensed there were holes in her story you could drive a Buick through, some of which could be explained by the fact that she herself was here on phony papers, but if that was the way she wanted to tell it, that was all right with me. There was enough truth in it to make a start.

"What about Walters? Couldn't he trace him for you?"

She looked away and shrugged. "He said to wait, that he was probably only delayed, but that he would come soon. I know that isn't true." She gave me a look that held all the certainty anyone could have about anything. "Herman would have gotten in touch with me somehow."

"Yeah, they have phones in Tijuana and a sort of a post office. What about the woman who was with Walters when he hired you?"

"I don't know her name. I never saw her again. She was very beautiful, but cold-looking, you know? Mr. Walters gave me his card long ago when he asked me to think about coming to work for him in the United States. The second time I saw him I agreed. The next day he sent a car for me. It brought me to the club. There was no trouble at the border. He gave Liz some money and asked if I could stay with her. Liz was very nice, of course. It was just temporary, he said. Soon he would get me my own place. That was some weeks ago. I've seen him once since then and I asked him about Herman. He told me to be patient. Herman would come. He said that he would soon have some news for me that would make me happy. He did not mean news about Herman, but some job for me. I haven't seen him since then. When I have tried to call him, there is a machine that answers his telephone and he has never returned my calls."

From her purse she handed me a business card with the name E. Walters embossed in gold and a number with a north county exchange. There was nothing else on the card.

E. Walters was the name on the liquor license at the Low Down. He owned at least two other topless joints, one in L.A. and one in Carmel. He signed my paychecks as head of Wolf Security Systems, which was an organization of doormen, bouncers, nightwatchmen, department store guards, ushers, repo men and professional witnesses for law firms.

"I'll tell you what I'll do." I sat her back down on the couch and spoke to her from the kitchen as I made the coffee. "In the morning I'll go to the detention center in San Ysidro. You said you have a photograph of Herman. I'll see if I can spot him. If he was arrested, he might still be there. I can't very well circulate his picture with the Border Patrol in case he's lying low somewhere and still trying to dodge them, but I can go to Coahuila and see if he isn't still hanging around—maybe find your Señor Morelos with the terminal acne."

"You would do that?" She looked up at me with eyes that weren't yet cried out. Her brother must be something special.

I would do that.

She brought my head down to her mouth and I stayed that way for a long time. After a while she said, "I will pay you." She reached into her handbag the way she did when she showed me her tips that first night. The bundle had grown. There must have been about a thousand dollars in twenties, fifties and tens.

"You're spoiling the moment. Put that in a bank somewhere."

"I don't like banks," she said defensively.

"Give it to Maynard. Tell him to put it in the house safe at the Low Down."

"He keeps my green card and he won't let me have it." She looked at me to see what I made of that and then said, "I don't like Maynard."

"No one does. Sorry, that was my dumb suggestion for the night. I have much better ones." I brought her closer to me.

She leaned back on the couch and I felt all of her beneath me. I supported my weight on my elbows and gradually brought myself down until she moaned and I felt her body against mine. She reached between my legs with her right hand and closed her fingers around the hardness there. My arms couldn't support my weight anymore, they shook like jade branches in an earthquake. It was my turn to moan.

Her tongue silenced me and I rolled to the side, gradually letting her down onto me as I lay on the floor. She straddled me and sat up lifting her skirt over her head with a fluid ruffle of soft beige. I had seen her take her clothes off before, onstage. But this wasn't a show. She looked at me now with an intensity and hunger that you always hope to find in a woman with that kind of beauty, but usually don't—settling for something close enough to get you through the night, but not close enough to want to remember the next day. She unhooked her flesh-colored bra and it fell away. She stayed upright for a moment just breathing and looking at me and for a while I didn't do anything because I knew that to begin meant that it would have to end.

"Nathaniel," she said, her breasts rising and falling as she tried to take in enough air to say whatever she thought had to be said. "This doesn't have to . . . I'm not . . . we. . . ." She bent to kiss me again. My mouth met hers and we finished the thought the only way that made any sense.

I slid her hose down from her hips and she pulled my shirt from my waist. Her lips played over my belly, the scar just above it, then back down. I felt her fingers on my belt and the buttons on my Levi's and in the next moment she had me in her mouth, all of me that mattered except for the little timekeeper existing somewhere in that cold place between the heart and the brain who kept pointing out that tomorrow or the next day or a year from now she would just be something else that I had lost.

When I entered her she bit her lip and laughed, shuddered and grew quiet. She said she was sorry that she laughed. I told her that I wasn't. I told her that was perfect.

We made love until dawn, and when it came time, I shook just as hard and laughed too—because it was perfect. And maybe because nothing else ever had been. I lay beside her tracing patterns on her cheek, still chuckling like a madman over some private joke. She kissed my forehead and my face until I stopped. She said, "You are a funny man."

"Ha-ha funny?"

"No."

"Then you mean strange."

"Different. A man who laughs when he makes love . . . and doesn't mind when I do. Do I sound stupid because I can't speak English well?"

"Not to me."

She said nothing for a while. A gray light came in through the venetian blinds; early morning fog that would burn off by noon. Then she said, "If you were a Mexican man, you would slap me for laughing and I would be humiliated if you laughed."

"That's what makes this country great. We're a funny people. We make the world safe for comedy." It was a bad substitute for what I wanted to say. The cleverness hung like body odor or old cigarette smoke in the room.

"You need to protect people, don't you?"

"I don't know about that."

"I think that about you, but I don't know why it is."

"It's a minor neurosis, I can deal with it."

"A what?"

"Nothing." I kissed her again because I wanted to and because it would stop me from talking about love and protecting people. She moved on top of me again.

I must have put the radio on because I remember music that isn't on any record I own. It probably isn't on any radio either.

We slept eventually and very late that morning she made me breakfast. Rice Krispies and papaya slices. We talked about everything: dancing and acting and movies and the regulars at the Low Down, Ronald Reagan and the Russians. We talked about the night before and how fine it was and then we talked about her brother, Herman Villez.

We talked about everything except love.

She gave me the family photo, taken, she said, after Easter mass two years ago in front of an uncle's ranch outside of Hermosillo. I drove her back to Liz's apartment around eleven o'clock. The hard strains of heavy-metal music came from an open window along with the too loud voices of people who had been up all night on cocaine and were too stoned to realize they didn't have to hold back the night anymore.

I kissed Juana on the tip of her nose and drove myself south to San Ysidro.

4

AT THE DETENTION CENTER a woman behind a sliding glass window asked me my business. I told her I was a reporter for the San Diego *Reader* doing a piece on the treatment of illegals by the San Diego Border Patrol. As just a curious citizen I could wait weeks or months to get clearance and then I would get only the sunshine tour, but as a representative of the press I hoped I would have a little leverage if I needed it. She told me to have a seat and wait for a Mr. Weintraub.

Weintraub's first name was Douglas. That's what it said on the plaque on his desk. Douglas Weintraub, Assistant Administrator. Doug looked like an old cop to me, maybe FBI, maybe military police. He had that dull look that comes with aging authority. He was about fifty-five with narrow eyes above coffee drinker's pouches and a whiskey drinker's nose. His sideburns were a little too long for his haircut and he looked like he would speak with a

Southern accent but he didn't. He was courteous but forgot to shake my hand. I put it back in my jacket pocket and sat down uninvited.

"So, you're with the *Reader,*" he said, standing.

"If I sell them this story, I am. I'm free-lance."

"Then the *Reader* didn't send you here?"

"Not exactly."

"You're writing this article on . . . whattyacallit? Speculation?"

"Right."

"You didn't tell the receptionist that."

"It didn't come up." I smiled, trying to look like a clever cub reporter.

He didn't smile back. "You mind if I ask who you've written for in the past?"

"I wrote for the *Village Voice* in New York. I did stringer stuff for the *Daily News* back there. I did a story on the American Nazi Party for *Rolling Stone* last year, a piece on male pattern baldness for *Esquire* . . ." I was just getting going when he interrupted me.

"I never read any of those . . ." He thought and then said, "publications." He said it as if it were a clever euphemism for toilet paper. "I don't read the San Diego *Reader* either."

"Over a hundred thousand people in this county do." I made up their circulation figure.

"Well, Mr. . . ."

"Hammil," I said. I don't know if it was some vague hunch I had that I should keep my real name from the Border Patrol's notice, a kind of clairvoyance about what was to come, or if I was just having fun. "Raoul Hammil."

"Mr. Hammil, before I could authorize a visit to the facilities, my office would require a letter from your superiors addressed to our public information officer in San Pedro outlining the exact nature of your article and the manner in which the Border Patrol would be represented."

"I told you, Mr. Weintraub. I'm free-lance. At the moment I have no . . . superiors." I smiled a gosh-shucks kind of smile. "The Border Patrol will be represented fairly, I believe. I could agree to submit the article to you before publication for your perusal." No reporter would agree to something like that, but I hoped he didn't know that.

Doug sat down and spread his hands to show me that they were empty, that he was powerless. "I'm sorry. That's not good enough. You understand." Now he extended his hand for me to shake. "It's a sensitive matter."

"Yes, it is." I stood up and started to go, leaving his extended and meaty hand poised over his desk. "Then it's okay with you if the article reads, 'The Border Patrol Administration Office would not permit an on-site inspection of the detention center'?"

"That would not be accurate." He closed his hands and sat forward.

It was my turn to spread my palms and shrug.

He glanced at his watch. "The morning is a bad time. Maybe if you were to come back after lunch I could get someone to take you on a brief tour. We've got nothing to conceal here. We don't mistreat these people." He was suddenly standing again. "They're a lot better off if we get them. We don't take their money or molest them or kill them the way their own people do. We feed them here. Your tax money buys them the kind of meal many of them could never buy for themselves. We take them back across the border and arrange for their transportation to wherever they say they've come from, which is more than their own government does for them. If we're a little cautious about who we allow into the place, it's because we're trying to do a job with no help from the media, who seem intent on portraying us as storm troopers. Come back this afternoon and you'll see beds for people who've never slept in one, quality food and medical care for people who'll never see it again unless they become regulars or graduate to the penitentiary. Come back after lunch, Mr. Hammer, and write your story." He dismissed me by screwing a True Blue cigarette into a white holder and lighting it. The witless tool of the commie fag New York press had been told off and shown largesse by one of the front-line defenders of Our Way of Life.

I turned to go. I was about to say thank you when he said, "Mr. Hammond, I don't think I like you or your way of doing business, but maybe you've got enough gumption to tell your readers the truth. I'm gonna count on that."

"I appreciate it, Mr. Weinhardt," I said as I closed his office door behind me.

Herman Villez wasn't at the detention center or "staging area," as they called it. The place resembled a well-maintained POW camp, which, in a sense, is exactly what it was. A hurricane fence enclosed a compound of numbered one-story buildings that looked like barracks only their cinder blocks were painted a cheerful yellow. The guy who showed me around was Agent Ybarra, a broad, pleasant-looking Chicano who probably lifted weights. He parked a turquoise-and-white Border Patrol passenger van that he had used that morning to bring the previous night's catch back over the border.

"You're not gonna see much," he said, unlocking a gate set into the chain link. "This time of day it's pretty quiet. We got three guys left from last night." He indicated a trio of tired-looking men squatting against the fence and smoking cigarettes. They didn't speak to each other. Their clothes looked dusty and cheap, their faces and arms had seen a lot of sun over the years. They could have been in their thirties or their sixties. I didn't get that close, but none of them were Juana's brother.

"One of these guys is a refugee from El Salvador. He goes to El Centro for official deportation tonight or tomorrow. This other guy goes to the marshal's office to be arraigned on charges of resisting arrest. He had a knife and tried to use it. Didn't do him any good. He'll probably do time at MCC."

"Metro Correction Center."

"Right."

"What about him?" I pointed to the third man. He wore imitation designer jeans that were too big for him and worn out at the knees.

"He turned himself in this morning. He was coming across last night and got separated from his daughter, just a kid, fourteen. They split up and ran from my patrol. He showed up here about nine o'clock to see if we picked up his little girl. We didn't. He goes back tomorrow with the ones we round up tonight."

"What about the girl?"

Ybarra turned and gestured out at the miles of valley stretching

out below San Ysidro along the Tijuana River basin. "We'll keep
an eye out for her."

"Yeah." I turned from the scenery. There was too much of it to
go along with the thought of a lost kid. I looked at the men in the
yard. If they gave a damn what happened to them, you couldn't
see it in their faces. "The guy who resisted arrest, you get a lot of
that?"

"Enough."

"Every night? Once a month? Anybody besides him in the last
couple of weeks?"

"Sure." He smiled. "There was a guy a few nights ago that bit
one of our people. Right here." He pointed to his inner thigh.
"He got away, though."

I wondered if Herman Villez was a biter. "You see the guy?"

"Oh, I know who he is. A regular. We'll get him again and when
we do, Caulfield is gonna bite his leg off. Then we'll just drive him
back to First Avenue in T.J., he'll come across again in a few
nights and get caught. It becomes a game after a while."

"Caulfield?"

"The guy he bit."

"I thought your regulars do a prison term."

"Not the everyday working guys. There's not enough jails,
man. No, our biter is an old friend. He picks fruit up here every
summer and spring, spends the money he makes on whiskey and
boys in T.J. He gets real pissed off when we catch him. He's okay,
though, you know."

"He got a name?" I brought out my notebook as though I were
taking notes for the *Reader.*

Ybarra grinned in a goofy way. Anybody who could make that
face had to be human as hell. I laughed before he even said
anything. "Juan Garcia, what else? Just like these other two guys.
Caulfield calls him the Tooth Fairy now."

"The Tooth Fairy?"

"He's an old queen, man. Too much." Ybarra looked at his
Casio watch. "You wanna see the barracks with the beds and all
that? You missed lunch for these guys. A restaurant down the
road caters their meals. Sloppy Joes today."

"Yummy. Thanks, Agent Ybarra. I've got enough for now." I
turned to go. Ybarra stopped me with a hand on my arm.

"If you're a reporter, I'm Marie of Roumania. Who are you looking for?"

"You've been a lot of help. If I was looking for somebody who was picked up, I would hope he ran into you."

"Don't let Weintraub get in your knickers, he's really okay. Most of the guys here are okay more or less. There are a few John Waynes and whatnot, what the hell? If you were looking for a wirecutter, they could do a lot worse than be picked up by the Border Patrol. A lot worse." I believed him.

"Yeah, they might miss out on the Sloppy Joes."

Ybarra laughed, then added, "If there's somebody out there" —he gestured at the valley, the DMZ between hostile countries in a quiet but nonetheless real war for the American dollar—"somebody we should know about who's liable to do more than just bite, you let me know. Okay?"

I nodded and walked back to my car. I would.

5

GETTING ACROSS the Tijuana border takes less time and is less trouble than entering Disneyland on a weekday morning during the off season. Coming out can be a little more of a headache, but nothing like the way it would be for Herman Villez. On an impulse I stopped and converted my money to pesos, though it wasn't strictly necessary. I took the highway turnoff for downtown and within a few minutes I was choking on exhaust fumes from vintage buses, dust from the side streets that would be rivers of mud in a few months and the odor of sewers gone wrong. Tijuana is less than a few miles from the shopping malls and Bob's Big Boys and the Best Western Motels of suburban America, but it might as well be light-years away; they have all those things in T.J., but they are grafted-on features that never quite took. There is no mistaking the fact that you have left the gaudy California dream of sun-bright promises behind you once you've crossed the border; in Baja the sun is just something that burns through the dust, scorching things and people.

I ignored the small army of guys hawking body and upholstery work along Third Avenue and parked at Tijuana Tillie's—260 pesos, or about $1.75, all day. Walking north along Revolucion, I passed blocks of ceramic figurines of everything from Darth Vader to the Virgin of Guadalupe, mass-produced blankets in Day-Glo colors, velvet paintings of crying Elvises and billiard-playing dogs, suede rifle cases and leather jackets. It was only late afternoon, but the discos were beginning to crank up for the night. Sailors from North Island and trainees from Miramar were already drunk outside The Long Bar. Marines from Camp Pendleton were smoking "Horseshit" cigarettes and leaning against taxicabs or having their pictures taken in madcap poses on zebra-striped burros. Families from Phoenix or Duluth or Sacramento paraded up and down the street with gag T-shirts, Japanese cameras and waxen expressions, pausing now and then to ask a vendor how much his wares were in "real money."

The heat from the day still lay over the street, congealing the smells of carbon monoxide, frying *carnitas* and American sunscreen oil into an odor that resembled none of those things, but something else, something foreign and smoldering.

I stopped at the Hotel Nelson for a cold Corona and listened to a tourist sing along with a mariachi trio for a rendition of "Spanish Eyes." When they finished, he pulled out a dollar bill from his wallet and waved it drunkenly at the guitar player. The guitar player grinned as if this were the most fun he'd ever had with his pants on or as if he were thinking of eighty-eight silent ways to kill when the drunken gringo ran out of folding money or maybe it was just a grin. They struck it up again. I wondered how long they'd been at it.

Two blocks later and I was walking downhill into the shadowed, crowded Barrio where the tourists don't find much that's quaint or charming: Coahuila, or "the little village." It lies between Revolucion, Constitucion and the bottom of the hill where the overflow from backed-up sewers silts up. This is the section of town where all the myths about T.J. originate. Like the one about bars where you can see a girl screw a donkey, or the one about every little kid's sister being available for a price, or the one about how you can get anything you want in the way of drugs, stolen goods and weapons from some sloe-eyed pirate. Myself, I'd never seen a girl screw a donkey—I suspected that that particular show closed somewhere back in the forties—but the rest were no myths.

I ordered an *El Presidente con aqua y lima* at a place called simply Delicias Bar. To get in you had to step up onto an old crate, duck a dripping air conditioner and push aside a set of greasy red leatherette curtains. If you could do this without falling onto the dirt floor, you were welcome to drink there. I sat at the bar next to a dusty *ranchero* and his wife with ten empty cans of Tecate in front of them. They swayed to some secret inner music they had memorized together years ago and watched *Roots* in English on a grainy black-and-white set over the cash register. Behind me, a boy who sold paper flowers and Chiclets to the tourists sat on a rickety table eating a *churro* and commenting on the movie to his father, who lay across the table with his head on his arms.

"The big one," the boy was saying, "he runs away and gets his foot cut off. I saw that part before on a color television."

"Eat your *churro,* little bat," his father advised him.

The bartender was tall, thin and not young by anyone's standards. He looked like a scholar who had discovered too late that his life's work contained some fundamental error. He ran his bar as if it were the Oak Room in the Plaza, leaning forward at regular intervals to inquire, *"Bueno? Basante lima? Okay?"* and cleaning ashtrays with the grim disapproval of a respiratory therapist. Into my second drink I presented him with the photograph and asked him if he had seen the young man in it.

"Policia?" He lifted his nose, skewed his head to the side as if he really didn't believe it but had to ask anyway.

"No. I'm a friend. He's missing. I'm worried."

He squinted at the picture again, shook his head. *"Yo no se. Los siento."*

I asked him if he knew a man named Morelos with a bad complexion. He seemed to think. The boy eating the *churro* scurried off his table and darted out the door. His father called after him but let him go.

"I'm old," the bartender said, "I don't know. So many faces." His eyes moved up and down the bar suddenly looking for new

customers or drinks to refill. *"Morelos. Morelos. Yo no se."* He
looked over at the boy's father behind me and started washing
glasses that he had already washed.

I drank my brandy and laid out about a thousand pesos on the
bar before I ordered another one. The bartender looked at the
money, then looked at the man behind me. He leaned forward
and said softly, "Come back tomorrow, maybe I will remember."

"Gracias." I got up and left without the drink I had ordered. I
left the money on the bar.

Outside I saw the boy. A large man wearing a tailored suit was
handing him a soda he had just bought from a vendor with a
pushcart. The boy looked at me and turned to the man, saying
something. I walked across the street to La Charrita.

I looked too much like an American, my Spanish wasn't as good
as Juana said it was and I just showed too much money to blend in
with the woodwork, but I had a buzz and considered it a calculated risk. I was playing detective.

Inside La Charrita I bought one of the hookers a beer and
shared my Marlboros with her. She'd never seen Herman Villez.
She'd never seen anyone with pockmarks either, didn't even
know what they were. One of the girls said she knew him and
would tell me where he lived for fifteen dollars. Another one said
she knew a lot of other boys I would like better for only ten
dollars. I could see that cash spent on information was probably
down the toilet. You could buy any fairy tale you liked for a few
bucks and to hell with the sales tax. I had enough money to keep
me hanging around the neighborhood for a day or so with my
eyes open. That was plan A.

I sat and burned Marlboros with the hooker—her name was
Reina—and watched the other girls lead down-and-out street
boys who couldn't afford them around the dance floor just for
practice. It was Saturday night, but that didn't make any difference. In Tijuana's Zona Norte or Coahuila there are so many
people out of work that weekends just blur into the sameness of
torpid days and shabby neon nights.

The big man in the suit who had bought the soda for the boy
outside came in and seated himself next to another man at a
shadowed table near the door. The other man was thinner and
shorter but also wore a jacket and tie. I figured them for pimps. I

figured the boy eating the *churro* must have made me for a client and tipped off the stablemaster. I figured wrong.

Reina was a big-boned girl with long wavy black hair to her waist. She didn't wear much makeup and she had a soft tired laugh that I liked. She chain-smoked my cigarettes and drank the beers I bought her as fast as I could get the money on the bar. At fifty pesos a bottle I could be Diamond Daddy all night.

"Why are you looking for the boy?"

"Why does anybody look for anything? He's missing."

"He's a wirecutter? A *pollo?*"

I drank my beer.

"Then he's dead. Otay Mesa is full of unmarked graves. Look for him there."

"Why do you say that?"

She laughed and shrugged. "That's the best information you'll get here. I won't charge you for it."

We took the air and found ourselves at the Copacabana around the corner. We listened to a rock group singing Blondie songs half in Spanish and half in English. The place smelled like old leather and urine. Sagging balloons hung from dusty rafters still decked out with faded crepe paper streamers from last New Year's Eve or maybe the one before that. Mutilated *piñatas* turned slowly in the colored lights like surreal carcasses.

Up until now I seemed to have been in the wrong places. I had seen nothing that might have been *coyote* activity in either the Delicias Bar or La Charrita. Here were three tables occupied by men, women and children carrying small bundles and bags. They had no drinks in front of them except for a few Cokes for the children. The tableau had the feel of strangers waiting in a bus station.

Reina got bored with me after a few dances and decided I wasn't going to spring for a night of *passion insaciable.* When I returned from the men's room, she was gone. I stayed for two hours getting beery and tired, but not as beery and tired as the band.

It was a little after twelve when a man wearing a new white cowboy hat and a windbreaker with the collar turned up stuck his head in the door. He gestured to the people seated around the tables cradling their sleeping children.

They got up and began filing outside slowly. I couldn't make out the *coyote*'s face because of the hat, the windbreaker and the lighting in the club. I needed to see if it was Morelos—nobody's that lucky, but what the hell. I didn't think it would be the slickest possible move to get up and show any interest in things, but I had to check it out and there was no good way to do it.

When the band finished whatever they were trying to play and the sound of a distant siren died, I could hear several car doors slamming outside, low voices and then someone saying, *"La avenida,"* which I took to be instructions to a driver.

I got up, patting my pockets as if I were looking for a cigarette. I walked to the front door. There was a cigarette machine next to it. While I fished for change, I looked outside. Across the street the guy in the cowboy hat was getting into the driver's side of a Datsun pickup truck. In the back were four adults and two kids. A minute ago they had been sitting in the Copacabana. The dome light in the cab of the truck came on when the driver opened the door and I could see the lower half of his face. No pockmarks.

I went back to the barstool with my pack of Fiestas. I heard the sound of three small car engines starting up outside. I wondered about the other drivers.

The Fiestas tasted like smoldering dung and brown paper bags.

On Sunday morning I woke up with a headache and watched a cockroach crawl around three of the baseboards in my room at the Azteca de Oro Hotel before I tried to sit up.

It was nine o'clock in the morning and it was already hot. The fan over my bed turned sluggishly and wobbled, steadily working its way out of the plaster in the ceiling. It was only a matter of time before the thing fell, crushing or impaling whoever was under it.

I got out of bed and threw some water on my face, brushed my teeth and shaved. I went downstairs to the café to try some coffee. The place was too hot and too full of flies. The coffee burned my tongue and made my headache worse. I left it unfinished on the counter and walked across the road to the Delicias Bar.

The father of the boy was still in the same booth he was in the night before only he was sitting up now and drinking coffee from a water glass. His face was perfectly round, chubby rather than fat. His eyes disappeared beneath his brows into the flesh of his cheeks as if they were puncture wounds. He grimaced into his coffee and gave me an uninterested look as I came in.

Three middle-aged men with dapper haircuts and *Guayabera* shirts studied the Sunday paper and placed bets on today's jai alai, the dog races and the bullfight. They were drinking Sangrita with salt. It seemed like a good idea.

The old woman behind the bar had to be the wife of the scholarly-looking *cantinero* I had talked to the night before. The lines of her face were set into a permanent defiant frown; no matter how bad the news was, she was ready for it.

I ordered a Sangrita, some salt and a beer. I asked her about the gentleman behind the bar last night.

"He's at mass." She jerked her head toward the door and up the street. "It's Sunday," she explained.

I tossed off the Sangrita, chased it with the salt and the beer and felt my head shrink. "I was talking to him last night about this boy." I showed her the picture. "Do you know him?"

"No." She barely glanced at it before shoving it back at me.

"A man with a bad complexion, holes in his face like from smallpox? His name is Morelos, maybe. You know where I can find him?" I put a five-hundred-peso note on the bar and finished my beer.

I noticed her eyes shift momentarily from mine to the money and then over my shoulder to the round-faced man in the booth just as her husband had done the night before.

"No," she repeated, and turned her back to me. She began to take cans of Tecate out of a case and place them inside a cooler.

I wrote down my room number across the street on a matchbook cover. "In case you remember. Or your husband." I placed the matchbook cover on the money.

She ignored it.

I got up and went outside.

Both the old man and his wife had checked out the kid's father with their eyes as soon as I had started asking questions. That bothered me. The kid's father was more than just the neighborhood drunk and they were afraid of him. It didn't mean they knew anything, but it meant that if they did, they probably wouldn't spill it now.

Congratulations, York. Way to go.

I walked back up Revolucion to Tijuana Tillie's and paid to park my car another day. I had breakfast *alfresco*, leaning on the hood of my Maverick with a half-dozen *carnitas* from a street vendor and a quart of orange juice. I couldn't decide whether to stay and keep my eyes peeled for another day, pack it in and drive back over the border, or go to the bullfights. The chances of getting anywhere doing what I was doing weren't as bad as the Padres winning the pennant that year, but almost.

I threw the napkins and the orange juice container into my car and walked back downtown to Coahuila, where the elite meet.

The Padres get paid for playing out all their bad seasons, but I was in it for True Love. Fuck it.

I sat outside the Hotel Nelson for a while in the sidewalk café watching the happy tourists on one side of the street and the cripples, winos, dope dealers, junkies and existential desperadoes on the other. It was a real study. As I sat there sipping coffee and Sangrita, I thought about what it means to be on the border. The border between one thing and another: the United States and Mexico, IRA accounts and just getting through the day, being human and being something else, the Optimist's Club and the Heart of Darkness, the few miles between going out for Chinese food on a gay impulse at one in the morning and a whole church congregation praying out loud that the government doesn't raise the price of tortillas another peso. I watched Ed and Evelyn Mastercard take pictures of Yaqui mothers in colorful native garb and their artfully dirty-faced beggar children against the backdrop of Mariachi Square. That was on one side of the street. On the other side, out in front of the Dragon Rojo Bar, were pensioners from the Federalis, deserters from the Sandanistas missing parts of themselves and illegal migrant farmers too old and too tired to make the run anymore, drinking their disability compensation out of bottles of bad mescal.

On the border.

I thought about Juana and I thought about myself. Love and loneliness.

I thought about Herman Villez and the unmarked graves in

Otay Mesa. Reina was probably right about that, but I wasn't
going to tell that to Juana unless I was sure.

After sitting there for an hour I got up and walked back toward
the Delicias Bar. Ten o'clock mass was over by now and there was
a chance I could intercept the old bartender and talk to him
without an audience.

The old woman was still there. The place had filled up a little,
but there was no sign of the scholar, the kid or the kid's father.
The old woman gave me a steely look and jerked her head toward
the door. Several regulars followed her gaze and gave me more of
the same.

York had eighty-sixed himself with his Sergeant Friday routine
and his pile of pesos.

I nodded and left.

I decided to check out of the hotel, get my toothbrush and my
jacket and just walk. Later I would go back to La Charrita or to the
Copacabana or somewhere. This time I would just keep my eyes
open and my mouth shut.

It was a little too late for that.

When I turned the key in my hotel room door, I discovered it
was no longer locked. I tried to swing it open but something was
blocking it about halfway. I stepped back from the door and to
the left as the cops do in movies when they pull their .38s and yell,
"Police!"

I didn't have a .38 and all I could think of to yell was, "Hey!"

The silence was something I could feel high in my chest and on
the back of my neck.

After a full ten seconds had passed, I knelt on the floor of the
hallway and craned my neck around the bottom of the doorjamb.
I was looking at the sole of a size-ten shoe, toe pointed downward. Beyond that I could see a liver-spotted hand stretched
palm upward toward the bedpost on the floor. A silver cufflink
glistened against a patch of starched white shirt. The shoes were
polished wing tips, the pants were charcoal gray with permanent
polyester creases. Sunday best. I stood up and shifted position so
that I could see that the room was empty except for the old man. I
got up and stepped over him. I knelt and put a finger against the

scholar's neck and saw where he had been hit in the back of the head. There was no blood, just an ugly mark that looked like a bruise on a grapefruit. His skin was colder than a San Francisco summer.

His other hand was closed over a matchbook cover from La Charrita. In pencil I had written "Azteca de Oro #4."

I picked up the phone next to the bed. It was as dead as the bartender but that didn't mean anything. It was just a telephone in Tijuana.

I went out and closed the door after me. When I looked down the hall, I saw someone peering around the corner of the stairwell at me. He was wearing a white cowboy hat. He turned and launched himself down the stairs.

I ran after him.

As I passed the desk I shouted at the clerk, "Call the police." But the desk clerk was taking an early siesta.

I lost him almost immediately in a sea of cowboy hats on Constitucion. I chased two of them down but they were the wrong cowboy hats.

When I thought to look for a Datsun pickup, I saw one. It peeled out of the parking lot of Silva's Auto Body and headed down Constitucion going the wrong way.

I thought I had let the old man's murderer get away and then realized that I hadn't really. I was wearing his clothes and I was going to wake up with him tomorrow and shave him in my mirror.

The police were there only forty-five minutes after I called from the desk. The clerk woke up when they arrived and seemed worried. The cops probably came around only once a week to pick up their envelopes and this wasn't the day.

One of them was a motorcycle cop, a flabby kid of about twenty-three in an imitation CHiPs outfit. He stood around outside striking poses of macho authority and saying, "Stand back," to anyone who happened to walk by.

I showed his partner the room and the dead man.

The partner was from the *judiciales,* or felony police, dressed in plainclothes; a white *Guayabera* shirt, white slacks and *hurachis.*

With one hand he played pocket pool with himself and with the other he examined my ID.

"So you're a play cop," he said, handing me back my wallet, still looking at the Wolf Security Systems card. "I hope you weren't playing cop around here."

"I'm looking for a kid."

"You *were* playing cop around here." He shook his head sadly and sat down on the edge of the hotel bed. He pointed at the body with his foot. "What about him?"

"He runs the bar across—"

"I know who he is. Why is he dead?"

"He had some information for me, I think, about the guy I'm looking for. That's my writing on the matchbook cover. Maybe somebody decided to kill him before he could tell me anything, but I don't think so. I think it was an accident."

"An accident," he repeated, and nodded somberly in an exaggerated way. He lifted the few gray strands of hair away from the large discoloration on the back of the corpse's neck. "Why didn't I think of that?"

"He must have decided to wait for me and had the clerk let him in for . . . a small consideration, but somebody had beat him to the idea of waiting for me. When he walked in, whoever was in here thought it was me returning and caved in his skull. My guess is they wanted me unconscious long enough to go through my ID and see who it was that was asking all the questions in the neighborhood last night and to put me off asking any more. But the old man couldn't take it. It killed him."

The cop laughed as if at some private joke. He started shaking his head again and picked up the phone. It seemed to work. He announced himself as Detective Bevilaqua and asked for the other cop, whose name was Manosa. He told him to send for a car from the morgue. As an afterthought he told him to send up the desk clerk.

"You want to start again? From the beginning? I'm just an ignorant Third World law enforcement officer and I didn't understand a fucking word you just said. Try hard to make me understand. Think about a long sentence in a Mexican jail and make it clear to me how you didn't kill this guy."

Bevilaqua didn't think I killed him, but unless I satisfied him that there wasn't something going on in his territory that he should be on top of, he could put me away indefinitely. He didn't want to be embarrassed and he didn't want to be insulted with bullshit so I didn't give him any. I told him about Juana and her brother. I told him about "Morelos" and his pockmarks. I told him about the bartender and the kid and the kid's father. I told him about the *pollero* in the white cowboy hat and his Datsun pickup truck. He took all this in with an unhappy expression. He showed a brief flash of interest at the mention of Morelos and his pockmarks but went back to looking like a tired father listening to his daughter tell him she was pregnant.

"You know," he said, peering at me as if I were far away, "You don't look so fuckin' stupid. What's the matter with you?"

"I'm in love."

"What?" He looked at me as if I had just stood on my head and started singing "Embraceable You."

"I'm in love with the girl who's missing the brother."

"Shit."

"Yeah."

Bevilaqua looked at the body, touched the part of its head that had been crushed by a blackjack or the butt of a gun. "He was hit sometime in the last couple of hours, say between ten and now. It still just looks like a bruise. It won't in a little while."

The desk clerk showed up and Bevilaqua asked him if I was in my room this morning between ten and twelve. He said no.

"Who else did you let in here besides him?" He indicated the body.

"No one."

"You're lying." He spoke very quietly. "I'll find out if I have to arrest you and every whore in this roach farm. When someone is murdered in our 'little village' without my permission I want to know who did it. You'll tell me here or you will tell me in a cage."

"He wore a hat," the clerk said, "a cowboy hat. He had bad teeth. I see him around sometimes, but I don't know him." The words came slowly as if each one cost him a lot. They probably did.

That was good enough. Either Bevilaqua wanted corroboration on my story or recognized the description of Wild Bill Tooth Decay or both.

"Get out of here," he said to the clerk. The clerk got out of there. "He wasn't robbed," he said. It was a statement, not a question. Neither of us had checked, but it was a safe bet.

"If he was, it was just to make it look good," I said.

Bevilaqua reached into the dead man's pants pockets and produced a few crumpled peso notes. He pointed to the cufflinks, a turquoise ring and a Timex watch. All of it might have been worth thirty dollars, but people have been killed for less.

"You think it was an accident, Mr. Play Detective York? Let me tell you something. You know what you're fucking around with here? You know how much money there is on the border waiting to get across? You think the local businessmen wouldn't kill you or him"—he jerked his head at the body—"over a few stupid questions. People as stupid as you should wear a bell around their neck so that everyone can get out of your way before you get them killed."

We walked downstairs and stood around in front of the hotel for a while smoking cigarettes and not saying anything to each other.

When the station wagon from the morgue arrived and the attendants carried out the old scholar, I saw his wife. She watched the attendants put the body into the car and then walked over to where I was standing next to Bevilaqua's car. Her expression hadn't changed, her eyes were drier than a Mormon wedding.

She spat at the ground between my feet and walked back across the street.

Bevilaqua came out and got in the driver's seat. "Get in."

"Where to?"

"Just get in. You got a car?"

"Tijuana Tillie's."

"It figures."

I watched the morgue wagon pull out ahead of us and said, "I didn't even know his name."

"His name was Caruso, like the singer, you know. He started out very young running booze during prohibition when they had the tunnel. When prohibition ended he would run the *alambristas* but that was still in the days when it wasn't work for animals.

When they started the *Bracero* program, he retired and opened a bar. He didn't like the new blood in the *coyote* business and he never shut up about it. He didn't have any friends left on the street. He was ripe for some asshole like you to get him killed."

"His wife didn't seem surprised."

"No."

"Am I under arrest?" I asked as we pulled into the parking lot at Tijuana Tillie's. I noticed that Manosa followed us on his motorcycle.

"Get in your car."

I got in the Maverick. The *carnita* wrappers had been frying in the sun and it smelled like a charnel house.

Bevilaqua walked over to my window. I rolled it down.

"We're going to escort you to the border. You will never show your face here again. Not while I'm here. If I see you in Tijuana I will just have to figure that you are going to get someone else killed. I'll put you in a cage and you will die there. The Pope couldn't get you out of my jail. You understand?"

I didn't say anything, just nodded.

"The quiet American," he said. "You come back here, you die. Got it?"

"It's a nice switch from 'Don't leave town.' "

"Move."

It took ten minutes to the San Diego turnoff and forty minutes in line for the inspection station. It was Sunday afternoon and all the tourists were heading back for cocktail hour, barbecued burgers, the Disney channel for the kids, a little Johnny Carson and bed. Bevilaqua and Manosa inched their way up in line along with me. Bevilaqua behind me and Manosa right alongside.

When I got to the U.S. inspection station, a girl with a red pony tail and a customs uniform asked me if I had anything to declare.

"Memories," I told her, "just memories."

She waved me through. I waved goodbye to the cops but they didn't wave goodbye to me.

6

THE CODEINE and the Ancient Age were making me sleepy. I sat at the bar in the Low Down and listened to the Police sing "Every Breath You Take" while I waited for Juana. The bridge of my nose was a distant point of pain and my right eye was completely closed. While I waited, I tried to think of a way to tell Juana that I had found nothing. I wondered what was taking her so long. I was so tired I was having trouble keeping my other eye open.

I caught Suzy Lee on her next trip to the service bar and asked her what was keeping Juana.

"She traded with Liz so she could go on now. She wants to show you her new routine. I helped her with it."

"Right." I leaned back, lit a cigarette, held the cold glass of Coke against my eye. I would have thought she'd be eager for news of her brother, but since I didn't have any, it could wait all right. When the Police had finished the song, Larry the DJ announced Juana.

The opening bars of Billy Idol's "White Wedding" chimed crazily through the room and the galloping bass line got my circulation going again. Juana burst onto the stage in a flurry of white lingerie and a wedding veil that reached to the floor. White shoes, white textured stockings sheathing her thighs, white garter belt and G-string, white corset and the headpiece all swirled around her as she danced with a kind of manic energy. It was startling, almost surreal somehow. The white against the smooth brown of her flesh was undeniably sexy. Maybe I was just stoned or punchy, but there seemed to be something vaguely wrong about it and I suddenly felt even more tired than I thought I was.

I noticed her hair had been cut and styled in an angular, new wave chop. She had also added some radically different moves to her routine such as bringing her arms together, hunching her shoulders forward and shaking her breasts out of her corset. In only two days she had taken huge strides in turning pro and I didn't like it.

I wondered what the hell was the matter with me besides having had a beastly day at the office.

When she finished dancing to three songs and had nothing left on but her G-string, she blew me a kiss and motioned for me to wait for her.

I noticed another mannerism she had developed over the weekend—she kept bringing her hand up to her nose and sniffing.

She emerged from the backstage area along with Liz. They both ran toward me. Juana hugged me quickly while Liz jumped up and down saying, "Whattya think? Whattya think?"

"Ah . . ." I tried to grin. Juana reached out and lightly touched my eye.

"No. Oh no. What happened, York?"

"It's okay. Just a stupid accident."

Juana kissed me on the temple. "Did you get in trouble in Mexico?" she whispered. Her hands fluttered nervously.

"No." I took her hands and held them to keep them still. "It's really embarrassing. I walked into a sidewalk, that's all."

Liz said, "What a spastic, York. Hey whattya think of Juana's act?"

"It's fine. Liz, I've got to talk to Juana. You mind?"

She turned abruptly, her hand to her nose, sniffing. "Why should I mind?"

Juana had thrown a kimono on and wore sandals. We walked to the back of the room where the pool table was. No one was using it at the moment. "I'm afraid to ask you about Herman," she said.

"I didn't find him, but I'm not finished looking."

She surprised me again by taking a cigarette out of my shirt pocket and lighting it. She didn't inhale.

"The best thing to do is to get in touch with Walters," I continued. "Maybe he can turn up Morelos. I couldn't, but I got close without knowing it. Give me that card he gave you."

"No, York. That would just cause trouble for me. You too."

"What makes you think so?"

"He owns this place. We both work for him. He has made it clear that he does not want to discuss my brother. He gave me the name of the *coyote* and as far as he is concerned his hands are washed of the matter. He said it was more than he would have done for someone else."

She was speaking faster than usual and waving the cigarette, pausing now and then to wipe at her nose. I kept telling myself it was none of my business if she wanted to do coke. I kept telling myself I wasn't going to chew Liz out for giving it to her.

"When did he say all this?"

"He was here last night."

"Did you tell him I was looking for your brother and Morelos?"

"No. I told you, he did not want to talk about it at all." She brightened, put out her cigarette. "He says he is bringing an agent from Los Angeles to see me dance. I've been working hard, can you tell?"

"I bet you've been up all night." I smiled at her. "Juana, give me the card. Let me talk to him. The worst he can do is hang up on me."

"York, this means a lot to me, this agent coming. I don't want to get Mr. Walters mad."

It was my turn to get mad. "Your brother may be in trouble, Juana. Walters is the only link to Morelos on this side of the border. Now, do you want me to find him or not? Make up your mind."

She looked into her lap and said, "Yes, I do. Of course I do. Wait here and I'll get the card."

I caught her arm and turned her toward me. "I'm sorry. I'm tired, that's all. Don't worry about it. I'll be the soul of discretion with him."

She went backstage again to get her purse. Liz had come on and was spinning around the stage at 78 rpm to the theme from *Flashdance.* Juana gave me the card and wiped her nose again.

"How about lunch tomorrow?" I asked her.

"I can't, York. I have to rehearse all week. I'll see you at work tomorrow night."

"Sure." She kissed me on the lips and I went home to bed.

I had warped codeine dreams about bartenders with death's heads, cocaine, Conan the Barbarian, cops and white weddings.

In the morning I fixed myself an omelette with scallions from my neighbor's garden and some cheese from my refrigerator that wasn't all green. I didn't eat much of it because I couldn't taste anything with my nose full of swollen tissue and coagulated blood. The swelling had gone down some on my eye and I could see out of it, but it was going to be a classic shiner. Halfway through my second cup of coffee the phone rang. It was Gordon, the night man at the Hillcrest.

"Where the fuck is my car, man? I had to take a cab to Mission Valley. If there's anything wrong with it . . . if there is one little fucking scratch on the motherfucker . . ."

"Sorry, I forgot about it. It's okay."

"You owe me six bucks for cab fare and I need my car back now."

"You owe me ten bucks on the Padres-Mets game. Take another cab to the Hillcrest and pick up your car. I'll still owe you a drink, okay?"

"Not okay. Fifty on the Dodgers next Sunday."

"The Dodgers and who?"

"Chicago."

"Jesus."

"Hey, man!"

"Okay. Okay."

I drove to the Hillcrest in Gordon's TransAm and parked it. From the phone booth outside the check-cashing place I called the North County number on the gold-embossed card that said E. Walters on it.

It rang three times and then a taped voice that might have belonged to a disc jockey on one of the "mellow stations" said, "No one is available to take your call at present, please leave your name and number and someone will get back to you at the earliest opportunity."

I waited for the tone and said, "My name is York, I work at the Low Down in San Diego and I need to speak to Mr. Walters about Nabor Morelos." I left my phone number.

It took fifteen minutes to start up my Maverick.

I drove it back to my apartment and played my guitar, an old Gibson acoustic, until I could go back to sleep again. I played Sonny Boy Williamson songs and Muddy Waters songs and Robert Johnson songs, but they didn't sound the way I wanted them to. They never did. I put down the guitar in the middle of "Love in Vain" and slept on the couch.

When I woke up, it was time to put on my uniform and go to work.

I figured something was wrong when I arrived at the Low Down about seven-thirty and Dick Holster was standing at the door again. It was supposed to be Dick's night off and my night on. He looked comfortable in the steel blue, epauletted shirt and matching pants in a way that I probably never did. "What are you doing here?"

"I got a feeling you're being rotated out. Maynard wants to see you." He jerked his head inside.

"Rotated out. Quaint, Dick, quaint."

"Hey, York." He stopped me as I brushed past him and a carload of drunken businessmen guffawing their way into the club. "I don't know what's going down, but I'm working, you know? Whatever happens . . . don't get . . . pissed off or something. Not while I'm on the door. Okay?"

"And go up against Audie Murphy?" I crossed the bar area toward Maynard's office, looking around for Juana. I didn't see her. I knocked at Maynard's door twice and then opened it.

The room smelled like aftershave and coffee. The walls were

hung with autographed pictures of former dancers who had gone on to greatness in diet soda commercials and porno films. Maynard sat behind a desk piled with liquor invoices, empty coffee cups, a telephone, a calculator and paperweights with little figurines of naked people inside who would ball each other if you jiggled them just right. Maynard was watching the news with the sound off and listening to Neil Diamond on the radio. He looked up at me and smiled grimly, leaned forward and massaged the bridge of his nose as if to say, "It's lonely at the top . . . uneasy lies the head . . . a man's gotta do what a man's gotta do." What he said was, "Sit down."

I said no thanks.

Maynard's eye started twitching. He did that whenever there was trouble in the club, something nasty for the bouncers. He was pudgy and balding and looked forty though he once told me he was only twenty-nine. "Don't spread it around" he'd advised me conspiratorially. "My mature looks inspire confidence, you know?" I never told him that his looks wouldn't inspire confidence in a neurotic three-year-old. I just stood there staring at his little David Niven mustache, knowing what was coming, but trying to think of some way to get it out of him without a lot of mealy-mouthed bullshit. "What's going on, Maynard?"

"York, I'm afraid that—"

"Don't be afraid, Maynard."

He looked up at me squinting, his left eye twitching away. "What's wrong with your eye?"

"What's wrong with yours? Maynard, why is Dick Holster out there working my shift?"

"York, I'm afraid . . . York, I'm going to have to let you go." He stared at a bill from the Coors distributor.

"Why?"

"I got a call from Mr. Walters this afternoon. I don't know what it's about, but he asked me if you worked here, I said that you did and he told me to let you go. Now, you probably know more about this than I do. He sent a car, a limo, for Juana and she's gone too. It's always bad when an employee gets involved with one of the girls. I told you that when you started here and obviously this is something that—"

"Where did they take her?"

"I don't know and if I did—"

I reached across the desk and pulled his fat necktie toward me. With my other hand I picked up a letter opener that had "No news is good news" carved into the blade and a magnifying glass pommel. I stabbed his tie and drove the blade into the desk, pinning his face six inches from the Coors bill. "Where did they take Juana?"

"I don't know. Goddammit, York!" He worked his necktie loose and started to reach for the buzzer under the desk. I grabbed his wrist.

"When did they come?"

"About an hour ago. When Juana came in they were waiting for her."

"They?"

"A chauffeur and you know, a guy."

"A goon. Okay, one more time, Maynard. Where?"

"I swear I don't know."

"Did they take anything else? What about her papers? You keep her phony green card in the safe, don't you? Did they take that too?"

He pushed himself away from the desk and stood up. "You're in trouble, York. You know I'll call the cops."

"Call them. They might like to see the safe too."

"You can't intimidate me. You're a fool if you think that I'm going to deal—"

I hit him with the back of my hand. Not hard, just enough to mottle his face a little. He stood for a moment staring at me rigidly. His eye had stopped twitching, but now he started looking back and forth between the door and the desk where the buzzer was. "Don't think about it, Maynard. And please don't say something like, 'You'll pay for this.' " He sat back down. "Now, let's say you don't know where they took her. Fine. Tell me about the green card, Maynard."

"Yes. They took it with them."

"Good. We're doing good, Maynard. Tell me the name on her card. Is it a hot card with somebody else's name on it or is it a phony with her name?"

"It says Juana Villez. Her own name." He was mumbling.

"Now you're going to give me Walters's address, not Wolf

Enterprises, his home address." I picked up one of the paper-weights and started making the little figures bounce around the liquid in the glass like drunken acrobats.

"I can't," he whispered, "I can't possibly do that." He looked really frightened. I was beginning to depress myself. Anybody can bully someone like Maynard. Anyone at all.

"Try. I figure it's in this office somewhere and I'll get it anyway. You know what I mean?"

"Shit," he said. "Oh shit." He slowly opened the Rolodex on his desk to the W's. I found the address in Rancho Santa Palma and pulled it out of the file.

On my way out I said, "I could use a letter of recommendation, Maynard. I've been with the firm for three months now and this misunderstanding could reflect on my résumé. If you could find it in your heart to kind of weasel-word something nice for me, you know, about my punctuality and personal grooming, that kind of thing, well, it might come in handy if I find myself looking for work in a sleaze pit like this again. No no, don't say anything, take your time and think about it. I understand how these things are." I closed his door and left him staring at the television set as if I'd never been there.

Dick Holster stopped me by the cigarette machine and said, "What was that all about? You got canned, right? Something about the Mexican girl, I figure."

"You know where they took her?"

"No, man, I don't. But she was hot. She'll probably be dancing up in L.A. Here." Dick handed me a cocktail napkin with something written on it. "You've worked behind a stick before, right? This place always seems to be hiring."

I took it from him and said thanks.

"Keep in touch," he called after me.

I drove up 15 to Rancho Santa Palma. It took about twenty minutes. The sun had set but the clouds were still stained with the color of cheap California rosé wine. I passed General Dynamics and Miramar Naval Air Station, reminders that paradise is ground zero. Fighter planes floated gracefully toward or away from the landing fields like slow, outsized and deadly insects.

Rancho Santa Palma was the place for money. New or old, it didn't matter. Coronado and La Jolla had the old money in San Diego, places like Rancho Bernardo and Carlsbad had the new money, but none of them had as much of it as Rancho Santa Palma. I drove through the town itself, which was nothing but a dozen banks and twice as many liquor stores, until I found the street I wanted. The address on the Rolodex card took me to a winding country road lined with eucalyptus, manicured yucca, oleander and hibiscus trees dotted with wrought iron gates and tasteful mailboxes at the mouths of discreetly shaded driveways. Santa Palma Drive snaked its way up the mesa and the driveways got more manicured, tasteful and discreet.

Walters's house was at the top of the hill, set back from the cul-de-sac "vista point" that looked out on Lake Hodges, Escondido and Mira Mesa. The mailbox was guarded by a pair of small jockeys with their faces painted black. The gate was de rigueur wrought iron and locked. A wolf's head was fashioned into the spiked bars and the name "Walters" was emblazoned in gold leaf above the intercom box. I got out of my car and pressed the talk button.

"Yes?" a woman's voice answered.

"I'm from Neiman Marcus in Fashion Valley. I have a package for Mr. Walters."

"One moment please." I waited and watched the lights come on in the valley below. It was fully dark now.

"Yes, what is it?" It was the disc jockey voice on the answering machine I had heard that morning.

"Neiman Marcus. I've got a box, it's pretty big. I think it's a, you know, like a planter or something. It's from a Mr. . . . I can't read the tag, it's too dark."

"You're delivering a package at eight-thirty in the evening?"

"Look, my truck swallowed a valve this afternoon and I'm using this guy's car. I've delivered everything except this one. If you want it tomorrow, that's okay with me. I've got the overtime anyway. Sorry to bother you."

There was no answer except for a harsh electronic tone. The gate snicked open and I pushed it wide enough to drive through. I got in my car and took it up the driveway. I was a little disappointed—the grounds weren't much bigger than Balboa Park and the house had fewer columns than the Parthenon. At the head of the driveway, I could see the Mexican maid in the light from two carriage lanterns. The lights were on either side of a Mediterranean, dark-paneled door that probably cost as much as a decent used car but didn't match the colonial theme of the rest of the place. She waved me toward the back of the house. I ignored her, killed the engine on my car and got out of it.

"No. Bring it around to the rear please," she said in perfect English.

"I want to see Walters, excuse me." I brushed past her into the hallway.

"Wait, you can't go in." She ran after me. I stopped.

"Did a limousine bring a young Mexican girl here tonight? Very pretty, couldn't have missed her."

"Who are you?" She didn't wait for a reply but started calling for someone named Carlos. I kept right on walking. I walked through a sunken living room with animal skin rugs and uncomfortable-looking furniture, climbed back up and passed through a dining room which was separated from the patio and pool area by sliding glass doors. The lights were on out there and someone was in the pool.

He was treading water in the deep end and his blond hair wasn't wet. He looked at me and opened his mouth just a little in surprise. Something about him reminded me of an overfed David Bowie. "Where is she, Walters?" I said.

He didn't answer, but climbed up the rungs on the other side of the pool, his back to me. He was taking his time.

I started to move toward him, but I was grabbed around the armpits from behind in a full nelson. I couldn't turn my head far enough to see who was holding me, but he was at least my size and in good shape. He was wearing a black or midnight blue velour jacket and he smelled as if he had been interrupted smoking a joint.

Walters put a robe over his milky pink body. He wasn't fat so much as shapeless and doughy. "You must be York," he said in his mellow voice. He smiled and put on his square, rimless glasses. Now he looked like a Hollywood Nazi . . . or an Orange County evangelist. "If I tell Carlos to let you go, will you sit down and behave yourself?"

"Tell me where Juana is and I'll think about it."

Carlos lifted me a foot and a half and, still holding me by the armpits, drop-kicked me, his knee digging into the small of my back. "I'll kick your ass up and down, shitheap. Just give me a reason. It's my job and I like it and I don't get to do it often enough."

From inside the house the phone rang. Walters stood and watched me with real amusement while I grimaced and then the maid came out and told him a Mr. Lyons was on the phone. Mr. Lyons was Maynard.

"Have a seat, York. You boys behave for a moment, eh?" He turned and left me to Carlos, who let go of me and shoved me toward a barca lounger. I sat down gingerly on my tailbone and grinned at Carlos. He had long, straight black hair and a beefy face with Indian features and wore mirror sunglasses though the only light came from lanterns around the pool. He grinned back at me and pointed his finger, working his thumb like the hammer of a pistol.

"You got that from Charles Bronson," I said.

"Shut up." His grin evaporated.

"Why don't you smoke another joint, you'll be in a better mood. I won't tell your boss."

He started to walk toward me strangling fistfuls of air. "I told you to shut up."

Walters came walking back out carrying a whiskey and ice in a glass the size of a child's sandpail. "You boys getting along? That was Maynard warning me that you might be on your way. He must have sat there squirming for forty-five minutes trying to decide whether to call me or leave town. Leaving town would require too much in the way of assertion for Maynard, don't you think? I always employ predictable people, Mr. York. You can have your talented people, your loyal people, your qualified people, give me someone predictable every time and it won't matter if they're incompetent or greedy or"—he smiled at Carlos—"psychotic. You see, you can count on them, make plans around them." He sat down at the poolside table across from me and folded his robe over his lap like an old spinster entertaining the vicar. "That brings us to you. You are enamored of Miss Villez. I have plans for her, perhaps she told you something about them. They are sizable plans, very sizable. Now a man in love is about as unpredictable as you can get, wouldn't you agree, Mr. York? And I've just told you where I stand on unpredictable employees." He tossed off a good third of his drink. "Which leaves you out of the picture."

"I want to know where she is, Walters. I also want to know about the *coyote* you told her about that would bring her brother across."

He got to his feet and slammed his glass onto the metal table. "You will *not* concern yourself with Miss Villez, her affairs or mine. I am seeing to all of that business about her brother and doing a better job of it than you can, believe me. Now I welcome this opportunity to put it to you nicely, civilly, but it's the only time it will be that way."

"I'll find her, Walters."

"You don't understand me." He leaned across the table and put his face close enough to mine so that I could smell the mints and Scotch on his breath and the chlorine in the towel around his shoulders. "You will *not* find her. You will never get close to her. I will see to that. I'm finished talking to you." He got up, wiped at his forehead with the towel and sucked at his drink again. "Carlos will explain further and see you out." He nodded to Charles Bronson's understudy and walked through the sliding doors to the kitchen. He paused, stuck his head out the door. "I really hope we never see each other again, Mr. York. For your sake."

No puckish retorts presented themselves. I was too pissed off to think and Carlos was moving closer. I turned to him and started crabwalking toward the dining room. "I'm going, okay? Take it easy."

He walked me back through the house. I took my time and looked around. Zebra-striped African shields decorated the walls of the dining room, clashing with what might have been a genuine lead-lined Tiffany shade over the table. Around it were antique mahogany captain's chairs that might have come from an old clipper ship, but didn't belong. Nothing did, at least not with each other. When we got to the living room, I saw a full-sized portrait of Walters over the fireplace. It looked as if some Tijuana street artist had done it. Red velvet drapes and bolsters and flocking paper gave the impression of too goddamned much red, like a Nevada whorehouse. I hoped Lenny Bruce wouldn't mind and I said, "It looks like some queen went nuts in here with a staple gun."

"The door's this way, shitheap."

He escorted me to my car and then pushed my face into the window on the driver's side. It hurt my nose. He leaned against me pressing my face into the glass. I brought my heel up against his knee and raked downward. He made a noise like he was trying to swallow a rusty door hinge and a bicycle horn. I turned and punched through one of the lenses on his sunglasses. I cut up my knuckle doing it. He staggered back, but came at me again too quickly. He hit me in the stomach and I doubled over. Then he brought his knee up against my face, which was already bleeding again and I almost passed out. He opened the car door and piled me into the front seat.

"Dig this," he said. "Walters doesn't want to see you again. Me, I'd love it. Adios, shitheap."

I started the car, trying not to black out, and backed it up. I threw it into forward and hit the gas. Gravel spun out beneath me and Carlos dove out of my way into a hedge. The gate was still open at the end of the drive, but it closed just as I passed it.

I drove too fast back to my apartment trying to get to the goddamned icepack again.

Over the next few days I ate a box of NoDoz and put a thousand miles on the Maverick. I drank my rent money at Walters's joints in L.A. and Carmel and looked for Juana. Asking anyone about her at either club was probably not a good idea since Walters had a Wolf Security Systems ID photo of me he had probably passed around to his bouncers and bartenders, probably the girls too. Of course I had a mustache now, and a beard on the way, but they would still be alerted to anyone asking about Juana at all. So I just sat, drank a lot of beer and ate a lot of microwave burritos and potato chips. Every once in a while, I would go out to sleep in my car, but not before I had given some likely-looking drinking buddy a few bucks to come and wake me up if a Mexican girl that looked like a cross between a young Joan Baez and a younger

Sophia Loren came onstage. After four days I was convinced Juana wasn't at either place. Walters had her stashed somewhere.

I spent ten dollars in change in a phone booth in West Hollywood calling every acting school, dance or voice instructor whose name I could turn up. I figured Walters's "sizable plans" had to do with making Juana a star of some kind. I was counting on the fact that he was too greedy to waste her on porno films. If I was wrong, of course, I'd kill him.

Before I had left, I'd gone to Liz's apartment. She jabbered at me about how wonderful it was; the limo and Juana headed for the big time and all. She had told Liz especially to tell me that she would call as soon as she knew where she would be.

After four days of bad food, too little sleep and no luck, I headed back to San Diego. Maybe Juana could get a phone call past Walters after all. The first thing I did when I got home was to check my answering machine. She hadn't. Not yet.

I stood in line at the unemployment office and went to the beach a lot. I ate a lot and drank a lot and watched television too much and slept too much. A few times someone had tried to call while I was out and had hung up, but people do that all the time. Liz hadn't heard anything either. When I got a final disconnect notice from the phone company, I knew I had to go back to work somewhere. I remembered the cocktail napkin Dick Holster had given me with something about a bartender's job. The information would be three weeks out of date, but what the hell, I didn't have any other ideas.

I found my old uniform in the bottom of my closet where I had thrown it the night I had gotten back from Walters's place. It was still full of blood from where Carlos had opened my nose. In the shirt pocket I found the cocktail napkin. It said, "Silver Sands Yacht Club/Bartender. See Big Bob," and gave a phone number. I called it.

7

THE SILVER SANDS SHORES is what they call a "waterfront community." It was built on a landfill road between Coronado, an island full of wealthy retired admirals living with their parents, and Imperial Beach, a shabby border town full of bikers and rednecks. The Shores was the kind of place you might like to live after your first million if boats and Bloody Marys were your idea of a good time. The houses were all too close together as if they were huddling and afraid of something, the lawns looked like postage stamps and the trees and shrubbery were as calculated as a corporate tax return. Outside of everyone's sliding glass kitchen door was a ramp leading to a slip with a boat that was hopefully bigger than the neighbor's boat. There was no one on the streets or the patios, all the Chryslers and Lincolns were in their garages behind remote-control doors, I didn't see any bicycles or roller skates and no one was on the boats; they just sat there in a row, covered with canvas like half-beached white sea elephants, skewered by masts and cobwebbed with rigging.

It looked like everyone had died and gone to Republican heaven.

The yacht club was situated at the end of a street called Whispering Winds Boulevard in a lonely spot on top of rocks and landfill just beginning to sprout clover and Bermuda grass. On one side was the bay and on the other was the channel. The club itself was a one-story building with picture windows facing out onto a parking lot and a real estate office. On the sides that afforded a beautiful view of the channel and the bay were walls covered with trophies, stuffed swordfish and flags and a bar with a dozen stools flanking it.

I walked in and was greeted by the man closest to me. He must have weighed three hundred plus pounds and his freckled ass hung out of his white duck pants between his belt and his XXLarge polo shirt with all the coyness of high noon. "Can I help you find something?" he said.

"You're Big Bob?"

"Bob Glenson." He nodded, looking down his rum blossom nose at me as if he were used to wearing bifocals or maybe just looking down his nose. "You have the advantage of me, young man." He had five empty martini glasses in front of him. A three-toed sloth would have had an advantage on him.

"My name is York and I'm here about a job." I looked meaningfully at the guy behind the bar. He was maybe seventy years old and his hands shook spilling Beefeaters all over himself. He went to spray some tonic from a soda gun into a glass and it erupted, spraying everyone near him.

"Then get back there and serve up a few deep-dish martinis. Hey, everybody, here's our new bartender. Looks the part, doesn't he? Clean-cut."

I had trimmed my beard, but it was still a beard. My hair was long, clean and blown dry, but it was still long. I wore my Hawaiian shirt. Big Bob considered himself a wry old devil, a master of ironic wit.

"Let me introduce you." Big Bob waved his cocktail shaker full of gin at the other boys while Marv doddered out from behind the bar. "That's Marv and this is Bill and here's ole Tom and this is Dwayne. Everyone of them bad niggers at boss dice."

I went behind the bar and checked out the speedrack, replaced the tank full of quinine and studied the price list taped to the old Sweda cash register. It was a toy bar and I could run it in my sleep. I made a few deep-dish martinis and handed them around. I listened to the sounds of dice rolling in leather cups, a lot of jokes about sheenies, polacks and beaners and laughter that was too loud and hearty.

I had a job again. Whoopee.

Two weeks went by and I still hadn't heard from Juana. I drove back up to L.A. and Carmel twice and made more phone calls. Nothing. Liz hadn't heard either. It was as if the earth had opened up and swallowed her. It seemed to run in the family. After a while I stopped eating and sleeping too much and seemed to lose interest in both. Everything tasted like cardboard, and when I slept, my dreams had a mocking quality to them. I still drank. One night, I drove back up to Walters's place in Rancho Santa Palma and rattled the gates, shouted incomprehensible threats and smashed a half-empty fifth of bourbon against his intercom. On my way back down the hill, I passed two squad cars that the maid had threatened to call. Walters hadn't even been home for all I knew.

I couldn't understand why Juana hadn't tried to reach me. Unless Walters had her under guard every minute, which didn't seem likely, she could have made a call or mailed a letter. Maybe Walters had sold her on his ability to find Herman and the idea that I would be bad medicine for her career, in which case he would have another "predictable employee" on his hands. Walters knew the extent of her ambition . . . and would know how to use it.

Once, on the phone, Liz told me, "Look, honey, I'm sorry, but she's doing what she wants to do, you know. Walters can do a lot for her. A hunk like you, what are you worried about? Ask Suzy Lee out for Chrissakes."

My anger and the hollow, sucking pain in my chest turned to a sour numbness. I felt the way an amputee must feel, knowing there's nothing you can do about it.

The yacht club was always a whirlwind of parties: trophy awards dinners, commodore's balls, Las Vegas nights, weddings, annual regatta regalia roundup-oramas, country and western nights, chili cookoffs, birthday parties, divorce parties, Monday Night Baseball parties, Super Bowl video tape parties, morning-after brunch parties, doodah parties, dingdong parties.

One Friday night a fight, if you could call it that, broke out or rather erupted slowly like a viscous boil between Big Bob and a short, paunchy guy named Eddy. Eddy had been coming on to Big Barb—Big Bob's wife—with gin-soaked double entendres that seemed pretty pathetic and harmless to me, but not to anyone else. Being pathetic and harmless was the last thing anyone of them considered themselves. I was drunk that night; no one seemed to mind if I poured myself tequila at regular intervals and that made it a swell place to anesthetize myself while making eight bucks an hour. When Big Bob and Eddy, thrusting their guts at each other like some kind of cartoon characters, squared off and started calling each other names like "adulterer" and "coward," I couldn't stop laughing. They looked annoyed and each demanded that I throw the other one out. I told them no way, I wouldn't miss this for the world. They started slapping each other with open palms and butting each other with their stomachs while the wives looked on nervously.

I was disappointed but not surprised when they collapsed into each other's arms and bought drinks for each other, hugging and crying and calling each other "the best goddamned guy on the block," drinking to "good fellowship!" All this probably would have gone down without comment like all the incidents of wife groping and drunken boat accidents if Rachel Cole hadn't arrived on her eighty-foot Hadderas that night.

I had never heard of Rachel Cole and neither had most of the members, but when somebody ties up with a boat that size, the idea was to put on your best face and suck up. Her party debarked and entered the club just as Eddy was enjoying a last spasm of righteous anger and machismo. "I still say you're an adulterer,

Bob. You gotta admit, you're an adulterer." He took a sloppy swipe at Big Bob and knocked over his "shipwreck," which is a triple martini with both vodka and gin. Big Bob stuck out his gut again and put up his dukes when Commodore Knox announced a visitor.

"I'd like you all to meet Mrs. Cole from the very beautiful craft outside, the *Ponce de León.* Mrs. Cole, I'd like to welcome you to our humble and beautiful spacious club." The Commodore was shit-faced and trying to bow while keeping his feet under him. He introduced the boys. Eddy slurred a quick "pleasetameetcha" and staggered outside to puke in the bushes and get in his DeLorean to drive home somehow.

Big Bob saluted and said, "Welcome aboard, me beauty."

The wives oohed and purred and elegantly refrained from scratching her eyes out.

Everyone fell all over themselves to present a picture of genteel dignity.

I figured Rachel Cole for her early fifties. She wore her chestnut hair tied back tightly in a bun, gold hoop earrings and a white jumpsuit that was probably real silk. She had a figure that would turn the collar on a Jesuit and she knew it. She ignored all the introductions and looked at me. Her party consisted of an aging blond muscle boy, a tall, gaunt, dark-haired man with eyes like brackish wells full of stagnant water and a complexion like paste wax and another man with a yachting outfit—double-breasted navy blue jacket, matching hat, white ducks and topsiders—who was introduced as Rear Admiral Something Retired. Knox almost blew his Tanqueray through his nose, being an old navy man himself.

I wasn't introduced, but when Knox took their drink order and I asked for proof that they were members of some reciprocating club, he bristled, the admiral harrumphed and Rachel Cole gave me her first smile of the evening. There was something dark and skeletal in that smile, but I felt it below the waist.

"Okay," I said, making the drinks. "I guess we waive the rules for any boat over sixty feet full of movie stars, bodyguards and admirals."

Rachel squinted at me and said, "You're refreshing."

I handed out champagne, Paul Masson. She wrinkled her nose

at it and ordered a Rémy Martin. The pale guy in the turtleneck asked for orange juice. I gave him some. He asked me if I knew I had a powerful aura.

"Sure," I said, and made a muscle. "I press my karma every day."

Rachel Cole's party made arrangements with the commodore to raft up over the weekend and invited both him and his wife down to the boat for cocktails. Knox didn't slobber any more than a Saint Bernard and accepted.

I stayed open until midnight. I got Big Bob out the door along with Marv and Ole Tom and was about to close up when Rachel Cole came in the door alone. She held an empty snifter in her hands by way of explanation.

"Last call," I said.

"Rémy please."

I filled her glass and started closing out the register. She seated herself at a barstool and watched me. "You don't like rich people much, do you?"

I lit a cigarette and studied her face. There was nothing sympathetic or kind about it, just very expensive good looks. She might have been carved from teak except for an air of sexual hunger that could be lost only on a dead man. "Oh, I don't know," I said, and counted tens and twenties. "They're not any more unlikable than poor people, they just have more money."

"Such a cynical young man." She tried to pout, but it would have come off better twenty years ago.

"I'm not all that young and as far as cynicism, I consider myself an amateur."

"A young man on a quest, that's what you are. I find that very attractive, even if you are so boringly unhappy."

"Excuse me, I've got to put a lot of other people's money in a safe and get home to feed my roaches." I smiled. "Enjoy your weekend, but not too much. Someone around here is bound to complain if it looks like you're really having any fun."

When I came out of the office, she was gone. I stayed in the bar until 2 A.M. watching MTV on the big screen and drinking tequila. As I walked to my car after locking up, I could hear the urbane strains of Guy Lombardo coming from the *Ponce de León*. I could see the silhouette of the commodore waltzing with Rachel Cole against the drawn curtains of the main cabin. His wife was a dim shadow on the bow staring into the bay.

I drove home and played my guitar: "Love in Vain." I played it until four in the morning because it finally sounded right.

The next day I was hung over. Business was brisk, as they say. Word had gotten out that the *Ponce de León* was parking for the weekend at the Silver Sands. I served a lot of Bloody Marys while the members ogled the Hadderas, waiting for someone to step off of it.

Rachel Cole and her entourage came up the ramp about 4 P.M.

She wore a coral cocktail dress slit up to midthigh with a neckline that plunged like Oldsmobile sales in Japan. Her breasts rode high and proud, her legs were sleek and belonged to a younger girl. Her skin was smoother than twelve-year-old whiskey. Admiral Something Retired ordered bourbon and seven, she and the bodyguard had Compari and soda, the pale and aesthetic aura expert had Perrier. She smiled at me and seated herself at a corner table.

A half-dozen yacht club wives joined her uninvited, pulling up chairs and discussing her gown or the latest fund-raiser while their husbands hovered and made what they hoped were canny and sophisticated remarks about local politics, dropping names of congressmen and bank presidents. She stole little glances at me over her Compari and I found myself returning them.

I don't usually entertain ideas of bedding women who consider me a young man—on a quest or on anything else—but I found myself doing that. In a way it was nice to know that my sex drive hadn't died or moved to Montana.

Commodore Knox arrived, still looking fried from the night before just as Happy Hour was peaking. He was a nervous little man who got patriotic, maudlin, racist and horny on gin. Sometimes he managed it all in one breath. After guzzling three drinks in the time it took him to chain-smoke two cigarettes and then fawning over Mrs. Cole, he took me aside. "So, just what are you doing?" he asked, fixing me with his best dead-eye look, which he probably hoped resembled Richard Widmark in *The Enemy Below* though it came off like Georgie Jessel on drugs.

"Making drinks and taking people's money. What am I supposed to be doing, parking cars?"

"I see." The little man looked as though he'd shake himself apart. "I have something to discuss. I've had some complaints about your attitude and the way you've been handling things."

"I've been getting them for years. I know what you mean." I turned to go back to the bar. He followed me, trying to keep from wringing his hands.

"That business last night. That altercation with the members, you know who I'm referring to." We stepped away from the bar again. "Well, Mrs. Cole walked in while all of that was going on apparently and it's not the kind of thing that represents us well. Some of us feel you could have handled that better. What do you have to say about that?"

People wanted drinks. I went back behind the bar and made them. He followed me, to show everyone he was important enough to be there by the cash register and the booze and everything. I edged past him in the small space and he followed me like an old basset hound.

In a hushed voice he said, "Mrs. Cole sits on the Coastal Commission, and she's tight with the mayor"—he paused for emphasis—"*and* the governor. Here." He crossed the room and grabbed a magazine from the stack of free ones on the Welcome Aboard table. There were magazines like *Senior Citizen, San Diego Log, Yachting Life* and *Golden Years*. He opened *Bridge and Bay* to a spread of pictures. There was Rachel Cole with the mayors of San Diego, La Jolla and Coronado. "She's very, very important, my friend . . . and last night, well . . . you're in a position of responsibility here and what she saw going on . . ."

"Relax, Commodore. She thinks I'm refreshing. She's having a great time, loves the place."

"You think so?"

I winked. He seemed satisfied, almost.

"Uh, the thing is, York, if you'd just smile a little, you know? Couldn't kill ya, hey?"

I exposed my teeth.

At the other end of the bar a woman who'd been there all day was waving an empty wine glass and whistling through her lipstick-stained teeth at me. "Hey, you!" she shouted at me, and then snapped her fingers. "Who you gotta know to get a drink around here?"

I pointed at another full glass of wine I had put in front of her five minutes ago. She looked at it in drunken surprise and then continued to wave the empty at me. "Well, I'm a two-fisted drinker! Give me another one, handsome."

The commodore had his hand on my shoulder. "Whattya say, smile and the world smiles with you, right?"

The woman started snapping her fingers at me again. I turned to the commodore and told him, "Look, I left my red rubber nose and my seltzer bottle at home. Why don't you just hire a clown that juggles and eats shit?"

I said it a little too loudly. Heads turned and it got quiet except for the two-fisted drinker.

"Hey, handsome. I'm talkin' to you, honeybunch!"

"Excuse me," I said to the vice commodore.

I walked over to the soda gun and lifted it. I placed a finger over the Coca-Cola nozzle and aimed it at the fading beauty with the big mouth. I sprayed her. Her hairdo collapsed and she winced as the stuff played over her makeup. She whined like Lucille Ball and staggered back off her barstool. I put down the gun and stepped out from behind the bar.

There was a general silence around the room except for the whining of the Coke-drenched woman.

"Get yourself a new clown," I said to the commodore, and walked outside to my car.

At the Maverick, I stopped to light a cigarette and noticed that someone had followed me out. It was Rachel Cole's bodyguard. He crossed the parking lot and handed me a piece of paper. He was an over-the-hill pretty boy with dead blue eyes and lips that you could call either generous or indulgent. He wore a khaki leisure suit with epaulets and safari pockets. He wore it open so it wouldn't bind against the gun on his hip. He watched me coolly while I read the note. It said, "I loved the floor show. I'd like you to work for me next Friday night. $200.00."

"You want the job? It's a pretty big-assed party. Two or three hundred people." His voice was a lazy Beach Boy tenor.

"Sure," I said. "Why not?"

He wrote directions on the back of the note. The address was

way the hell out on Route 18 in the foothills full of high pasture-
land and lonely, rambling estates.

"See you Friday about seven-thirty, okay?"

"Okay," I said.

"You're from Jew York, right? That's why you call yourself
York?"

"It's my name. I also happen to be from there."

He grinned. "I knew it. You talk too fast."

"Maybe you listen too slow."

He turned his head to look at me from a new angle. "You're a
Jew, right? A Sephardic Jew, I bet. I know about you people.
God's gift to women, huh?" He didn't wait for an answer. There
wasn't one coming anyway, I was suddenly too tired for this
conversation. "Wear a white shirt, black tie, black pants, you
know. You gotta vest?"

"Am I going to be dealing blackjack or slinging cocktails?"

"You're gonna be looking nice. What you won't be doing is
douching anybody with Coca-Cola."

I held up the note. "Rachel Cole seemed to think it was the
cat's pajamas."

He looked me up and down once more and still didn't find
anything he liked. "Rachel has weird tastes." He left me standing
there and went back into the club. I think I was supposed to bleed
to death or go blind, but I got in my car instead.

I drove to Liz's apartment and bought a gram of cocaine.

8

I SMOKED A JOINT as I drove northeast from Escondido on State Highway 18. I passed miles of orange groves, roadside beer bars, acres of avocado trees growing upright on the sides of sharply sloping hills, truckers' cafés and mobile homes sprouting TV antennas like inverted roots. The joint took the edge off the coke I had snorted that afternoon while playing pool with some bikers in an Ocean Beach bar. I was singing along with the radio. It was oldies weekend on KFMB and hits from the sixties kept on coming. I knew them all. Smoky Robinson and Marvin Gaye, Credence Clearwater and Procul Harum, even the goddamned Monkees. There was nary a tune on which I sounded less than superb. My car had a huge dent in the right front fender, one shoulder was bruised and numb, and I didn't know how either had come to pass, but the wind was hot and exhilarating, the night was young and I was going to a party.

I glanced at the directions and the map that the blond tough guy had given me and put my foot to the floor. It was a long drive along hypnotic country mountain roads and the Byrds were singing "Hey Mister Tambourine Man." A fine sweat had started soaking my white bartender shirt beneath my black vest. I was cool. I was fine. Yes indeed.

All in all, it hadn't been a bad week. I had gone on a tear for a few days with Dana, the singer and harmonica player with the blues band at Mandolin Wind. Dana was tall and gawky with Raggedy Ann–striped stockings, leather skirt and a vodka-eroded voice. We did a lot of coke and she let me sit in with the group on Sunday night. I even got some applause. She was a great drinking buddy and she helped me forget everything, including my own name. I forgot if we made it or not, but it didn't matter. Dana took off for a gig in L.A. and I slept through the middle of the week before going out again. I forgot a lot, but not Juana Villez or the old man I'd gotten killed for nothing. I was working on it.

The Maverick started to wheeze at two thousand feet.

The Skylark Lounge, Fat City, the Low Down with some new guy at the door, Liz and Suzy telling me to go home. Funorama.

The Rolling Stones came on KFMB doing "Sympathy for the Devil." I didn't sing along, just sort of nodded superbly to the music and watched the world outside my windshield turn to scrub desert.

The sixties. For a lot of people they were bright, jangling guitars heralding the Age of Aquarius, incense and idealism, righteous causes and mystic crystal revelations. Some just slept through it all somehow and for others it was all only fashion; but for a lot more of us, and it didn't matter what side of the world you were on, it was the realization that you just weren't adjusted to the modern world or thinking clearly about what was happening if you weren't wrenched out of your face. It was a crash course in the science of oblivion. A dress rehearsal for an apocalypse that didn't quite come off. It had been a dream and when it was over it was 1958 again.

I passed a caravan of RVs going up the mountain.

I still had a little coke left. Liz's boyfriend wouldn't extend me any more credit and I tried to reason with him with a lamp in my hand. He had a .357, I had a lamp. I don't remember leaving, but I seemed to have done it without getting shot.

I took another hit on the joint. Jimi Hendrix complained about manic depression from my dashboard. Strange things come to mind when I hear that song: euphoric nightmares from the war. An ugly nostalgia, but it was mine.

I skirted Los Coyotes Indian Reservation and began to climb the eastern rim of the Lake Henshaw basin toward Rachel Cole's estate. Tumbleweed flew across the one-lane blacktop on the Santa Ana wind. It would be a good night for a brush fire.

I could see the three-story Spanish mansion, the terra cotta–tiled roof and the bell tower two miles from the front gate. There was no intercom or mailbox, no sign that said "The Coles" or "Happy Hacienda," just a soldered hatchwork of three-inch steel pipe on hinges that swung outward from a high Cyclone fence crowned with barbed wire. A golf cart with a fringed top was parked at the end of the driveway and two Mexican men wearing dark suits leaned against it. One of them held a piece of paper that was probably a guest list.

The closest one greeted me. "Good evening, sir."

"Yeah, good evening. The name's York. I'm the bartender."

He glanced at the paper. "Yes." He dropped the sir, I was the help. "Up the drive to the right of the fountain and around the side of the main building. You'll see the caterer's truck. Park there, go inside and ask for Mr. Ryder."

"Thanks."

The grounds were neglected. Manzanita bushes and cholla cactus poked around boulders and the occasional stunted fir tree. As I headed up the drive, things got a little better. Rocks had been cleared to make a stone fence along the road and cactus gardens gave way to a grove of cyprus trees and a scorched lawn beyond. A tennis court overgrown with hibiscus came into view on my right. I could see that the net sagged in the middle of the cracked court. The fountain at the head of the driveway was a stone carved figure of an Indian woman balancing a water urn on her head in the middle of a dry tiled basin.

The mansion was tiered with arched galleries on the first two floors made of stone and stucco. The third floor had leaded glass windows framed with dark old wood and walls that looked like real adobe crumbling in spots. The bell tower rose fifty feet from the roof on the north side of the building and had a bell in it. Scaffolding clung to the south side of the tower and I could see where someone had been retiling the roof of the tower. The whole place had an air of half-hearted maintenance and grand decay. It looked like an abandoned set for a Zorro film or a spaghetti Western.

I pulled around the side and found the caterer's truck. I parked and killed the engine. The Rolling Stones died, echoing off the walls of another courtyard beyond the arched entranceway to the house. I got out of the car and realized how wrecked I was. I also realized that I had been smelling sulfur all the way up the driveway. It was carried on the Santa Anas from the hot springs that ran through these mountains. It gave the old mission an air of having died and gone over to the other side.

I grabbed my black necktie out of the backseat full of crumpled, slept-in clothes and twisted it around my neck. I walked through the arch and into the courtyard. Someone had installed a pool years ago, but now it was a scummy, algae-filled haven for oversized carp with gold flaking scales. When Cole's bodyguard had told me that she had weird taste, he hadn't said it just to be clever.

I walked into a kitchen that had been renovated with tiles, stainless steel tables, a grill, a long oven with a dozen burners on the range and a walk-in refrigerator. Three girls wearing red vests and aprons were laying out cracked crab on sterling trays, a cornucopia ice sculpture decked out with fruit and melon balls, wheels of cheese, chopped liver molds and fondue kits. I asked one of them for Mr. Ryder. They directed me through swinging doors and up a flight of stairs and I found myself standing in a long room with a table draped with linen supporting a candelabra that Liberace would have envied. Count Basie and Oscar Peterson came from concealed speakers somewhere. I approved. A bank of windows to the left looked out on Lost Valley, the Indian reservation and the Lake Henshaw basin. I was checking out the art on the walls: portraits of conquistadors, the governor of California, one of Aldous Huxley, a Klee painting, a pen and ink of Marcel Proust, a woodcut of George Bernard Shaw and an impressionistic acrylic of the strange, pale man I'd met at the yacht club with Rachel Cole.

"I don't know art, but I know what I like. That's an awesome portrait of Ian." It was the bodyguard. He crossed the room, extending his hand to me just like I was a white man and every-thing. He wore his hair blown back showing his tan to good effect, a white tuxedo and, under that, a gun. A bigger one than he wore at the yacht club, maybe a long-nosed magnum. I didn't take his hand but pretended to study the portrait.

"It's a funny thing," I said, not shaking his hand, "I minored in fine art for two years and I still can't figure out what I like or why." It sounded off-the-wall even to me.

"Yeah, well." He couldn't decide if I was needling him. "I'm Ryder. Sandy Ryder. The bar area's this way."

"Ah, of course, indeed, yessiree."

Ryder showed me to a living room with high beamed ceilings, polished wood floors and sparse antique furniture. The bar was hand-rubbed oak, sunken into a rust-carpeted well and framed with wine racks on two sides. There were no barstools, but it sported a fine brass rail that would have done any pub proud. Ryder gestured at the racks of French, German, Italian, even Algerian and Australian vintages. "Rachel's a wino." He chuck-led.

I chuckled.

"I think . . . you know"—he pointed around the sink, the ice bin, the cases of Smirnoff, Red Label and Jack Daniels, the liters of soda—"you've got everything there." He fixed me again with that aren't-you-pathetic look. "Jesus, awesome outfit, Ace."

"Why, this old thing?" I touched my vest. "Why, Mr. Ryder, how you do carry on."

He looked at me as if I were a bent surfboard. "Uh, don't think about doing anything weird, here. Rachel might like you, but that doesn't buy you anything with me." Unconsciously he touched the bulge at his hip, grinning like one of the Beach Boys.

"You mean you'll shoot me?"

"Just set up and do the job, man. Okay?" He walked back across the dining room giving orders to a small legion of ser-vants.

"Right. The job." I placed antique colored highball and rock glasses on the bar, filled them with ice. I lit a cigarette and listened to cars arriving outside.

Rachel appeared while I was downing a tumbler of Jack Daniels. She was accompanied by an underaged, pretty Mexican boy wearing a white linen jacket and bow tie. She wore black silk pants and silver high heels, a beige calfskin halter above her suntanned navel and muscled stomach. Draping her shoulders was a fringed peach shawl. Her hair was up, revealing a jawbone and neck that had fine smooth lines unmarred by age. I looked for evidence of plastic surgery, but I didn't find any. Her eyes held the only indication of the years. They were gray-aqua, the color of an ocean filled with drowned men.

She seemed surprised to see me. "Why you're . . . oh, I remember now. I'm so sorry you came all this way, you'll be paid of course, but you can see I have a full staff after all. Eduardo, go on back there." She gestured for the boy to take my place. I didn't move. The boy looked back and forth for a minute between us and settled on a spot at the edge of the bar.

She looked at me. "I've forgotten your name, you'll have to forgive me. I was bored to distraction last weekend." She gestured vaguely all over the room. "I do appreciate your coming, though. Somehow I supposed you wouldn't." She smiled briefly and signaled to Ryder, who was conferring with another Mexican in a tuxedo with a pearl-handled .45 in his cummerbund. "Sandy, please write out a check for this man." She tried to look all dizzy and silly, but her type was never more dizzy or silly than a barracuda. "I had forgotten I asked him to come, you know me."

"The name is York. I drove for an hour and a half to get up here. I'll take cash for the gas money and that's all." I finished the whiskey and let the kid come back behind the bar.

Ryder stood looking foolish holding a checkbook and looking back and forth between us the way Eduardo had a moment ago.

Rachel said, "You're very proud. I remember now." She looked at me as if I'd shown her a card trick once. "Still, you must take a check for—what was it?—the full one hundred dollars, or whatever I said . . . so I don't feel so badly. Please indulge me."

"It was two hundred, but I'll take ten for gas unless you have an extra rumpus room you might have misplaced that needs a bartender. You never know, you being so silly and all. Of course, you could just invite me to the party. I'll put a lampshade on my head for the two hundred. You'll love it."

She threw back her head and forced a laugh as if she were practicing for the party. Her teeth were perfect.

Ryder walked across the room, putting away the checkbook in his jacket. "Rachel, this guy's big. Manny's out sick and we could use somebody on the east road by the old garage and servant houses tonight."

"Oh fine. That's just fine. You two talk it over, will you? I really have to run. Oh my God, there are people arriving. They all make me nauseous, you know, but I must start looking delighted." She left in a swirl of peach shawl, her heels clacking on the varnished hardwood floors.

Ryder took me outside. He got in a black Jeep Renegade and told me to follow him in my car. I brought the bottle of Jack Daniels with me and got in the Maverick. I ate his dust on the way up a gravelly road that climbed another five hundred feet along a wire fence that enclosed nothing as far as I could see except more dust and gravel. I took my tie off and watched steam pour out of my radiator. The road ended at a promontory overlooking a ravine, Cole's estate below and wooded mountains on three sides. Directly in front of us was a chain-link fence with a locked gate. Beyond that was an outbuilding that looked like a run-down apartment house over a five-car garage. The last rays of sunlight fled over the mountains far to the west beyond the Lake Henshaw basin, but the air didn't cool. Hot winds and the smell of sulfur springs collaborated with a sudden chorus of crickets and the decayed cocaine in my system to put my nerves on edge.

Ryder left the engine running on his Jeep and walked over to my car like a blond ghost in white evening dress. He tore off a name patch from a sheet of adhesive and placed it over the left tit on my vest. It said "Manny" and beneath it "Estate Security."

While I read it, Ryder told me, "Just sit up here and turn away anybody who comes up looking for a place to fuck or whatever. You know, if somebody drives up and feels like taking a moonlight stroll, just point 'em back down the road."

"Sure," I said. "Why?"

"Two hundred bucks, for one. For another, well, Rachel's an

investor, you know, heavy duty. There's agricultural machinery in that building. You heard of industrial spies?"

I grunted.

"Well, it's an off chance, but certain characters she's invited tonight might like to see what's what in there." He jerked his head at the building beyond the gate. "There's nothing in there that makes any sense to me or you, but some of these guys might want to check it out and . . . I don't know, I guess if they saw the stuff it would mean something to them and they'd try to develop something like it and Rachel's edge would be jeopardized. Can you handle it?"

"Gosh, spies and stuff? I don't know."

"Here." He handed me a walkie-talkie. "Anything you can't handle, just call in. I'll come up."

"Don't I get a pearl-handled .45?"

"You wanna do it or not?"

I got out of the car and saluted. "They'll never get near those fucking milking machines. You can count on me."

"Yeah, well, just hang around and discourage the tourists. I'll radio up in a few hours."

He got in the Jeep and drove back down the mountain. I listened to the crickets for a while and drank whiskey. Peering down the road at the house, balconies and courtyards lit by torches in stained glass, I tried to make out the songs that the jazz combo was playing. Snatches of something by Sergio Mendes, something by Herb Alpert and a song by Barry Manilow wafted sporadically up the mountain on vagrant back currents of wind. The crickets sounded more interesting. I looked at the gate and the building beyond and wondered how stupid I really looked.

An hour went by, no one came up the road and I did some more coke. It kicked in like an icefall on the back of my head, giving me grand ideas. I took my flashlight out of the glove compartment, dug my old denim jacket out of the backseat and tied the arms around my neck. I walked to the gate. There was no one around, but there had been recently. Large tire tracks, two sets of them in the dust, still hadn't been scattered by the Santa Anas. They might have been trucks moving farm machinery. I don't know why I cared, but I was bored and stoned and I resented being lied to.

I climbed the gate and then took my jacket, doubled it over and spread it across a section of barbed wire large enough to grip. I swung my legs over one at a time and climbed down the other side leaving the jacket. The windows on the garage had been whitewashed over from the inside. The doors were locked. A set of stairs on one side led to the apartments on the second floor. There were three doors, presumably leading into three apartments. I pried open a dry-rotted shutter on the first of the windows and played the flashlight inside. The beam was weak but I could see that all the walls had been knocked out, forming one long room. It was empty except for some graffiti on the walls that I couldn't make out and a stack of mattresses near the door.

I replaced the shutter and went back down the stairs, looking for a way into the garage. I moved the light along the walls, doors and windows and found a rusted fifty-five-gallon drum filled with trash. Inside were chicken bones, paper napkins, ten empty soda cans, oil-soaked rags, an empty can of STP and a Kotex box filled with its used contents.

One of the small panels of whitewashed glass set at eye level on the garage doors was cracked at one corner. With the butt of the flashlight, I tapped out the small fragment and looked inside. Two identical panel trucks painted blue and white sat next to each other. On the sides were painted the name of a fertilizer company, Vita-Gro Farms. A workbench littered with tools lay against the opposite wall; above it hung hoses, saws, cans of paint. Three other spaces for vehicles sat empty except for a recent brownish stain on the cement, still wet, that could have been paint or blood. Maybe there was some kind of truth to what Ryder had told me after all. Maybe the trucks carried cow shit synthesizers invented by some mad scientist on the rag.

I snapped off the flashlight and walked back to the fence, climbed over it and got back in my car. I lit a cigarette and drank from the bottle, wondering again just what I was doing there. I turned the radio to KFMB and tried to stay awake.

Some party.

The walkie-talkie Ryder had given me woke me up. "You there, York? Answer me." It was Ryder's voice.

I pressed the talk button. "Yeah. I'm here."

"Where've you been? Most of the guests are gone. You can head back down."

"Right."

"How'd it go?"

"Quiet."

"Come get your money."

I started the car, turned on the headlights and tried to drive. I was seeing two trees for every one that was really there. I looked over at the seat next to me and saw that I had killed almost half a quart of the Jack Daniels. It took forever to get back down driving like a blind little old lady.

The car got parked somewhere and I walked through open French doors at the front of the mansion. Couples were mumbling good nights and taking shawls or hats from a gray-haired and mustachioed Mexican woman in a maid's costume. I walked past her, staggering a little, and tried to see into the room that I found too bright after being out on the north forty all night. Rachel Cole was seated in a sunken conversation pit off to the left. Her fingers played with the hair of some Hollywood starlet I had seen on television, but whose name I couldn't remember. The starlet had her hand on Rachel's thigh. They were both listening to a man whose back was to me. Another man next to him nodded gravely. He was the Republican congressman from my district.

The man with his back to me wore a powder blue leisure suit with puku shells around his neck. His hair was blond. He was saying, ". . . and it seems likely that the project may merit the kind of funding you're talking about." The voice was mellow, a low tenor, and belonged to E. Walters.

The congressman got up and shook his hand. "I know we can count on you, Gene. Rachel told me that you were the kind of guy who should get the inside track on what we're doing. It was a pleasure meeting you and you'll be hearing from me."

Walters remained seated and shook his hand.

Gene? E. Walters. Eugene.

Rachel saw me standing in the middle of her living room trying to find my center of gravity. "Yes?" She arched her eyebrows and let go of the girl next to her. "Are you looking for Sandy?"

Walters and the congressman looked at me. "Jesus Christ!" Walters said. "What the hell is he doing here? Rachel, is this some amusing party game of yours?"

"You know him? I'm sure I had no idea. I found him at some tacky little South Bay yacht club and hired him for tonight."

Walters regained his composure, even smiled a little. "Well, as it happens, this young man used to work for me. Quite a coincidence. How are you, York?" He walked cautiously forward, extending a chubby little rabbit's hand with four rings on it that were too big. I let them hang in the air. "No need to be that way, my friend."

"Where's Juana?"

"Not that again." He ran his hand through his hair and tried to chuckle tiredly, but he was afraid.

Rachel seemed to sense it too and leaned forward on her seat, her eyes flashing, her teeth parted. She drank in the tension and the threat of ugliness in the room as if it were tonic to her bored nerves.

"Where's your big buddy, Walters?" I asked him. "Give him the night off?" My words slid into each other like a freeway pileup.

"You're a loser, my friend. Why don't you go sleep it off?"

He turned his back on me and I spun him around to face me.

I swung and hit him along the side of his left eye. His glasses flew across the room and he went to the floor of the conversation pit, head first.

I went after him. The congressman tried to stop me and I pushed him aside. I lifted Walters by his lapels. "Get up," I said. "Where's Juana?"

Rachel clapped her hands. "Yes, get up, Gene, and tell us about this Juana."

I could see Ryder running toward me from across the room, but he was too late. Walters was out cold and I couldn't keep my knees locked under me anymore. I let go of Walters, but we both went down together. I heard Rachel Cole say, "Put him in the white room, I suppose." And then I didn't hear anything anymore.

9

I WAS DREAMING about Juana Villez. She was straddling me with a finger to my lips while we made love. I tried to speak, it was important that I tell her something, but she kept shushing me. I tried to be quiet and love her, but the room was on fire.

I sat up and opened my eyes. Rachel Cole was leaning over me wearing a white, midthigh negligee. Her hair was loose around her shoulders. She sat cross-legged at the foot of the bed and held a snifter of Sambuca in her hand. It was burning. She took the match she had used to light it and held it over me. I was lying in a huge bed with off-white satin sheets. The room was lit by a dim chandelier that cast soft light on an expanse of white walls, curtains and some small, blanched sculpture. She dropped the match on my chest. I picked it up, still burning, and tossed it away.

"Are you too stoned?" she asked in a husky voice.

"Too stoned for what?" The curtains billowed with warm wind and I could see that it was still dark outside. "What time is it?"

"Sex. And it's four-thirty." She blew out the flames and drank the liqueur. With her other hand she gripped me between the legs. I was naked and hard.

I had been asleep for only a couple of hours and I was still twisted. The only thing I could focus on was that she was not Juana and I wanted to punish her for it. She was responsible for the dream. I grabbed her wrist and pulled it toward me, squeezing it until she dropped the snifter over the side of the bed and breathed hard with the pain. She didn't cry out.

Her face was down next to mine and I found myself pressing my mouth hard up against hers. I bit her bottom lip until I tasted blood. She moaned and pulled her wrist free. She grabbed me again between the legs, digging her fingernails hard into the taut flesh around my balls.

I pulled her negligee down to her waist and took hold of one of her breasts. I kneaded it, pinching her nipples between my thumb and forefinger, and shifted my weight on top of her. She was breathing like a marathon runner.

I was talking, snarling things I don't remember, things that probably made no sense. When I pulled her crumpled negligee up over her hips, I saw that there was no tan line, just an even, smooth brownness beneath me. Her pubic hairs had been cut short.

Pinning her wrists to the side, I entered her and thrust upward. She arched her head backward on the pillow and hissed through clenched teeth, sobbing, laughing, mumbling.

She was tight and wet, but without warmth. Her body was hard and facile as she met my hips again and again. If I had been in my right mind I would have been amazed considering her age, but all I could think of was fucking her lights out. I hated her and I didn't know why. I hated everything and everybody, and if I couldn't kill somebody, I'd just fuck myself and her to death.

I moved mindlessly against her for an eternity, thinking about that and thinking about nothing. A current moved through me with dark pleasure, a grim instinct that fueled a perpetual motion machine only death could stop.

She flooded the sheets twice and then I pulled out of her and pinned her biceps with my knees. I made her take me in her mouth and she was eager.

She worked until my back and thighs locked and stiffened like a dead man's. The muscles in my neck grew tight and I shuddered with a spasm that brought reds and blacks to the insides of my eyelids. A bitter satisfaction made a rictus mask of my face and I could see it mirrored in hers beneath me. Repelled and hungry, she bit and tongued and played her face over me as if it were something mad with a life of its own, cut off by my weight from her body. Her fingernails raked my calves and thighs.

I let myself roll to the side and sank into the bedclothes.

She lay still beside me for a while and then got up. I didn't watch her, I didn't care what she did. My mind was moving down black corridors full of slithering things.

She shook my shoulders and I sat up looking at her. She held out a snifter of Sambuca. "Maybe you'd like cognac?" she said.

"Beer. Get me a cold beer." I sat up and found my clothes folded over a chair next to the bed. I went through the pockets and found the last of the coke. I laid it out on the surface of my wallet and snorted it with one of the hundred-dollar bills I had found inside.

She spoke to someone over an intercom and then walked back across the room, still naked. "I'm having some more of that brought up too." She gestured at the empty foil. "You'll stay here with me. I have everything you want. Everything."

When I woke up the next afternoon, my nose was bleeding, my head was pounding and my back and legs were covered with deep scratches. There was blood on the pillow from Rachel's lip. On a tray next to the bed was a tall glass of orange juice, some toast, four aspirin, two Valium, coffee, a Bloody Mary in a miniature carafe, another gram of cocaine in a crystal vial and a bottle of St. Pauli Girl beer in an ice bucket. There was also a note.

It said, "Darling, Come and have a sauna. There's an intercom by the door. The staff will tell you where it is. The sauna, I mean. —Rachel."

I swallowed the aspirin and the orange juice, found a shower with a toothbrush and a bathrobe conveniently my size, or close

enough. Then I went to work on the Bloody Mary. When I could
see, I checked out the room. It was bigger than my apartment, but
it was probably a small room in that house. I discovered all the
long-forgotten clothes from the backseat of my car, laundered
and folded neatly in the top drawer of a white bureau. The sculptures I had noticed last night were all nudes or representations of
Pan and Dionysus, Priapus, nymphs, satyrs—like that. There was
a white shag rug, the chandelier controlled by a rheostat, the
bureau, a full-length mirror I avoided that was framed in ivory
and two curtained windows. I opened the curtains on one of them
and looked out at late, slanting light that transformed the Laguna
mountains into a Parrish painting. Lake Henshaw looked like a
sea of molten brass. Sometimes nature has the taste of a Greek
restaurant decorator.

I turned from the window and then turned back. I heard something I hadn't heard in a long time. The toy ticking sound of
automatic rifle fire in the distance. There were short bursts of two
or three rounds at about two-second intervals. It sounded at least
a mile off, but I didn't know from which direction. The staccato
cricking could have been echoing off any of the mountains and
the Santa Anas were still blowing.

I put on some clean Levi's without underwear, a white shirt and
my running shoes. I picked up the vial of coke and went out to see
about some breakfast. I didn't want a sauna. It would just precipi-
tate a hangover I was keen on putting off for as long as possible.

I walked down a short corridor that ran perpendicular to a
longer one flanking the courtyard with the goldfish pool. I turned
right and looked down from the arched balcony. The courtyard
was half in shadow. On the other side was the pale guy that Ryder
had called Ian. He sat in a lotus position wearing only a loincloth,
the kind fakirs wear, at least in movies. Next to him was an open
book and an orange. His eyes were closed, and while my Pumas
didn't make any noise on the tile floor, he looked directly up at
me.

"Won't you join me?" he asked in a quiet voice that somehow
carried across the courtyard. "The sun is warm yet."

I looked for the stairs and found them to my right. I walked
down and around the edge of the pool. "What are the chances of
getting some breakfast, or dinner or whatever?"

"I have an orange." He offered it to me.

"Thanks, but I'm trying to quit. How about some bacon and eggs?"

"You'll find no meat here, I'm afraid. We are vegetarians."

I brought out the last cigarette from a crumpled pack and tried to find a match. I didn't bother to ask Ian for one. I looked at him instead. He looked back at me with eyes like cloth buttons. He was pushing forty or so, but despite his paleness, his sunken cheeks and chest, he looked boyish. The kind of boy he looked like was the kind that pulled wings off of flies.

"My name is Ian Broctor and you are . . . York . . . ?"

He was waiting for another name. "That's right," I said. "York."

Ian Broctor. The name was very familiar. I looked at him and mentally shaved his head, put a beard on him and couldn't believe it. *"The* Ian Broctor? The Children of Light and Darkness and all that?"

He smiled. "That was a long time ago." He seemed happy that I remembered. The Children of Light and Darkness was a cult commune out of Santa Cruz or Santa Barbara that made headlines in 1970. Just after Altamont; the year of Kent State and Charlie Manson. At the time he was the media's favored candidate for the next most likely guru to axe-murder middle-class people in their sleep. When the rock star Rod Ash of Dogsbody went berserk and slashed his girlfriend, his mother and the family dog, he left a note before driving a bayonet through his own throat. The note said that Ian Broctor had instructed him in a vision—To "cleanse his set and setting with blood" was how he put it, I think. Broctor testified at an inquest that was a media circus. There was talk of kidnaping and brainwashing cult members, animal sacrifices and whatnot. He had never been convicted of anything and had quietly disappeared from the public eye since then. If I worked for *Rolling Stone,* I would have a scoop for a where-are-they-now story.

I said, "No shit?"

"Your aura is muddied, but it is, as I said when I first met you, a very powerful one." He began to peel the orange. His fingernails were long, like a Chinese mandarin's.

"It's due for a dry cleaning, yeah. So what are you up to these days? Times must be lean in your line of work."

"I live here with Rachel. I advise her. I meditate and continue my work."

I looked around at the half-renovated mansion, the dragon palms and potted orange trees, the neglected swimming pool filled with fat, slow carp. A Mexican man in a San Diego Chargers cap was hosing the cigarette butts from last night's party across the cracked tiles of the patio. "Just what is that, your work?"

"It is what it has always been, to free the mind from evolution's stranglehold, to sieze the reins of immortality from the chimera, death. To transcend this plane, utilize the forces of chaos and creation, orchestrate them, harness the maelstrom within, shed the skin of the beast while assimilating its power and embracing the wisdom of the serpent. . . ."

I could see that I had pressed his button. He went on like that, staring into the dull surface of the pool. I looked at the book that was opened in front of him. It was Ouspensky's *Tertium Organum*. In the margins were scrawled words with exclamation points, like "Fool!" and "Blood!" or "Yes!"

I got up to go find some food. "Look, I'm sorry I asked." I said. "We must chat over another orange sometime."

He went on. "The fish, you see them? No one really knows how long carp live. Some of them die, but others seem to go on for hundreds of years. It is the flora in their intestines, some say. I am attempting to synthesize that flora, but I am convinced it goes beyond that."

"Interesting. Look, I've got to eat or I'm going to pass out. See you around the campus." I started to walk away.

"I permit your presence here. Go without fear. I understand Rachel's needs." He smiled as if he were sharing a locker-room joke with me. ". . . the skin of the beast."

"Right." I winked at him and crossed the patio. I got a light from the guy in the Chargers hat and found the kitchen.

After two fried eggs, half a cantaloupe and some fried fish I couldn't get down, thinking about carp intestines and all, I tried to strike up a conversation with the young Mexican girl who seemed to be the cook. Her name was Maria and she didn't speak English as far as I could tell. She wasn't very talkative in Spanish either. She was about twenty years old with a nice figure, sleepy eyes and a guarded smile. I gave up being friendly and laid out two lines of coke on a stainless steel counter. She almost ran out of the room when she saw the stuff.

I was feeling passably all right when Rachel came in.

"There you are. Why didn't you buzz someone and tell them you were up and about? Let's have some champagne. The sun is over the yardarm." She wore green khaki shorts, a T-shirt that said "Beverly Hills Polo Club" and what women's magazines call a radiant afterglow. Her hair was in a whimsical, girlish pony tail.

I followed her through the house. Maria followed me with an ice bucket and glasses.

Rachel spread herself out on the beige sofa in the sunken conversation pit where I had left Walters last night. She patted the cushion next to her. I sat on the other side of the glass coffee table instead. It was where the congressman had been sitting last night only there had been no coffee table. Rachel sat back up, smiling at me meaningfully. She leaned forward with her elbow on her knee, her fist under her chin, and looked amused.

"You don't seem any the worse for wear today," she said. Maria brought a bottle of Mumms and placed it in the ice.

"I've been training for a while."

Shadows grew around the room. The only light came from an orange smudge of sunset beyond the curtains. Maria went around the room turning on lights. She asked Rachel if there was anything else.

"Yes, Maria. Come here." Maria walked hesitantly to the edge of the pit. "Sit down, dear. York, why don't you open the champagne?"

I opened it and spun the bottle in the ice while I watched Rachel place her hand up underneath Maria's peasant blouse. While she smiled at me, she worked her fingers slowly over Maria's breasts. Maria closed her eyes and bit her lower lip. I couldn't tell if she was enjoying it or not.

With her other hand, she brought Maria's head down to hers. She kissed her and played her tongue over Maria's lips. Maria's tongue appeared and then disappeared in Rachel's mouth.

I popped the cork on the champagne and poured some into the two glasses. Rachel pulled her face away from the Mexican girl and said, "That will be all, Maria."

Maria got up and walked back to the kitchen, her lidded eyes expressionless.

Rachel picked up her champagne and studied me, all of me, to see how I had reacted to the show. She found what she was looking for and sat back satisfied. "So," she said, "what shall we do to amuse ourselves?"

"Let's talk about your friend Walters."

She looked disappointed. "Oh, Gene. Well, I would like to know why you hit him. It was over a girl, I gather."

I told her about it and then I asked her if Walters was still here.

"No. He came to long before you did. His driver took him home."

"Carlos?"

"I think that's his name."

"So where would Walters have stashed her?"

She rolled her eyes and stood. She stepped up to the main floor level and paced slowly. "I'm sure I have no idea. Gene is involved with so many things. He has a lot of friends in show business, he backs projects. If he wanted to make someone a movie star, I suppose he could do it. Why don't you just let her alone. Gene wanted to have you killed last night. He was insanely angry of course and probably didn't mean it, but he could have it done. He's a dangerous man to have as an enemy, as many people have found out. He's pissed as hell at me for keeping you here last night."

"What's your connection with him?"

"Not that it's any of your business, but we've known each other for years. We have interests together—real estate, joint ventures, investments."

Something she said half triggered a connection. I waited for it to click, but it didn't come. It nagged at me while I drank my second glass of champagne.

"Really," she went on, "Gene is a dear friend, but he can be maddeningly dull and boorish." She continued to pace around the edge of the pit and then stopped behind me where I couldn't see her. She knelt and began massaging my shoulders. "I didn't mind you hitting him, he probably deserves it just on general principles and besides, it was the most interesting thing that happened at the party—but must we continue to talk about *him?*" She slid her hand down under my shirt. Her tongue ran around the edge of my ear, the hand continued down beneath my belt.

I took her hand out and leaned forward over the coffee table with the vial of cocaine. I poured out four lines and rolled my hundred-dollar bill again. "Join me?" I invited.

She got up and walked around and down to the table to pour herself another champagne. She sighed. "No. Why don't you use one of those little spoons? It's disgusting what you're doing. You never know where money has been."

"I found it in my wallet. I figure I got it from you."

"You see what I mean?" She smiled and licked her top lip.

"Where do you get this stuff, anyway? Just keep it around the medicine cabinet?" I did all four lines. My face and throat froze. The room came into impossibly sharp focus.

"Oh, it's just a party favor. I serve pâté too, but I don't eat it."

"That's right, you're a vegetarian. I ran into your resident Rasputin this afternoon." The coke made me restless. I got up, found a cigarette in a Russian lacquered box and lit it. I started pacing the room the way she had a moment ago.

"Ian. Yes." She seated herself on a blond piano bench in front of a matching Steinway grand. "You can make jokes if you like, but he is an extraordinary man."

"No argument there. Ordinary men don't go around spouting from the *Necronomicon* when you ask them how's tricks. How did you find him, cruising homes for retired psychopathic messiahs?"

"That's enough! I won't have you being clever at his expense. He's the greatest man I've ever met and I don't have to defend him to you."

"I take it he's not the greatest in bed."

She walked briskly toward me, covering the distance in four strides. She lifted her hand to slap my face and I caught her wrist. She brought up the long tulip glass of champagne with her other hand and tossed the contents in my face. I slapped her hard and she liked it. A strange spark seemed to glow brighter in the back shadows of her slate eyes. She lifted her face toward me, her eyelids eclipsing slowly, and opened her mouth. The image of her and Maria came back to me and I clamped my mouth over hers and lashed her tongue with mine.

After a while she said, "The very idea of Ian and I . . . sexually is"—she shook her head—"out of the question. Not something for your sarcasm." She paused and then whispered, "Just don't, that's all."

Someone cleared his throat. I let go of Rachel and turned.

Sandy Ryder stood in the arched entryway wearing a camouflaged utility fatigue flak jacket without the lining. He held a CAR 15 in his hand. It was pointed at the floor and didn't have a clip in it. On his head was a black baseball cap with a happy face on it. "Sorry to interrupt," he said. "I was out shooting with some of the boys up by the treeline. I thought I'd check in with you before I went into town tonight."

Rachel was still breathing heavily. "Well, you checked in," she said impatiently. "You can go now. I want you back by tomorrow afternoon."

"Fine." He curled his lip at me. "You almost got your ass handed to you last night. Gene Walters wanted you strung up from the bell tower."

I poured myself the last of the champagne and toasted him. "We're almost even now."

"I wouldn't bet the ranch on it." He sneered. It was a good sneer. He had the lips for it.

"Sandy, I don't want you traipsing in here with guns and dust all over your shoes. Is there anything else?"

"I'm going. Good night."

He left and Rachel turned back to me. "Where were we?"

"We need more champagne."

"It's over there." She gestured at the bar. "Why don't you chill a bottle while I slip into something easier to take off? Take it out on the veranda. I'll meet you there and we'll have some dinner brought out." She kissed me and walked up the stairs trying not to run.

I found the champagne and drank the first glass warm. I was stoned again and feeling philosophical about being in a mansion in the mountains with an overage bisexual nymphomaniac and her little family of psycho spiritualists and gun nuts and her swimming pool full of carp. I took the ice bucket and the glasses

through the French doors and looked out at the mountains silhouetted against the evening. The Santa Anas felt like the breath
of some distant dragon drying the pores in my face and raising
the hairs on the back of my neck.

I nearly finished the warm champagne in my glass and felt the
need to make a toast to something. After a while it came to me. I
lifted the glass and said it out loud as I looked at the stars. "To
California." The stuff went down with a deceptive, gentle flat-
ness.

10

I STAYED PAST the weekend.

Bits of memory, isolated images, fragments of conversations floated on a sea of champagne and whiskey, tossed on whitecaps of cocaine.

Juana Villez became a receding ache. I could remember her face and I could remember her touch, I could remember loving her and maybe I still did, but I didn't poke at the scab to find out. She had been reduced to a handful of memories and sensations disconnected from any nerve; just something else that had gone wrong some time ago. Or so I told myself. Sometimes I believed it. In a way, I had started to say goodbye to her that night just before we had made love, the night she told me about her brother. It was as if I knew, in some secret part of myself, that she would be in and out of my life all too quickly. When she disappeared in Walters's limousine, I sensed she was gone from me forever in any way that mattered, but I couldn't admit it to myself. The real bon voyage party started when I arrived at Rachel Cole's estate, though, and by that time I was saying goodbye to myself, or at least a big piece of me, as much as anyone else. It was a hell of a send-off too.

After all, every time I checked I seemed to be having a good time.

Once I woke up to find that Maria had been in bed with us. One of my prime fantasies since puberty, but I couldn't remember any more about it than the Spanish-American War.

I didn't learn much about Rachel Cole (other than how she liked it and where and when) or her business and I probably wouldn't have been able to even if I had been interested. She told me she owned the San Diego *American*, which was the second-oldest newspaper in the county and a little to the left of the *Neo-Nazi Bugle*. She had a lot of *Forbes* magazines around which she never read and a locked library and office no one was allowed into. She spent a lot of time in there on the phone or dictating to Maria, who, tireless and versatile girl that she was, also acted as a personal secretary.

Rachel screamed in her sleep more than once and disappeared with Broctor in his rooms (also off-limits) only to come back and fuck as if it were the only thing between her and the Grim Reaper. She would go off in the afternoons sometimes in her Mercedes and be back by nightfall.

I tried wandering around the estate, only to be turned back by a lot of Mexicans with guns and diplomatic or not-so-diplomatic smiles. The kind of thing I was supposed to do the night of the party. Ryder came back from town when he said he would and seemed to spend his time driving around the property in his Jeep wearing fatigues and a hunting vest and armed with exotic weapons including a crossbow and an Israeli Uzi. For a while, with the particular kind of insight one can achieve on cocaine and liquor, I thought I had the whole bonzo bin figured out. The farm machinery in the outbuilding was the cheapest and most efficient kind. People. They were smuggling and housing illegal migrant workers to harvest vast, hidden marijuana fields. This explained Sandy Ryder and his Captain Guts act—or so I thought. I kept thinking of these dope growers I had heard about up around Northern

California somewhere who had arsenals of LAWS rockets and even Burmese tiger pits with real tigers in them to discourage the feds. Of course I hadn't seen a single joint anywhere near the place—though I would have liked to.

I also gathered that Ryder was one of Cole's discarded lovers, still carrying a torch. I got this mostly from Ryder's trying not to let it show.

The blackout periods were more pleasant than the drugged dreams I had that featured echoing screams and minor-key chanting—the sound track to some bad Vincent Price epic.

I held a long, nonsensical conversation with Ian Broctor one dawn that seemed to make sense at the time, but had to do with Rachel's being an avatar of Cybele, a seer or goddess, and Broctor's being a kind of metaphysical midwife in some cosmic process. Great stuff. I listened to all of it the way you might listen to one of the Hare Krishnas while waiting for a flight to Chicago. I downed cognac and "shared intuitive impulses." Rachel refused to discuss her relationship with him. The very idea of talking about Ian Broctor with me was sacrilegious.

All in all it was wonderful. The kind of long weekend for anyone interested in poisoning himself, learning the trade of pet stud and rubbing elbows with the insanely wealthy and the wealthy insane.

By Thursday the Santa Anas were over and a late summer storm was coming up from Mexico. The sky had turned the color of ash and lard and was pregnant with rain. I had drunk myself sober, which is a biological impossibility though you can't tell that to someone who has done it. I was staring out the dining room window with a glass of Chivas Royal Salute in my hand. It tasted like greasy kerosene. I could see my reflection in the window darkened by roiling clouds. My face was puffy and swollen, my eyes had almost disappeared, but on the whole I was amazed that I didn't look worse.

The night before, I had been too loaded to do Rachel any good. As the booze stopped getting me high and just fucking me up and the coke raked my nerve endings, inspiring cheap nightmares, the touch of her had begun to sicken me.

I wanted a steak, to go to a ball game, to discuss politics with Bananas at the Hillcrest, to put on a Sonny Boy Williamson record. It had been fun, I supposed, and maybe I belonged in a madhouse, but not this one. It was time to drag my ass down the mountain, back to my apartment and what I called my life.

Apparently Rachel thought so too after last night.

The old Mexican woman with the mustache who had taken hats and coats at the door during the party came in the room behind me and placed a canvas travel bag on a chair. On the floor next to them she set my boots. I was wearing my track shoes.

"Dese are your clothes," she said. "Meesus Cole say to tell you Mr. Walters is coming. You go now."

"Do I get a pink slip?"

"*Mande?*"

"*Nada.*" My résumé was really turning to shit. I would have to get Hunter Thompson to write up the next one. "Consuela"—I remembered her name—"*cerveza, por favor.*" I set down the glass of whiskey thinking that I really should say goodbye to everyone, especially pay my respects to Gene. I was suddenly tired and annoyed at being pushed around, even though I'd let her do it since I got there and even though leaving was my own idea. The thought of Walters was like poking at the scab around the wound I thought was healing. I wanted to poke back a little. Maybe more than a little.

I might have just got in my car and driven away and forgotten about the whole goddamned summer if the maid hadn't come to kick me out because Mr. Walters was coming.

In the words of Leroi Jones, "There is some shit I will not eat."

"You go?" Consuela didn't want any more trouble than she'd already seen in her years. She reminded me of the dead *cantinero*'s wife and I wished I hadn't started thinking about that again too.

"*Si, me voy. Una para el camino.*" She made no move to go. I smiled. "*La caminera,*" I joked. It meant "the roadrunner." She looked unhappy, but went to the kitchen anyway.

I seated myself on the sofa in the living room, put my feet up on the glass coffee table and smoked cigarettes from the lacquered box. I had two more beers for the road while I waited and watched the room and the sky outside darken.

Exhaustion can sometimes bring a kind of clearheadedness, even if it's bracketed by toxic mania and depression. It's like being in the eye of the hurricane, or in the motionless center of a

merry-go-round. I remembered what had bothered me that afternoon when Rachel had been talking about her joint interests with
Walters. She had mentioned real estate. I thought of the hotel in
Ensenada where Juana was working when she was "discovered"
by Walters. Juana said that there had been a woman with him,
"beautiful, but cold-looking." That was Rachel Cole. I don't
know why I cared or what difference it could make now, but it
seemed to me that given Rachel's penchant for beautiful Mexican
girls, she probably wasn't as oblivious to Juana's existence as she
had pretended.

Rain lashed the windows. The wind blew like notes from a
demented oboe player through the drainpipes, whistled around
the bell tower and set something up there creaking like the bed-
springs in a honeymoon suite. By six-thirty it was nearly pitch
dark. I didn't turn any lights on.

Ryder came in through the kitchen wearing a plastic poncho
and dripping water. His hair was plastered to his forehead.

"You were invited to leave. C'mon, let's haul ass, meatloaf." He
walked to the chair with my clothes on it and threw the canvas bag
at me. He held the boots in his left hand.

I caught the bag and put it on the couch. "Sit down, Ryder.
Have a beer. I'd never forgive myself if I didn't say goodbye.
Besides, look at it out there. I could kill myself going down that
mountain. My tires are bald."

He examined me with disgust and amusement as if I were a
talking cockroach. "You're moving out, Jew York." He liked that
and started chuckling. "You ought to get cards made up, Jew
York: Hired Hard-on, Circumcised." He was really cracking himself up now.

He started to walk toward me and I stood up. I motioned for
him to come closer.

"C'mon. Throw me out, Sergeant Rock. You know how Rachel
doesn't like to be surrounded by her old stuff. Only she made an
exception in your case, didn't she? You're such a loyal little lap-
dog and she appreciates a good grovel. Besides, you provide her
with laughs running around here in your GI Joe costume." I felt
adrenaline up through the backs of my arms and legs. He could

kill me, but not right away. It would cost him. "You're a joke, Ryder. That's something else she appreciates, a good joke."

He came forward. He had stopped laughing and I couldn't see his face in the dark.

Headlights distorted by the sheets of rain on the window moved the shadows around against the far wall. "Walters," he said. "And Rachel. You're out of here."

He turned his back to me and then spun, lifting his leg to his shoulder and swinging it around to where my head was. Karate. I threw my head back and missed most of it, but I caught the heel of his canvas laced boot on my right cheek. It didn't hurt. Yet. I staggered two steps and tripped on the first stair of the conversation pit. I reached for the neck of the beer bottle on the table. Ryder bent and grabbed my wrist. I took hold of the front of his poncho and pulled him down to me, butting him in the head with my own. It sent a bolt of pain clear to my shoulders. He let go of my wrist and I brought the bottle up against the side of his head. It broke in three or four pieces. I had a scrap of jagged bottleneck in my hand and waved it in front of his face.

The lights came on. I was holding Ryder's poncho and the broken glass. He was holding a bayonet in his right hand, but his eyes were dull and glazed. I could see Rachel Cole standing in the foyer removing a disposable plastic rain bonnet. Consuela was standing by the kitchen entrance with her hand on the rheostat switch for the living room chandelier. Behind Rachel, Eugene Walters made his entrance shaking a black umbrella. He wore an off-white trench coat that matched his pallor and the kind of stingy-brimmed hat you put fishing tackle on.

"Uh oh," I said, "Mom and Dad are home. We're gonna get it." Then Ryder's fingers loosened on the bayonet, his eyes fluttered and he dropped to the floor like a moose on ether.

Walters was the first to speak. "Goddammit. Him."

"What the hell is going on?" Rachel said.

I stayed where I was and crossed my legs on the floor. I began to feel the pain in my face. Blood dripped from my bottom lip. My tongue found a loose tooth.

"Manny?" Rachel turned and called out the front door that was still open. I heard a car door slam. My hand crawled under Ryder's parka and searched his waist. My fingers closed on a snapped holster. I fumbled with it and drew what felt like an automatic. I couldn't find the safety on it. Footsteps clattered on the tile outside and then Manny appeared. He was one of the guys who had pointed me away from the east forty the other night on my evening stroll. It took him three or four seconds and then he had a gun in his hand. I lifted mine. I was right, it was a Walther P-38. I found the safety.

"Mexican standoff, you should pardon the expression. And to think I was your understudy the other night, Manny."

Manny glowered at me above three or four chins. He wore a blood-colored Members Only jacket.

"What do you want?" Rachel said through clenched teeth. "I thought I made it clear that you were to leave here."

"I wanted to say goodbye," I whined. "Talk over old times with Gene, shoot the shit, wait for the rain to settle down. But he wouldn't let me, Mrs. Cole." I looked at Ryder. "What the hell ever happened to Mr. Cole, anyway? Fuck him into a cardiac arrest? Or didn't he like carp in the swimming pool? I got it. He didn't want to go into the alien-smuggling business, right? He probably wanted to use the old servants' quarters above the garage on the east road for his den. Maybe put some model airplanes together up there."

"Are you always drunk?" Walters looked genuinely curious.

"Lately, Walters. Lately." I was still holding the gun and pointing it at him. Manny was still pointing his gun at me. "Actually it dates from about the time you whisked Juana Villez off to some sleazy show-biz twilight zone." I pulled the hammer away from the chamber on Ryder's gun. "You're going to tell me a little bit about that now. Before you take your raincoat off and sit down, you're going to talk about that little thing. Now Manny could shoot me dead where I sit from there, it's true. But I guaran-fucking-tee you I'll put three or four in you before I go. I've got Ryder's automatic, Manny's holding a .38 revolver. I'm good with guns," I lied. "Manny probably is too, but you can only be so good with one of those things and you don't have to be very good at all with one of these."

"What could you possibly offer her?" Walters looked disgusted.

"A few nights is about it, I'd say." Rachel smiled contemptuously. It made her look her age for a moment.

I braced the pistol with my other hand around my wrist. "That's not the point right now, is it?" I moved the gun toward Rachel.

Her calm began to crumble. The harsh overhead chandelier showed up her rain-streaked makeup and dead gray eyes in a way I hadn't quite seen before. I felt my stomach turn. My hands shook. I was suddenly afraid. But there was fear on Rachel's face too. I liked it. I hated myself for liking it, but I liked it.

"You know, I was about to pack up my tent and steal away into the night like a good little Arab, forget I ever heard of either of you, but you had to push my buttons one more time, didn't you? It got me mad and started me thinking all over again. Something I'd worked real hard on not doing for a long time. Maybe you're right, Walters. Maybe Juana is better off without me to screw up whatever kind of career you may or may not be able to give her. And she may not miss me, but just to satisfy my curiosity, I'd like to know where she is. I'd like to make a clean goodbye of it, without eating myself up anymore. I'd also like to know what happened to her brother, not because I think it would buy me anything with her, but because I said I would find out and I didn't and I got somebody killed trying to do it. I've discovered that even unlimited amounts of expensive booze doesn't wash that down. What about it, Walters? You can chime in, too, anytime you want, Rachel. Don't look so puzzled. Juana Villez was the maid you both recruited out of your hotel in Ensenada. You couldn't have missed her, Rachel, she makes Maria look kind of plain."

I felt like I was jabbering. I was out of the eye of the hurricane and I felt dizzy. This was going to end badly and I knew it. When you hold a gun in your hands, you're supposed to feel an icy grim control over things. In the war I'd learned that that was bullshit, but I'd seen a lot of movies before and since then and they seemed more real than the war ever was.

"Look, I don't give a shit what your scam is here with all these boys running around with guns and your fertilizer trucks and your joint ventures, whatever they are. I figure it has to do with illegals and phony green cards—yeah, I was just guessing about that, but Maynard confirmed it for me, Walters. I hope he doesn't lose his job or anything over it—but I can't figure how there can be enough money in that to interest you, Rachel. I don't know or care what Broctor has to do with it, if anything. Like I said, I just want enough of the picture to trace Juana's brother, even if it's just a shallow grave somewhere, and to see Juana one more time."

Walters shot a glance to the windows.

"Gene, I'm talking to you. Is your boy Carlos out there? It won't help you." I lowered the gun a little. "You'll lose a kneecap if he so much as sticks his head in the door." But there were a lot of doors and windows at Rachel's cozy hideaway. I had my back to the hallway leading to the north wing and there were several doors opening onto it. I realized I was fucked. I started to get up and back myself toward a corner where I could see all the entrances. It seemed to take more time than it should. The room was suddenly much bigger than it had been an hour ago.

Walters started to breathe easy. "She's in New York," he said. It was bullshit. He was stalling. Waiting. "She's working hard and doing well. Her prospects are very good. She's happy, can you understand that? I won't put you in touch with her. Even if I thought she wanted that, I wouldn't do it. No matter how many guns you point at me. Look at yourself, York. You are a sick, dangerous man. I don't know anything about half of what you're raving about, but you'd better get some help, my friend, before you end up drooling on yourself in a corner of some state institution."

"You're such a righteous prick, Walters."

I think I was going to shoot him when I backed into the muzzle of something big, metallic and cold.

"Hey, shitheap," Carlos said behind me.

"Don't tell me. Charles Bronson, right?"

Ryder groaned and started to get up off the floor.

11

I GOT BEHIND the wheel of the Maverick soaking wet. Ryder was on the passenger side pointing the Walther at me and Carlos held his .45 right up against my head. My car keys were in the bottom of the canvas valise—compliments of Rachel. They had even brought out my boots for me.

The car wouldn't start.

Ryder looked pale and unsteady standing there in the rain. Now and then a little blood would run along with the rainwater down the side of his face where I had hit him. Carlos looked pissed off. He wore a nice beige linen jacket that wouldn't be good for anything except the children's section of a thrift shop after tonight.

I kept telling myself, *I'm not dead. Nobody shot me. God looks out for drunks and fools. Thanks, God.* But I was beginning to get pissed off too. If my car wouldn't start soon, they were going to kill me. It was just a wild, fey hunch I had.

Manny stood beneath an overhang out front and held his pistol negligently in folded arms.

The engine ground and wheezed.

"Piece of shit." Carlos kicked a dent in the door.

When it finally turned over, they both stood aside. Manny jumped off the porch and into Ryder's Renegade. He started it right up.

"Manny and I are gonna follow you down," Carlos said. "Make sure you get off the property."

Ryder walked slowly up the front steps and into the house. He held the iron railing to support himself.

" 'Bye, Sandy!" I called out. "Hey that was fun. We'll be talking about it for weeks I bet."

Ryder turned and pointed his gun unsteadily in my direction. He fired and the bullet went wild into the rain somewhere. If he had meant to hit me, he would have. I shifted into reverse and spun out in a puddle, threw it into drive and headed down the driveway. When I got past the gravel, I slowed down. I made out the lights of the Jeep following me not too far behind. Just as advertised. I skated and swerved on mud, my headlights playing wildly over the trees, the tennis court, ice plants and cactus. I alternated my foot gingerly between the accelerator and the brake.

The clay and sand that make up most of the ground in Southern California won't take more than a quarter-inch of water before turning to goo. By the time I got to the gate at the bottom of the incline, I might as well have been driving on chocolate pudding.

I hit the paved road beyond the soldered gate I had entered three days ago. Lightning lit the sky and I could make out the bell tower in the distance for a moment.

The Renegade's headlights disappeared behind me and I took the winding mountain road at a sober, careful pace.

People in Southern California don't know how to drive in the rain; they don't have much practice at it. During the rainy season, the conventional wisdom seems to be to speed up, beat the rain home or drive between the drops maybe. An inch of rainfall between dusk and dawn usually means overtime at the emergency wards in a dozen counties, carnage up and down the Sunbelt freeways. Jackknifed semis, overturned school buses, chains of accordioned Datsuns, Subarus and Toyotas. But this was something else. It wasn't the rainy season, but a freak, late-summer tropical storm, and more than an inch had fallen in the past hour. Someone probably had a name for it like Gladys or Myrtle in the weather bureau offices. I started thinking of all the people who were going to be dead tonight because of it. The fact that I might be one of them crossed my mind. The rain was moving in solid walls over the mountains. Within ten minutes I began to come down from the adrenaline high. All the cocaine I had taken was suddenly clamoring for its pound of flesh and my thoughts came in paranoid cartoon balloons. I should never have started thinking about overturned school buses. It was seven o'clock at night after all and school buses wouldn't be on the road for another three weeks. There's no reasoning with spent cocaine, though. A dash of self-loathing began to set in with the onset of the hangover I'd been putting off God knows how long. I started to shake with fear, disgust, residual impotent anger and a kind of disappointment that I hadn't, after all, killed myself over the long weekend or goaded someone into doing the job for me.

I was driving at ten miles an hour now. I couldn't see anything in front of me or behind me. Nothing. The shaking got worse.

I slowed to a stop along the side of the road that was eroding into the cliff face. I cupped my hands over my face to keep from hyperventilating. *Stress. That's what it is, my boy, just stress. Losing people you love—or might have loved—a marathon binge, religious maniacs, fucking old ladies and, of course, all those guns being pointed around. Why, you're just under a strain, pal. Pull over and catch your breath and then stop at the nearest Howard Johnson's for a bracing cup of coffee after this monsoon lets up. You'll be as right as rain. . . .*

Rain. There was just too much of it. I couldn't even see my headlights. The car shifted as the shoulder of the road sagged. I had to get back on the pavement, find one of those vista points with the barriers. I couldn't stay there or I'd find myself at the bottom of whatever was down in that wedge of blackness that looked like a piece of the night sky driven into the earth by Mexico's displaced hurricane. I shifted the rod on the steering column into drive and nosed carefully onto the road. Something exploded alongside the Maverick and sent me skidding back toward the edge. My neck whipped sideways, and I hit the top of the steering wheel with my nose. Something black and vaguely shiny streaked past me, illuminated briefly in the lame light from my headlights.

It was the Renegade.

I heard a sound like wet earth sucking against rubber. I wasn't on the road anymore. I was back on the shoulder and losing ground. I threw the gearshift into first and hit the gas.

Gradually, I gained traction again. I kept the car in low gear and peered wildly out the windows for any sign of the Jeep. It was like looking through a shower curtain during a blackout.

I drove on the wrong side of the road hoping that, if the Jeep came back, I would keep it between me and the edge of the world. Hunched over the wheel like an old man, imagining that I saw things that weren't there, I watched a mile and a half click over on the odometer. I was beginning to believe that Carlos and Manny had just wanted to have a little fun, to throw one final scare into me just for kicks, when a pair of headlights appeared from a curve less than fifty feet ahead of me and closing rapidly.

I swung the wheel to the right and got out of the northbound lane. A Volkswagen sped past me at about sixty-five. In the brief time it took to pass in and out of my headlight beam, I recognized the bumper sticker it carried on the front fender. I'd seen several of them around town. It said, "Welcome to San Diego Now Go Home."

"Loosen up," I told myself out loud when I felt my hands cramping on the wheel. My voice sounded thin and ridiculous. I forced my hands to ease up and leaned back a little in the seat trying to work the tension out of my shoulders.

They appeared on my right this time from one of those vista point turnoffs I had been looking for. It was nearly invisible. I wouldn't have seen it at all except for another flash of lightning far away, out to sea maybe. The darkened Jeep sped behind me trying to get over onto my left. I zigzagged across the two lanes and increased my speed to keep from being rear-ended.

I was doing fifty-five, now sixty, sixty-five—hydroplaning down the two-lane mountain road.

I tried to make out road barriers in my headlights, but I couldn't see anything except a vision of Highway Patrol officers

gathered around the wreckage at the bottom of some godfor-
saken canyon in the morning fog, my body twisted like a blood-
spattered doll inside of it and one of the cops saying, "Course,
we'll have to wait for the coroner's report, but judging from the
smell, I think we'll find a good .25 blood alcohol level in this
asshole." And if they found a little black paint embedded in the
gouges along the side of the car, they wouldn't go to too much
trouble about it.

The Renegade got alongside of me while I was thinking about
that. Metal bashed against metal as we sideswiped each other like
charioteers in some film noir *Ben Hur.*

The Jeep rode a good foot and a half higher than the Maverick.
It had a four-wheel drive and sat on forty-inch tires. Mine were
bald. It was only a matter of time before they ran me off the road
unless I did something about it.

I tried to peer into the plastic windows looking for Carlos and
Manny, but I couldn't make them out. I didn't have to.

The Jeep hit me again. The door next to me buckled. The
armrest dug into my ribs and I could hear the sound of tires on
wet pavement, louder now, humming like basso synthesizer
notes. I caught a glimpse of oily black road water rushing beneath
me between the floor of the car and where it used to meet the
bottom of the door.

I took my foot off the gas and let them speed ahead of me. I
killed the headlights and hugged the sheer rock wall on the
northbound side. They had disappeared in the darkness ahead. I
continued to drive at a crawl until I saw that the rock curved away
to the left.

I stopped the car and kept the engine idling. When they decided to come back for me, I would hit the accelerator and try to
T-bone them over the edge of the curve. I would have to be very
lucky. If I hit them head on, I'd probably total myself. I might
anyway.

The rain let up. The night was quiet except for the drizzling on
the roof and the sound of a dozen little timeworn channels of
water running off the cliff face. They were the kind of soft, com-
forting, liquid sounds of a rainy night you learn to fall pleasantly
asleep to when you are a kid.

I wanted a cigarette. The thought made me start to laugh, but I stopped it. It would have been a dangerous, scary sound that I didn't want to hear.

They came around the curve in reverse, doing about fifteen. I hit the gas and sent my right front end dead center into the driver's side. The Maverick bucked and stalled, sitting across both lanes like a barricade. I prayed there were no other cars barreling along either side of that curve.

The Renegade slid sideways toward the shoulder of the road and stopped up against a tree.

Fuck.

Someone was screaming inside of it. I hoped it was Carlos.

I turned the key in the ignition and felt my heart try to scrabble its way out of my throat as the whining *uunngghh* sound of the starter motor tried to turn over a flooded carburetor.

I was about to give it up and take my chances on foot when the engine caught and roared like the Mormon Tabernacle Choir in my ears. I spun out and almost lost control, but didn't. I downshifted and tried to keep a steady, deliberate pressure on the pedal at about forty-five.

The odometer clicked off two miles, three. No one was behind me, not that I could make out. I began to breathe again and even reached for a cigarette in my shirt pocket. Of course there wasn't one there. The rain started up again with renewed fury and I had to slow to thirty.

Two cars passed me going up the mountain.

There was still no one behind me.

I was congratulating myself when they hit me on the left rear side. It sounded like a giant's fist punching through my trunk. It made me queasy for a moment and light-headed. It was maybe a second later, though it felt like twenty minutes, that I realized my head had hit the windshield and cracked it. The phrase came to me, floating up like a bubble through oil, "Whiplash. I'll sue."

I was flying, sailing off the edge of the world in a 1975 cream-colored, six-cylinder family car.

Lightning lit the sky, but nothing beneath me. It was black, null, void, antimatter. In the rearview mirror, as the lightning stuttered, I saw the Renegade without lights, gleaming wetly in the brief flash before the darkness swallowed everything.

* * *

Pain woke me.

I didn't swim up from a deep pool of unconsciousness or stumble down a long dark tunnel toward a point of light; I was catapulted back into the land of the living by a hundred burning points of fire: pieces of broken glass embedded in my right cheek, along my forearm and in the back of my hand.

I couldn't see anything. I didn't know which way was up or down. I tasted something metallic and sour and I seemed to be deaf, all I could hear was some hollow roaring noise.

Rain was banging against the underside of the car. It sounded like steel drums in a waterfall. There was no smell of gasoline. It might have all been washed away in the rain and, I realized, I'd had less than a quarter-tankful anyway.

It was still dark. I didn't know how long I had been out.

I rolled down the window. Or rolled it up actually. My arm felt as if it were made of oatmeal. Water rushed in the opened window, enough to snap me to without drowning me. I started to crawl out but my left leg wouldn't cooperate. It just wanted to lie across the ceiling of the car and catch a few Z's. I could see where the roof had buckled, pinning my leg against the headrest at the top of the seat on the passenger side. I felt nothing below the knee where it was pinned and I started thinking about severed nerves and gangrene and other cheery possibilities.

With my other foot I pushed against the shredded layer of upholstery and the bent metal of the car roof. My leg sort of fell out of the position it had been in. I ran my fingers lightly over the knee, up and down. It didn't seem broken. A rush of blood back into it nearly blacked me out again. I bit my lip and made noises until the pain subsided to a throb.

I began to slide slowly out of the window, careful not to move anything too quickly.

I must have blown it because I went out again. When I woke the next time, I was still half in and half out of the car. The rain had stopped and the sky had begun to lighten. I could see that the Maverick had knocked down a good-sized pine or fir tree and lay across it on its back like a comatose wrestler pinning his opponent. The tree had broken the fall, it was the only reason I wasn't dead.

I couldn't make out the road yet, it was still too dark. I started to crawl in a general upward direction. Using handfuls of roots and thorny bushes, I slid on mud that was already drying. A mist began to form at the bottom of the canyon and, as the sky brightened, wrapped me in a damp cocoon.

One hand after the other, left foot . . . right foot. I climbed through the mist thinking of Jack and the Beanstalk. Pain propelled me up the embankment like a steadily stoked engine. I passed an area where a huge gash had recently been carved out of the vegetation. It must have been where the car hit the earth for the first time, then bounced and flipped on its way to meet the fir tree.

Ten feet to the right I saw the canvas valise with my clothes in it. I debated with myself whether or not it would be worth the pain to go after it. Without ever making the decision I found myself almost standing, crabwalking toward the khaki-colored bundle. I threw it up the side of the mountain and when it didn't tumble back down, I climbed after it.

I threw the bag upward twice more and found it. The last time, it lay along the shoulder of Route 18. The mist lay below me as I stood. The day was overcast, but the storm clouds had spent themselves. The sound of a truck's engine in low gear carried on the still morning air across the canyon. I could see a green-and-chrome semi lumbering slowly down the mountain toward me. I was covered in mud and blood and I weaved as I stood, trying to keep my feet under me, but I stuck my thumb out.

I remember the trucker helping me into the cab—he had a tattoo that said "Roselle" on a heart—and I remember telling him I had had an accident. I remember him saying, "No shit," and then night fell all over again.

12

"How many fingers?"

I saw bright lights and a man wearing a puke green gown. He was holding three fingers silhouetted against the light. I said so.

He seemed satisfied and sat on a folding chair at the edge of the bed I was in. "What's your name?"

I told him my name.

"You know where you are?" He didn't seem interested in whether I did or I didn't.

"More or less," I said, and read the information on the tag pinned to his gown.

"You've got a concussion," he said. "That's the worst of it." His name was Paul Rice Resident M.D. Emergency at El Cajon Mission Hospital. "You've also got multiple contusions, likewise lacerations, none of them too bad, except for the one on your knee. You'll limp for a while, a couple weeks. They'll rent you a cane downstairs. I can give you a sheet with some knee exercise diagrams on it, they'll hurt and you don't have to do them, but they'll help. Let's see . . ." He looked at a chart. He was tan, a few years younger than I was, and wore his hair shaved at the sides, but long and curly at the collar. In his right ear he wore a simple, tastefully unembellished gold earring. He didn't look like anybody's idea of a doctor; he looked like a band member in a group that might have a name like Razorburn or Bile. "You're also missing a tooth: upper right canine. That'll be about half a grand worth of bridgework if you want to go that route. Not our department. Uh, sprained metatarsals, no biggie, but it'll drive you nuts for a while. Leave the dressings on your face and arm for three or four days. That's it." He tossed the chart and the clip-board onto the chair he had just been sitting in. He walked around to the left side of my bed. "The concussion could be serious. We didn't do a CAT scan, but there's always a risk of a blood clot in the brain. You've been out for twenty hours. You woke up for a while, didn't know who you were and couldn't tell three fingers from a quiche lorraine."

"I probably wouldn't have been able to three days ago either."

"Yeah, that's another thing. We did a blood test on you when you came in and you had a .13 blood alcohol level. Three hours ago it was only down to .09. I'd give the stuff up if I were you."

"Has anyone been here asking for me?" I started thinking about Carlos, Manny and Ryder. They would know by now that there had been no body discovered with my car.

"Not that I know of," Rice said. He pulled a cigarette from his pocket and lit it. It smelled like cloves.

"Can I get out of here?"

"My guess is you've got no medical insurance, right? Any way you could foot the bill for a week of observation and physical therapy . . . for the knee and everything?"

"No."

"That's what I thought." He blew smoke at the curtain drawn around the next bed. "You should stay right here. If you've got a blood clot, you could be killing yourself by walking out that door, literally. You move, the blood clot could move."

"You don't know that I have a blood clot."

"No."

There wasn't any point in telling him that my chances for survival dropped with every minute I spent in a hospital anywhere near the place I was supposed to have been killed but wasn't. It would just complicate things with cops and I would be a fixed target.

"What do I have to do to get out of here?"

"There are some forms. Look, if you split, you'd better take it easy, my man. I mean, lay around, watch soap operas and read dull books for a couple of days, a week would be better. If you start thinking you're Napoleon or begin to receive brain transmissions from Proxima Centauri . . . or forget your name . . . or start walking into walls, you'd better check back into a hospital. On your driver's license it says you live on Robinson Avenue in the city. You're near Mercy and University Hospital. I'll give you their emergency numbers. I'd suggest you tape them to the door of your liquor cabinet." He leaned over and wrote them on the chart.

"What about the guy who brought me here?"

"What about him?"

"You know his name?"

"No. You can ask down in emergency admissions. I'll have someone bring your clothes and stuff. You really should get some major medical coverage, you know."

"If I had it I would have known by now about that blood clot, wouldn't I? You would have gone ahead with the CAT scan and the bill to Blue Cross would already be in the mail, wouldn't it?"

"What do you want me to tell you?" He tapped his pen against his earring. "That this isn't a business?" He gestured around the room.

"How can I ever thank you, doctor? God bless you."

"Hey, maybe next time you'll get Marcus Welby." He coughed burnt cloves around the room and left.

I gave the cashier one of my hundred-dollar bills, my social security and driver's license numbers and a promise to pay the balance of my $818.19 bill at the earliest opportunity. I discovered that the trucker who had delivered me to the hospital was one Luther Warren, Jr., of Grass Valley, California. I got his number from information and reached his wife. Her name wasn't Roselle. I told her to thank him for me and said I would try and reach him myself in a few days when he would, she said, be home from a six-day run.

The woman cab driver shook me awake when we arrived at the address I had given her. I had fallen asleep again. Or passed out. That happens with concussions. She was saying, ". . . and she put me in touch with my whole brain. I discovered I didn't need doctors and hospitals anymore. I'll give you the number. You should call and share your experiences. It's a whole other thing. Diet: fiber and grains and whole-brain learning, left and right side, you know? You go through the birth process again with Jesus Christ and when you hug the other people in the group at the end of the sessions, it's total, complete, incredible. I cried and I found I wasn't sick anymore. I don't even have colds."

She helped me to my feet and handed me the cane. I thanked her and tipped her and accepted a card that read, "Holistic Sunrise Encounters," with an address in Santee. She told me to have a nice day. I said, "You too," and stood swaying for a while in front of the bleached pink apartment house on Oklahoma Street.

After a while I got my legs moving and found the mailboxes and doorbells that were hidden behind the snail-eaten leaves of a bird of paradise plant. I pressed number 3G. Dick Holster was home.

"Yeah?"

"York. Let me in."

"Well, whattya know?" The inner door buzzed, I pushed it open and climbed the stairs very slowly.

Dick stood in the open door of his apartment with a can of Coor's Light in his hand. He was a tall man with an air of autonomy about him that wasn't just aloofness. It was a rare occasion when he laughed or even smiled, but he wasn't a hard man. The lines of his face were drawn sharp, making him look as tough as he was, and the crow's-feet around his eyes gave him the air of someone who never takes anything at face value. His eyes were dark, intelligent and expressive; what they expressed was a controlled restlessness and a little sadness. It was strange to see him

out of uniform. He was wearing red jogging shorts and a San
Diego Zoo T-shirt with a koala bear on it. On him it looked like a
disguise. I could hear the ball game on TV behind him. He
looked at the bandages on my face, hand and arm, the cane. He
shook his head from side to side.

"You wanna give me a hand?" I asked him.

He came down and helped me up the rest of the stairs without
saying anything. He took me inside and cleared a stack of magazines from the couch. I sat on it and put my knee up on the coffee
table and some more magazines. It was dark and cool in the
apartment, the venetian blinds were drawn. The walls had bad,
motel art that probably came with the furniture. One wall was
covered by cinder-block bookshelves that held the kind of books
that you don't generally see in Southern California apartments—
they looked like someone had read them. Dick's place wasn't
modest, it was cheap and spartan. He had two acres and a cabin
built into the side of a mountain up around Jamul. He invested
what money and time he had on furnishing it as a fallout shelter
and fortress against the day someone pushed the button or the
economy finally went down for the count. I used to kid him about
it all the time.

On the television, the Padres were playing Atlanta but not very
well. Dick disappeared in the kitchen and came back with a can of
beer. He handed it to me, but I didn't take it. "How about a glass
of water?"

He set the beer down next to his own and brought me a glass of
water. I drank it and leaned back on the couch, closing my eyes.
Garvey hit a double driving in a man on third. Dick grunted.

"I need some help, Dick."

"Yeah," was all he said.

"Can you get me a small, lightweight but high-caliber automatic? Something I can conceal with a lot of stopping power."

"Why?"

I sat up and looked at him. He was watching the game. "You
really want to know?"

He drained his beer and then cracked the other one that he had
brought for me. "Maybe not," he said.

"There's something else. I can't stay at my apartment. If I go
back there someone is going to finish the job on me that they

started. I need a place to stay for a couple of days and I need to do it without anyone knowing. Especially anyone at the Low Down. Also, I can't pay for the gun. It's nice to see you, Dick."

He turned away from the television and looked at me. He belched. "You're not going to tell me what happened?"

"I got run off the road, up on 18, in the mountains. The only part that was accidental was my walking away from it."

"Okay. I won't ask what you're involved in, but I can guess. You're still looking for the Mexican girl and you went up against Walters, who doesn't like you. I told you a long time ago Walters was involved with some heavy people. Mafia or some shit."

"Some shit is more like it. What do you say?"

"Let me get this straight. You want me to put you up here for a few days and keep it under my hat, get you a gun you can't pay for and not ask any questions?"

"You can ask away, but I might not tell you much. The less you know, the better off you are. Me too."

"Either you trust me or you don't."

"I put my ass on the line by coming here at all. I had some idea I could trust you, yes. I don't think I'm wrong."

"But you're not all that sure."

I grinned. It probably didn't look very merry.

"Okay, but I'm curious." Dick got up and shut off the Padres game. Garvey was tagged out at third when Kennedy or whoever it was grounded to the shortstop, which retired the sides. Atlanta led by five runs and it was the top of the eighth. A lot can happen in one inning of baseball, but not if the Padres are playing it. A year later they would win the pennant, but that summer they weren't doing a thing that I could see. I'd been spoiled by New York, ask anyone. "I'll trade you. You can stay here. I won't mention it around in my vast circle of friends and confidants. The gun, I don't know, you're going to have to tell me more about who you're going to kill with it."

"The gun for the story, is that the idea?"

"Yes."

"Okay, look. If I can get into my apartment, there's a guitar in there. I can hock it for a couple hundred. Will that cover the gun?"

"It's not the money, York."

"What is it then, a question of ethics? Law and order? You want to be sure I don't shoot any cop friends of yours or a Libertarian or a loyal member of the order of Survivalists?"

"You're supposed to be buttering me up and you're not doing it. How about this? I'll trade you some news about your girlfriend and you tell me what the fuck is going on."

"Juana?" I sat up and toppled a pile of *Soldier of Fortunes* onto the floor. "What about her?"

"She called Liz at the Low Down last Friday night." Dick seemed to be enjoying his beer for the first time. He looked at it, drank from it and studied the label, turning the can around in his hands. He smacked his lips.

"Where is she? Do you know where she is?"

Dick held up the silver-gray can at arm's length and squinted at it. "Not a bad beer, for a light beer. Not great, but not bad. A nice grainy aftertaste without being, you know, foody or something. Watery, of course, but I guess that's the idea with light beer." He patted his stomach. There was no fat on him. He must have been pushing forty, but he was in better shape than I was in when I was twenty.

"Okay," I said. I was suddenly very tired again and felt the need to sleep, but I told him everything as best I could. I began with Juana and Walters and Cole at the hotel in Ensenada. I told him about Herman Villez and everything, roughly, that had happened to me since I had first heard his name. I cut it short and left out the bedroom details. I finished up by gesturing at my bandages and saying, "I think it was something I said."

"You hit a nerve with the alien-smuggling business." Dick lost interest in his beer again and set it down. He stared at the blank television screen. "It doesn't make sense, though. It doesn't surprise me that Walters might be involved in something along those lines—from a safe distance of course—but your Rachel Cole doesn't seem like the type to play around for bush league bucks."

"That's what I thought. Maybe there's real money in it after all, though. There's a lot of other things that bother me, like the small army around her estate. You don't need men with guns to keep a bunch of illegal Mexicans in line. They're usually frightened, have no idea where they are and are generally eager to please. They just want to keep a low profile and get some kind of work. Walters is too sensitive about it, so is everyone I contacted in Tijuana. Sensitive enough to kill people over it."

"So what do you plan to do?" Dick leaned forward and cupped his chin in his hand. "Go back and storm Cole's place with a handgun? Force the truth out of them? It seems like you tried that."

"What I plan to do isn't part of our deal. Tell me about Juana. You know where she is?"

"York, I don't mind helping you, but let's can the bullshit about deals. With you here, my ass is grass too the way I see it."

"I'm sorry, you're right, but I don't want you involved any more than you have to be. If you know what I'm going to do, it's just one too many people."

He crushed his beer can and threw it into a wastebasket across the room. "Fine," he said. "I figure that means that whatever it is that you're planning is illegal and probably crazy and in that case, you're right, I don't want any." He unlaced his running shoes. "Juana told Liz she was calling from Las Vegas. Said she had a job up there dancing. She asked about you, said she tried to call you, but you weren't home. According to Liz, she's doing great. Walters has her in a house with a pool, parties, hobnobbing with Vegas wise guys, like that. If you still have any ideas about her being a damsel in distress, I'd forget them."

"I just want to talk to her." It was getting harder to stay awake. "I don't want Liz to know where I am, though."

"No."

I was starting to doze off. "Your boss wants me dead."

"I don't owe him anything if that's what you're worried about. From what little I've seen of him I think he's a career scumbag. I take his money the same as you did, but all it buys him is a babysitter for horny sailors."

"I want to talk to Juana, just say goodbye maybe."

"You're beat to shit, York. You've got all the color of a cue ball. Sleep for a while." He threw an olive drab blanket over me and took the cane out of my hands. I eased my legs onto the couch and leaned my head back on a pillow that Dick had produced from somewhere. "I'm going out. I'll be back in a couple of hours. Try and stay out of trouble."

I slept and didn't bother to worry whether or not Dick would try and make brownie points with Walters by turning me up. First of all, I didn't think he would, and second, there was nothing I could do about it anyway if I was wrong.

I awoke in darkness except for a sliver of light coming from beneath a door several feet away. I heard the sounds of a shower running and someone singing "Midnight Special" out of tune. I got to my feet slowly and not without pain. The kitchen light switch was where they usually are, to the left, about halfway up the wall. The first thing I saw was a clock above the stove. It was only ten o'clock. I'd slept for eight hours. A can of Hormel chili sat on the counter. I took it and started to look for a can opener. The first drawer I opened had one. It also had a corkscrew, some silverware, some Safeway supermarket bingo cards and a Colt Python revolver. I grabbed the opener and a fork and went to work on the chili straight out of the can. I found milk in the refrigerator and a *Star Trek* glass in a cabinet. I made my way back to the couch and coffee table, found a lamp, turned it on and sat down.

Dick came out of the bathroom wearing a towel and wiping shaving cream off his face. "Why don't you let me heat that up? Put some Tabasco in it, some onions, cheese, you know?"

"It's okay," I said. He sat down on a recliner chair that needed reupholstering.

"I went to your apartment," he said. "The front door lock was broken. Somebody tossed the place."

I just looked at him and chewed.

"They smashed up your guitar, your stereo, the TV."

"The TV didn't work very well."

"I found this and they didn't." He reached down next to him into the pants pocket of a pair of Levi's. He pulled out a wad of money and tossed it at me. There were a thousand dollars in twenties and tens. "They were inside a box of Rice Krispies on the floor. I kicked it out of my way and the money fell out."

I looked at it and set it on the couch next to me. "It's Juana's," I said. "She must have put it there that morning. My fee for finding her brother. I told her I didn't want it."

"I went over there to see if your place was being scoped out."

Dick got up and went to the refrigerator. He took a can of beer out and cracked it. "There was a guy, a Mexican with mirror shades on, parked down the street in a Honda Civic."

"Probably Carlos," I told him.

"Okay. I can get you a Beretta 9mm if you want or you can take my .32. You can't have it small and with the kind of power you're talking about at the same time. By the way, it looks like you can pay for it, doesn't it?"

"You can have all of it." I shoved the money across the coffee table. "It doesn't belong to me."

"The Beretta will cost you three, the .32 you can have on loan."

"I could stash the .32 in an ankle holster, right?"

"You could stash it in your jockstrap."

"I'll take it. Thanks."

"There's something else." Dick got up and took his pants and shirt with him back into the bathroom. "I talked to Liz. She said Juana was going to call back next Tuesday night at eight o'clock. I didn't mention you."

"Did Juana?"

From the bathroom he called out, "Yeah, she said in case Liz saw you to tell you not to worry anymore about her brother."

13

IT WAS THREE DAYS before I felt like anything but an extra for *Dawn of the Dead*. I ate and slept, lay in the sun out on the apartment complex patio, staring at the bank of mailboxes, the snail-infested Bird of Paradise and a dying banana tree. Overripe peaches fell at slow intervals from a neighbor's roof. I drank iced tea, Diet 7-Up and a lot of tap water and listened to Dick's jazz records. I read one of Dick's books—it was by Nathaniel West, about the Trojan horse and a flea named St. Puce that lived in the armpit of Jesus Christ—while I waited for a blood clot to kill me. I had shaved off my beard, left a long Fu Manchu mustache, covered myself with Hawaiian Formula suntan oil and did the knee exercises on the sheet of diagrams I got from the hospital. My knee hurt and I thought more than once about sending Dick back to my apartment for the codeine there. It would have helped the headaches too, which came and went with the ferocity of rattlesnakes on amphetamines. Instead, I made friends with the pain, it reminded me of what I had to do.

Coming off a marathon liquor binge, two weeks of heavy co-caine and recuperating from a car wreck were nothing compared to the withdrawal I experienced from a much more powerful drug. Hate. It takes a lot out of you to go around hating some-thing even for a day or two. I had developed a bad jones, hating myself and the world, and as I lay in the sun in front of that shabby pink building for three painfully sober days, I felt it all go out of me. My muscles uncoiled, my nerves downshifted, the brackish metallic taste passed from the back of my mouth and all the hate seemed to harden into a specific pinpoint of diamond-bright resolve.

Dick and I discussed how I should get in touch with Juana. It didn't seem like a good idea for me to just show up at Liz's on Tuesday night. Dick told me that Maynard had passed the word that if I were to appear at the Low Down I was to be detained—it seemed that I had stolen money from the club when I was fired and Mr. Walters was eager to recuperate the funds and settle the matter without proferring formal charges if possible. Neither of us knew how Liz would react to this, but if I showed at her place, she would know that Dick had a line to me and she might just say so to Maynard or, if not, to one of the other girls who would. In the end, we decided that Dick would talk to her and ask her to call at a number belonging to a pay phone on Market Street in front of an Irish bar Dick was partial to but couldn't be connected with if Walters's Vegas people thought the number looked suspicious on their phone bill.

It went down as planned. He said he wanted to talk to her about something very important, but didn't say what. He also made it clear that she should place the call without anyone on her end knowing about it. If anyone was listening in at that point, it would already be too late, but Dick didn't seem worried. He was count-ing on the fact that Juana was making these calls behind some-one's back anyway. But if it did lead back to him, he'd just say that he had found the money that I had told him about a long time ago when he dropped by my trashed apartment and wanted to get it back to Juana discreetly. If he did run afoul of Walters, that story probably wouldn't do him any good. I owed Dick in a big way.

* * *

I stood in front of Delaney's on Wednesday night feeling a stray, cool breeze from somewhere east of the city. I watched the sun sink behind the Imperial Bank building and didn't lean on my cane too much. The knee was coming along. Dick was inside drinking Harp's Lager at the bar, not flirting with waitresses or chewing the fat with the bartender, but chomping nachos and stolidly drinking his beer as if it were damned serious business. I looked at my watch too much and tried to pace with a stiff leg in front of the phone booth and thought about Irish bars that served nachos and jalapeños. At five minutes past eight the phone rang. I picked it up and saw Dick squint at me from his barstool.

"Hello?"

"Dick?"

"No. It's not Dick."

"Nathaniel?" Soft, surprised, without an accent. She said it the way she had that night. It had seemed like such a long time ago, until now.

"Yes," I said, never at a loss.

"Oh . . . are you all right?"

"I'm fine."

"You are at Dick's? I hear cars."

"No. I'm not at Dick's. Does anyone know you're calling?"

"No. They are next door at a party. There are so many parties, it's wonderful. I get tired of them sometimes, though. Lately I have been sad."

"Juana, where are you?"

"Didn't Liz tell you? I'm in Las Vegas. Oh, York, it's wonderful. I have a good job dancing at a place called . . . well, I'd better not tell you. I have a lot of friends. I miss you, though, and Liz and Suzy and Dick. Oh, I have a car, York. I paid for it myself. It's a Pinto." She called it a "peento." It was the only heavily accented word I had heard so far. Her English had come a long way over the summer.

"Why can't you tell me? I'd like to see you, Juana."

"York . . . Nathaniel, I'm sorry. I can't. Mr. Walters has forbidden me to see you or talk to you. If he knew I was talking to you now, he would send me back to Mexico. He hates you, because you've caused him trouble. I don't want to go back, I'm sorry. He told me you had a girlfriend, an old woman with money, he said."

"He's a liar, Juana. He hates me because I've tried to find your brother. A man got killed because I was asking too many questions about the *coyote* he recommended to you. I screwed it up, but I got people that work for him nervous enough so that he had me fired. I went up to his house and he threatened me and had his one-man goon squad work me over. I gave it up and forgot about it when I didn't hear from you for so long. But then I ran into his partner, the woman who was with him at the hotel when he first talked to you. They're both running illegals and they're doing it damned strangely. I stumbled onto it and almost got killed five days ago, again courtesy of Mr. Walters. He wants me dead, Juana, and he's already got blood on his hands, some of it is probably your brother's." I was shouting, the little diamond of hatred was running its charge up through my neck and into the phone.

"York, stop it. I don't know what you're talking about. I don't believe you!" Her voice had risen too. It sounded stupid and shrill. "Mr. Walters *did* find what happened to Herman when you couldn't! Herman is dead. He was killed in a fight in a bar in Tijuana. He was always like that. He carried knives and he drank too much and always lost his temper. I know. Mr. Walters took the trouble and the time to make inquiries among his friends with the *judiciales* in Mexico. Herman is dead and buried in Tijuana. Mr. Walters paid for his grave and sends flowers every week and money to my family. He will take me to visit the grave himself soon. He has been very kind to me and you have caused him nothing but trouble. How can you say he had anything to do with Herman's death? Why would he do such a thing?"

"How was the body identified, Juana? You know what your brother might have been carrying. Was any of it mentioned?"

"He had his father's *Bracero* card." She was almost hissing, with grief or anger or both. "I have it now. I am looking at it. It was given to him for good luck before he left to come north. I told Liz to tell you, don't look for Herman anymore."

The card she was talking about was issued to immigrant workers during the forties as part of the *Bracero* Program under FDR. The idea was a kind of sanction or amnesty to registered Mexican nationals who would come north and fill the jobs of American servicemen while they were otherwise occupied. The cards still turned up in the Border Patrol roundups, usually among old men who were proud of the cards and didn't know or refused to understand that the program had been dead for over thirty years. It was just the kind of thing a Mexican father would give to his son for good luck before coming to the United States to make his fortune.

"I'm sorry, Juana."

"I am sorry too. Things are not so bad, though, for me. They are very good. I have a good job, money, a swimming pool and friends. I am going to be in a movie. Life is very bad for a long time and then it can become good. When it does, you must take it and enjoy it." She began to cry. "I don't want trouble, York. Not now. Herman is dead. That is the way it is. It can do no one any good to make trouble."

"Sure." My voice was distant and dry in my ears. I really didn't want to talk to Juana anymore but maybe because my goodbye hadn't come off the way I wanted it to, I found myself saying, "Could you call again?"

"No. I'm sorry." Her voice sounded flat like the last echo of someone who had already hung up on a bad phone connection.

"All right, then. . . . Goodbye, Juana."

"Goodbye, York."

The phone went back in its cradle with a plastic snick. I felt nothing at all except that icy little hardness I woke up with in the hospital room. My little diamond.

In Dick's car we smoked cigarettes and drove back up to his apartment. We watched television without seeing it or talking to each other. Eventually I told him what she had said about Herman and the *Bracero* card. He grunted and massaged his eyes. He moved some books out of the way on his shelf and produced a small black gun. It was the .32. He said, "There." It was his only comment on anything. After a while he turned out the lights and went to bed.

I stayed up burning tobacco and wondering why Juana had said "his father" gave him the card and not "our father." It probably didn't matter, but it's funny what you think about in a quiet room full of shadows when your life has turned to something like the spaces in between stars.

14

BY NOON the next day I had gathered a few things I would need from a thrift shop on El Cajon Boulevard. I laid them out on Dick's couch and inventoried my haul, trying to think of anything I might have missed. One brown-and-red-plaid Western shirt worn through at the elbows and with phony mother-of-pearl button snaps, one faded flannel jacket—again Western style and a reddish plaid—and a down-at-the-heels pair of dust-colored, size nine-and-a-half cowboy boots, soles intact, with pointed toes the former owner might have used to pick his teeth. One pair of faded Wrangler jeans and a pair of baggy black cotton pants that would fit over them. The last item of haberdashery was a straw cowboy hat curved at just the right angles on the sides. A block from the thrift shop was a darling little boutique called GUNS! GUNS! GUNS! Inside it I found the accessories I needed for my outfit: an ankle holster, a box of ammunition and an extra clip for the little black .32 Dick had given me.

With everything on, both shirts, both pairs of pants, the holster, gun and hat, I checked myself out in the mirror over the fireplace. To get the whole picture I had to stand on Dick's coffee table. My three-day tan provided the right finishing touch. I looked like I had just gotten busted picking strawberries without a green card in Imperial Valley.

In the mirror, I saw Dick coming out of his bedroom scratching his balls. He squinted up at me and said, "You're too tall."

"I'm standing on the coffee table."

He ignored that and walked into the kitchen to get some coffee. I stepped down and took everything off again. He leaned against the kitchen doorjamb and said, "You're too tall to pass yourself off as Mexican. Also your accent is a combination of border Chicano and New York Puerto Rican. You'd hang yourself the minute you opened your mouth, even if you weren't too tall. You can change your walk so you don't *seem* tall, but you can't change your talk. I'd suggest you keep your mouth shut as much as possible."

"Not all Mexicans are short, Dick. That's bullshit." I was thinking about Conan.

Somehow it didn't surprise me that Dick hadn't asked me what I was doing. He had tumbled to it as soon as he had seen the getup. I think maybe it was because in my place, Dick would have done the same thing.

He got his coffee, drank some of it and said, "You walk like a man with a hotfoot, in a hurry all of the time, even with your limp."

"I prefer to think of it as my purposeful stride."

"Mexicans don't walk like they're late for an appointment on Madison Avenue. Slow down, swagger a little, shoulders back. Macho, you know. They're in no hurry. They walk like they've got life dicked. Sometimes the walk is all they have, so it's important."

"Sounds vaguely racist. Besides, I think you're talking about the Logan Heights, East Los Angeles boys who have been here, legal or otherwise, for a while, not somebody who is turning his back on everything he knows, risking his life and the livelihood of his family by dodging bandits and border cops. Those men don't have life dicked, they're scared and they move the way scared men do, which is any way they can."

"Maybe you're right. You're still too tall, though. Try to walk . . . shorter. I'd get some heavy-framed glasses too. You don't want to be recognized by that cop down there or the guy who broke your nose or God knows who else you advertised yourself to. Yeah, glasses. Your eyes have to be scrambled a little, they're too distinctive."

"Aw shucks, Dick. You really think so?"

Dick looked at me from various angles as he drank his coffee. "Actually, I'd forget billing myself as Mexican altogether if I were you. Try Nicaraguan or Guatemalan, Chilean, anything. South of Chiapas, the average Mexican will believe anything about a person. But like I said, don't talk any more than you have to, you'll blow it."

"Okay," I said. "I think you're making too much of 'the average Mexican,' but you're probably right about keeping quiet mostly."

"You're not just going to walk into T.J. like that, are you?"

"No. I need a ride to the bus station down in Ensenada. The idea is I'll be getting off the bus in T.J. from *somewhere* south. Hopefully someone will approach me rather than the other way around. Ensenada will have to do, Nogales or even Mexicali would be better, but I don't have the time."

"I'll drive you because I know you're going anyway, but you shouldn't. You need more rest. You've got a concussion, remember?"

"Thanks, but you've done enough. Like you said, your ass is grass as long as I'm here. The concussion is obviously bullshit, I'm fine." I didn't tell him about what happened to me in the gun shop. It was frightening and weird. For a full five minutes as I pretended to study the racks of Springfields, Remingtons, Colts and Mannlichers I didn't know where the hell I was, what I was doing there or even *who* I was. It passed, though, and when it all came back to me, I almost wished it hadn't.

"I'll take you." Dick drained his coffee and got dressed.

The drive south took a little over two hours. We stopped at a department store in Imperial Beach where I bought a pair of

thick-framed reading glasses I could see through, some underwear, socks and a toothbrush. I changed five hundred dollars into
pesos at a *casa de cambio* in San Ysidro. We had lunch at McDonald's and soaked up the strange border atmosphere, where, it
seems, anything at all can happen. Hopeful Mexicans in a promis-
ing and plentiful new country chomped Big Macs next to Anglo-
Americans who were either tourists on their way south for a dirty
weekend of license and squalid color or residents who looked
desperate with their backs up against the Pacific Ocean and the
Third World. It was at that same McDonald's a year later that one
of those residents, an out-of-work security guard named Huberty
who had come from Ohio looking for a patch of paradise, had
found his own psychological frontier and massacred twenty some
men, women and children with an Uzi and a shotgun because
there was nowhere else to go, nothing else to do. It was the
border. The last McDonald's.

We were waved through the gate by the Mexicans and drove
the toll road as it wound its way along the rocky, barren coast that
had grown condos and hotels like weeds over the past few years.

Dick didn't talk much, but I tried to draw him out. He was
something of a mystery to me. A guy who was that into guns, that
alone and, from where I sat, looking forward to civilization going
down the toilet so that he could live his life the way he wanted to,
was not the kind of character I generally found myself calling a
friend. Of course, I don't find myself calling anyone that very
often. I don't really know why I gave the cab driver his address
that day or even why I had remembered it—but I was glad that I
had. The magazines he subscribed to were the stuff of macho
fantasies, of would-be tough guys getting their rocks off to images of themselves in camouflage fatigues, bandoliers full of bullets and the only fallout shelter full of canned peaches on the
block. Somehow, none of that quite fit, even if the name did, with
Dick Holster. When I asked him why he read that stuff, he said,
"There's a lot of information in those magazines you can't get
anywhere else. Tips on low-tech farming, fishing, the way things
work and how to repair them without metric tools or replacement
parts from Salt Lake City, how to cure hides, preserve meat,
herbal medicines . . . you know. It's not all 'How to repel the
commie hordes under fallout conditions' or whatever."

The conversation came back around to My Mexican Holiday. "I don't know what you expect to prove or what you can do about it. Do you?" he asked.

"I have a very vague idea about what I expect to prove and I don't know if I'll be able to do anything about it at all," I said.

"You're crazy. I know you already know that and I'm just saying it because I'd feel . . . remiss if I didn't."

"Okay, you said it."

The fact that he didn't try to talk me out of it somehow made me feel even better about giving that cab driver his address. It meant he already understood something about me that I couldn't have explained if I tried.

"Ensenada's just past these hills here. We'll have to ask directions to the bus station."

On reflection and general principles I had ditched the canvas valise I had received as a door prize at Rachel Cole's. Instead I had borrowed a ratty old green khaki backpack of Dick's and tore out the Montgomery Ward's label. Inside were the clothes and the gun. I fondled the bag as we drove through Ensenada and tried to wipe the sweat on my palms onto the shoulder straps.

Dick asked directions and too soon we were parked in front of a taco stand across the street from the Tres Estrella de Oro bus station.

"You got a name?" he asked me.

"What, oh . . . I don't know. José. What difference does it make?"

"José what?"

I looked across a vacant parking lot that was being torn up to provide a foundation for something else that would be torn down in ten years. I watched a backhoe with the word "CAT" written on the yellow plate above the engine housing rake dirt and brick from one place to another. Cat.

"Gato," I said, "José Gato."

"Good luck, José Gato."

I took his hand and clasped it without actually shaking it. With his other hand he handed me a piece of paper. It reminded me of when he had done that the day I was fired from the Low Down. "What's this, a yacht club in Rosarito that's hiring in case I fail as a tomato picker?" I looked at it. It said "Audie Murphy" in handwriting, his phone number at the apartment and the address of his place in Jamul. "Sometimes the *polleros* want the address of someone in the States who will pay for your delivery. It might buy your way out of something . . . maybe."

"Okay."

"Also, if you've got the rest of that grand along, I'd tape it to my nuts if I were you."

"I've got half of it, the rest is in the *Star Trek* glass in your cabinet."

"It'll be waiting for you."

"Use it if you need it."

"Let me know what's going on as soon as you can. Keep your ass down and your mouth shut."

I nodded and turned toward the bus station. Behind me I heard his Pontiac rumble up the street.

The Tres Estrella de Oro bus station was a shabby, square, cinder-block building repleat with broken plastic chairs, a bank of video games against one wall, a snack bar offering *papas, tortas, churros, jugo de pina, tamarind* and soda, a newsstand full of newspapers and comic books with names like *Ciencia Ficcion* or *Delito!* and titles like *Mi Esposa es sexomaniaca!* Angular graffiti covered the walls, and the smell of jury-rigged plumbing permeated the room. No one looked excited, hopeful, longing, happy or sad the way they do in airports. It looked like a bus station anywhere full of people who were being shuffled from one place to another on a low budget; it just happened to be in Mexico.

The men's room was too small, had no partitions between the stalls and looked to be a blow-job factory judging by the henna-haired boys who ran the soap and hand towel concession. I took my backpack across the street to the Pemex station and completed my transformation into José Gato. I strapped the ankle holster over the right pant leg of the jeans, pulled on the boot and let the black cotton pants ride over it so that I could get to it quickly. Most illegals coming north for work wear two sets of clothes. After running through canyons in the middle of the night dodging *La Migra,* piling into the trunks of cars with a half-dozen other people for hours on end and sleeping in drainpipes or dumpsters, they shed the outer layer to look as presentable as possible to an employer. With the *ranchero's* hat on my head, I walked back across the street and bought a ticket to Tijuana. I had forty minutes to wait. I read an Alfred Bester story in a copy of *Ciencia Ficcion* while I did.

The bus took me back over the same toll road I had come down on with Dick. I tried to sleep away the redundant two hours, but I couldn't. My unconscious kept asking my conscious mind what the hell it thought it was doing. There was no good answer. The question just kept bouncing around along with the rest of me on a bus that needed new shocks, new brakes and a new transmission.

It was late afternoon when I arrived in T.J.

15

THE ACT of getting up and slowly filing out of the bus between a drunk parrot salesman and a woman with twin little girls sent lances of pain through my knee. I coughed carbon monoxide and gritted my teeth as a familiar headache aggravated by the bus's exhaust and the glasses I was wearing tightened its grip around my temples. There were maybe two dozen people waiting along a bench that ran the length of an outdoor wall full of advertisements. I searched up and down for anyone who might be soliciting travelers for a trip north.

I don't know what I was looking for—maybe a guy in the shadows with a wide-brimmed fedora and a trench coat hissing, "Psst, chocolates, nylons, American cigarettes, feelthy peectures, a ride to Pasadena een the trunk of my Chebby?"—but I wasn't looking for a little Chiclets salesman with a fondness for *churros*.

He moved up and down the lines of people disembarking from

the bus that farted huge clouds of oily smoke into the twilight sky.
"Chiclets," he said. *"Norte?* Chiclets? *Norte?* L.A.? San Diego?
Chiclets?"

A boy of about eighteen who had been in the seat behind me
stopped, bought some Chiclets and talked to the kid. The older
boy stood in front of the little entrepreneur, so I couldn't see his
face, but I didn't really need to. I remembered the voice well
enough. . . . *the big one, he runs away and gets his foot cut off. I saw
that part before on a color television.*

It was the round-faced man's "little bat" all right. The kid who
ratted on me to Conan for the price of an Orange Crush. The kid
was what they called a *talon,* somebody who solicits customers for
the border racket. I had no idea whether or not he would recognize me with my new look, but it was too late to get out of his way.
He gestured for the older kid to wait on a bench inside the bus
terminal. I could see five others sitting there with paper bundles,
bowling bags or just the clothes on their backs. They were all
male, the oldest maybe thirty.

He stood in front of me, offering me a packet of fruit-flavored
gum. "Chiclets? *Norte?"*

I took the gum and gave him ten pesos, about twenty cents. *"Si,
norte,"* I said, and then, "Morelos. I must see a Señor Morelos."

He didn't recognize me. "Yes, yes. No problem, I am from
Morelos." He grinned at this happy coincidence. "If you have
four thousand pesos, I will take you to him. No problem. You wait
over there." He must have noticed the sweat standing out on my
face in spite of the cool evening. "Don't worry. Everything is very
easy. No difficulty. Just wait."

He continued making his rounds of the passengers and I found
a seat next to the others inside the terminal.

The suddenness of finding what, or rather who, I was looking
for, put me more on edge than I'd been in the first place. I had
expected to do some comparative shopping among what I assumed would be a highly competitive group of street hustlers,
talons, subidors, polleros, coyotes, whatever you wanted to call them,
all vying for illicit northbound traffic. I thought I would be wad-
ing past one after another saying, "No, I must find Morelos." The
fact that I ran right into the kid as I stepped off the bus put me in a
paranoid frame of mind. I couldn't get rid of the feeling that

somehow they knew what I was up to and were waiting for me. That was impossible, but the idea of just walking into the bull's-eye out of dumb luck scared me.

I pretended to scratch inside my boot just to make sure the gun was still there.

The eighteen-year-old kid who had signed on with the Morelos express ahead of me had a pleasant, open face, wide eyes and a scar over one of them as if he had done some boxing recently. *"Ese, que paso?* My name is Luna, Pedro Luna. It will be Peter Moon when I make it up north. I'm a singer. I sing like Elvis. You are going to L.A.?" He didn't wait for an answer, which was just as well. I hadn't really given any thought to where I was supposed to be going. "Me, too, then to Reno, Nevada. I can get a job there as a busboy easy. I have two cousins who make two hundred and fifty dollars every week there. They have good cars, man, blond girlfriends. They eat steaks all the time. Every day. Big steaks . . . and they drink Chivas."

My smile must have looked pained. My knee was killing me, I wanted to take off the damned glasses so I could see straight and I was giving some serious thought to just getting up, walking out of the bus station, hailing a cab to the border and catching happy hour at Fat City on the Coast Highway.

"Don't be upset, man. It's easy, everybody does it. I did it before. I worked in Santa Barbara for six months in a restaurant. *La Migra* busted me. So what? I sent five hundred dollars to my mother. I went back to Mexico. That's where I am from, Mexico." He meant Mexico City. "A real *chilango,* that's me." A *chilango* is a street-wise guy from the big city. "My uncle works on the ferryboat to La Paz, so I came up that way. Man, there is nothing in Baja. It's really the sticks. Where are you from?"

"Managua," I said.

"Where is that?"

"In Nicaragua."

"Oh yes. There." He looked around the room. I might as well have told him I was from Antarctica. On the other hand, maybe he knew something about the place and was afraid I'd start bumming him out by telling him my problems. It killed the conversation anyway and I didn't mind.

Another couple joined us, a man of about forty and a girl of maybe fifteen who was probably his daughter. They had high, Indian cheekbones and stony expressions. The bat came waddling in after them and announced that we were to follow him.

Eight of us filed outside onto the dimly lit Avenido Segundo. We marched in silence uphill toward the lights of El Centro and Mariachi Square. He led us a block west to First Avenue and then down into Coahuila. What was left of the sun was spread low across the sky like a fading bloodstain.

A group of boys lounging in a doorway called to us like a group of merry farmers summoning their chickens in for feeding. *"Pollos, pollos, pollos. Aqui, pollos!"*

It occurred to me that only twenty-four hours earlier I had been standing on Market Street in San Diego at a pay phone talking to Juana about her swimming pool and her new Pinto. It seemed like a lifetime ago and continents away, but it was only yesterday and fifteen miles from where I stood now waiting for a light to change with seven other people like myself with very little to lose.

A young man wearing a Jack Daniels cap came running out from the Copacabana and waved our group inside. He didn't look familiar and I was vaguely relieved. We all took seats at the tables I had watched two months ago. He collected four thousand pesos from each of us, gave the bat one of the thousand-peso notes and told us to wait. There was no band onstage tonight and very few people at the other tables. From the jukebox a singer shouted over manic accordion music. A waiter brought us Cokes. There was no charge.

"This is a dump. I've been here before." Pedro Luna produced a small bottle of Juarez whiskey from an old Aeromexico bag he was carrying. Inside I could see some clothes and a pair of patent leather, high-heeled disco shoes. He poured some of the whiskey into his Coke and offered it to me. I put my hand over the glass and shook my head. "See the girls there?" He gestured at the bar. *"Putas."* He grinned. "Rot your dick off."

I grinned back and drank my Coke. I was thirsty. Reina, the hooker I'd once shared my Marlboros with, wasn't at the bar. Even if she had been, she wouldn't have taken any notice of the ragged crew I was part of. No money in it.

"Callado," you should relax." He tried me with the whiskey

again. It seemed like an exceedingly fine notion, but I shook my
head once more. "What's your name?"

"José," I said, and finished my Coke.

"José Callado," he repeated. The quiet one. "You're a farmer, I
bet."

"*Si como no.*" I shrugged. "Farmer, mechanic, it makes no difference."

"Why do you look so worried?" Pedro chugged his drink.

"I'm not worried. I'm just surprised, that's all. I thought it
would take longer to find the man, Morelos. A friend gave me his
name and I thought there were so many coyotes, yet the little boy
says he works for Morelos. Everything is moving so fast. I'm a
little nervous, I guess."

Pedro Luna leaned forward. "Let me tell you something, José.
Morelos, sometimes he is called Kaliman here, or Nabor. He is
the man. He is the biggest *pollero* of all of them. A *pollero*, not a
coyote. A *pollero* takes care of the chickens, eh? And what does a
coyote do to chickens? You are a farmer. You know." I didn't
mention that there weren't any coyotes in Nicaragua, at least I
didn't think so. "You see, there is a difference. There is no one
else anymore. The frontier business is all his now. He is like—"
He made motions as if he were firing a machine gun. "Al Capone,
right? Any other *coyote* or two-bit hustler who tries to muscle in
. . . rat-tat-tat-tat-tat!" He said "two-bit hustler" and "muscle
in" in English.

I smiled, but looked blank. Pedro set down his drink and tried
once more to share his savvy with the bumpkin from the South.

"If you want to cross the Tijuana–San Diego border, you can
run across the fence past *La Migra* and maybe you'll make it,
maybe you won't. You can always try the next day if Kaliman's
boys don't beat you up. If you want to get there for sure, in one
piece, you go with Kaliman's people. You pay the *talon*, like we
did. You pay the *comprador* the most unless you have people in San
Diego or L.A. that will pay, then there is a little something for the
subidor who will take us right to the fence, not much, and boom,
you are there. You have people in the United States that will pay
the money to the *comprador?*"

"No. I don't know. Maybe."

"Then it will cost you sixty thousand pesos. You have that much?"

I nodded.

"No problem." He spread his hands.

When he saw that he hadn't put me entirely at rest, he said, "What's the matter?"

"It is difficult for me to understand. The *comprador?* That is Morelos . . . Kaliman?"

"Yes. Of course, Kaliman himself does not take you across. You don't see him. He is the big man. But there are many other *polleros.* They all work for Kaliman. *Comprador* is just a word from the days—not long ago, last year even—when there was someone on the other side waiting with cars to deliver the wirecutters. They would buy the people from the *talon* in Tijuana. This was bad because sometimes the *talon* would turn *coyote,* deliver the people to the *comprador,* find out when he would be taking them past the checkpoint in San Clemente and then call *La Migra* and tell them. Everyone would be arrested and taken back to Tijuana. The *talon* would then collect more money from the same people and more money again from the same *comprador.* 'After all,' he would say, 'it is not my fault that *La Migra* caught you. I did what I said I would, no? There is always a risk.' Now this cannot happen. Everyone works for Kaliman. On both sides of the border. There is a very big organization. If somebody turned Kaliman's *alambristas* into *La Migra,* he would be killed. Everyone knows this." He leaned closer and lowered his voice. "I think the Sicilians in the U.S. are the big money behind Kaliman. That's what I think."

"Sicilians?" I echoed.

"Italianos. Like Al Capone. Don Corleone, you know?" He started humming the theme song of *The Godfather.*

I smiled weakly and said, "I don't understand very much, I'm afraid. Italianos? What would they want with us?"

He sat back and looked at me sternly. "I can see that you don't know anything about the world. I'd better take care of you myself." He poured the last of his whiskey into his glass.

Another half-dozen or so people joined us at the group of tables. They arrived one at a time except for a father-and-son team. Either the guy in the Jack Daniels cap brought them in or the kid. After we had been sitting there for an hour, Pedro regaling me with tales of money and opportunity in North America, our numbers had swelled to an unlucky thirteen. The guy in the cap introduced himself with the manly, reassuring smile of an airline pilot telling his passengers about arrival time and weather conditions. His name was Jesus. Jesus wore a Rolex watch, a pair of new Penney's jeans, new cowboy boots and a blue jacket with the name of a Little League baseball team from Chula Vista across the back.

"First we will wait here," he told us. "Then we will be taken to a hotel nearby, put in a bus and driven to Colonia Libertad on the east side of the city. From there you will enter the United States, guided by professionals to a place where you may make further arrangements to travel either to Los Angeles or anywhere you wish in San Diego. The price will vary. For those of you with phone numbers in the U.S. of friends or relatives willing to pay upon your delivery, those arrangements will be made at the hotel and you will not be troubled for any further expenses. If you wish only to enter the U.S. safely, be brought to a place in San Diego, those arrangements you can also make at the hotel. There is only a small fee for this. All of you will be asked for two thousand pesos to pay the *subidor* who drives the bus. I see we have no small children in our group. That is good."

Abruptly, he turned and left, leaving us with the image of his competent, manly smile. He didn't explain why it was so wonderful there weren't any children. I suspected it had to do with the logistics of lying dead quiet in a canyon while Border Patrol jeeps cruised past.

Someone played a Spanish version of "For the Good Times" on the jukebox. One of the men, filthy, chain-smoking cigarettes and smelling like garbage, smiled desperately at everyone as if to say, "Isn't this fun?" He sang along with the record.

The girl with the Indian face who had come in with the older man put her hands over her face and cried softly. Her father, if that's who he was, held her and stared into the middle distance of the darkened room as if trying to envision what was in store for them.

The young turks joked with each other with abbreviated laughter, their eyes scanning the shadows to either side of them.

Pedro Luna motioned for me to lean closer to him. He put a finger to his lips and bent toward the floor. Lifting his pant leg, he showed me a seven- or eight-inch switchblade taped above his sock. He winked at me and smiled craftily.

I wouldn't have to worry about my nerves giving me away. I fit right in.

Jesus came back and told us to pick up our things and follow him outside. We shuffled after him and stood on the street corner. He waved the first four boys into a Chevy Love, counted the next six, including the young girl and her father, and motioned for them to get into a Datsun pickup truck across the street. Behind the wheel of the truck was a man with a white cowboy hat. I couldn't be positive from this distance, but it seemed likely that it was the guy who killed Caruso, the old *cantinero*. Bevilaqua hadn't been looking very hard for him. I started to join the four walking toward the Datsun. I don't really know what I had in mind, maybe just a better look. Jesus called me back. "No, my friend. This way."

"Where are you going, José?" Pedro called out. "Stay with me."

I stopped in the middle of the street. The dome light came on in the Datsun as one of the kids climbed in the passenger side. The driver turned his head and smiled at the boy. His teeth were jagged ruins. It was him.

"José! C'mon, man. What the fuck?"

There was nothing I could do there and then. I wanted to pull him onto the street and do some of the dental work he needed, but it would probably have been my last act on earth. I would have to wait and hope there would be another time.

Following Jesus, Pedro and I got into the backseat of an old Dodge Colt with the grinning, foul-smelling singer. In the front seat, in the middle, was our *talon*, the Bat. Next to him, Jesus sat in the driver's seat. On the kid's right was his father, the round-faced man with the sunken eyes. He turned to face us in the backseat. I looked down, letting the brim of my hat cover my face, and heard him say, "Good evening, my friends. We are throwing a little going-away party for you. I hope you like it." He chuckled. It sounded like he was gargling broken glass.

Jesus stuck his head out the window and called to the killer across the street in the Datsun, *"La Avenida!"*

We rode in silence up to First Avenue, turned south and drove ten or twelve blocks. We turned right again and headed back down into Zona Norte. This was all residential, if you could call it that. Here were slums that made Harlem look earthy, funky or just lived-in. This was world-class poverty here. Shacks made of corrugated tin, packing crates and cardboard leaned against banana trees or grew out of the sides of junk cars. Children darted in and out of the tortured cobblestone streets, pitted and washed away in huge chunks by sewage and rain. The smell of burning garbage, stagnant water and shit hung over the streets and choked me. I noticed Pedro wrinkle his nose, but no one else seemed to mind. The driver took the sharp hills, potholes, ditches and all at about thirty miles per hour, sending us bouncing against the roof and each other.

At the end of the street, on the corner facing the old road that climbed toward Rosarito and Ensenada, the same road I had traveled twice that day, was the Hotel Londres.

Cars were parked at every possible angle up and down the side streets and the main road. Hundreds of people milled around, shouting, laughing or dancing to the music from a live band that poured into the night from somewhere inside the three-story, rose-colored building. Every light in the place was burning and brightly colored lanterns were strung outside, illuminating taco stands offering chicken, *carnitas, papas* and goat's head. Jesus pulled the car behind a delivery truck that had been burned and abandoned years ago. "Follow me," he said, and got out.

We followed him into the hotel, weaving and threading our way through the revelers. A desk clerk was swinging a broom at a boy who was dancing on the desk in the front office. On our way up the stairs, we passed someone asleep in a pool of vomit. Jesus took us to the third floor and let us into a small room where there were maybe thirty other *pollos*, all standing upright because there was no place to sit. Babies were crying, women jabbered and prayed, men smoked and leaned against the walls. We were told to wait here until someone came for us. An old woman came in behind Jesus carrying a cardboard box full of warm soda and Tecate beer and packages of Del Prado cigarettes, which she handed out, compliments of Señor Morelos. "Kaliman," she smiled.

Pedro and I found ourselves a patch of wall to squat against. Pedro took a beer and a pack of cigarettes. I joined him in a smoke and drank a pineapple soda. "Now they will come for us, the ones who have just arrived, one by one. We will each make our arrangements. You stick with me. I will go with you so you are not cheated."

I gestured at the hallway outside and shook my head. "Is today a feast day of some kind?"

"No," Pedro scowled knowingly. He got to his feet. "I'll show you, c'mon."

We edged past bodies until we came to the windows overlooking the main road. He pointed across the street at a tall fence, cut and trampled in several places that I could see. Beyond it was the Tijuana River levee, bone dry. Beyond that, on a ridge, sat four Border Patrol Ram Chargers. Though I couldn't see it, behind them, at the bottom of the ridge was Monument Road, a winding dirt track with farmhouses. In the distance beyond, I could make out the lights of Imperial Beach.

"That is North America," he said. "That's where we are going. But we will probably not cross here. The party, I think, is to fool *La Migra.* You see them?" He pointed at the pale green vans in the distance. I nodded. "Look." He pointed at the bottom of the levee. A group of boys ran across the concrete being chased by Border Patrol cops with flashlights. A helicopter roared into view and raked a searchlight over the fence below us. Pinned against the beam were the figures of twenty or more boys, perched on the fence and shouting. Some of them jumped and ran a few yards into U.S. territory, ran back or broke for the drainage pipes that extended for a hundred yards, coming out just above Monument Road. The border agents were running all over the place. It was a scene from the Keystone cops.

Below, on the street, the crowd was cheering the helicopter, the boys, *La Migra* or all of them. It was a good show.

"You see," Pedro explained further, "Kaliman keeps *La Migra* busy here, busy there, while he moves his people across somewhere else where there is no *La Migra*. The runners down there are paid by him. They get caught, they come back, get their money. It is a game for boys. Only a boy would think it is fun to be a professional *alambrista*, eh?"

But I was no longer listening to Pedro. I was watching a group of men gathered around a new Lincoln Continental and a police car with the seal of the *judiciales* on the door. There was the guy in the white cowboy hat talking to Jesus and two other men. Inside the Lincoln, in the backseat, was a man, his acne-ravaged face illuminated by the garish lantern light. He was leaning out the window and handing something to another man in a pale green *Guyabera* shirt. An envelope. They laughed together for a moment and then Morelos leaned back inside the car. It started up and slowly moved away from the hotel.

Detective Bevilaqua waved the envelope at the retreating car and then turned to climb into the police car. He disappeared up the street driving in reverse.

16

WE WERE KEPT in the room for only half an hour or so, though in the heat and closeness it seemed like half the night. Lowering myself against the wall, I rested on my haunches with my arms hanging loose and straight down between my thighs. It was a restful posture I had learned from the Vietnamese though it had taken fourteen months to get the hang of it. I leaned my head against the wall and closed my eyes. Taking off my glasses was out of the question, but my eyes needed a break or I would be paralyzed with a migraine and blind before the night was out. Pedro hunkered down next to me and jabbered merrily away over the sounds of crying women and children, the reverberating Farfisa organ of the live band and the occasional shouts from the street below.

". . . the place where I worked in Santa Barbara. They're all like that. You always get plenty of warning before *La Migra* comes around. You just split, that's all, and you come back later. They're always trying to bust these empty restaurants, man. It's funny."

I was thinking about Bevilaqua. Of course you couldn't run a smuggling operation on this scale without the cooperation or at least the blind eye of the Tijuana police and on the face of it I couldn't find anything wrong with that idea. After all, it probably supplemented the income of overworked and underpaid cops and didn't harm anyone except the theoretical and probably non-existent U.S. citizen who wouldn't do farm labor for Mexican wages anyway. What made me feel stupid and angry was that Bevilaqua had allowed Caruso's murderer to go unpunished. He and Wild Bill Tooth Decay's boss had been yucking it up together down on the street a moment ago. Nabor Morelos aka Kaliman really did run this town if the *judiciales* were afraid of him. Pedro's comparison to Al Capone wasn't so ridiculous when you considered the size of Tijuana. It compared favorably to Chicago in the twenties and was just about as wide open. If you substituted bootlegged liquor for a huge illicit labor force . . .

Jesus in his Jack Daniels cap stuck his head in the door and motioned for several people to follow him. I got up and looked out the window again. He led them down the stairway we had come up and dispatched them into various cars and one of two city buses. The room had thinned out by half now. Outside vehicles arrived and left from and to all directions. If the Border Patrol were on to Kaliman's diversion tactics, which undoubtedly they were, they still would be unable to trace any coherent movement around the Hotel Londres. It was chaos outside, choreographed chaos.

When Jesus arrived back upstairs, he motioned for all of us who had come with his party to form a line in the hallway just outside a door to the right. The old Indian and his daughter were first, then Pedro and myself. It took them only two or three minutes inside and then it was Pedro's turn. He said we were together so we were waved in by a man with red-rimmed eyes who smelled of rank mescal. Tucked into his belt was a .45. Another man lay sprawled on a broken couch covered with nameless stains. He looked both of us up and down and fingered a sawed-off shotgun in his lap. At the far end of the room was a desk with a ledger, a cash box full of money and sheets held to a clipboard. The man behind the desk was the mongooselike man who had been with Conan that night at the Copacabana and then again at the Hillcrest the next afternoon.

I didn't look into his face—the last time I had done that I was strangling him—but studied his hands on the ledger. He wore three rings, diamond, turquoise and gold. His nails were trimmed and clean. His cuffs, emerging from camel hair beige jacket sleeves, were held together by black cuff links in the shape of wolves' heads.

Pedro did the talking as I'd hoped he would. I tried not to think about how close I was to an abrupt death if the mongoose recognized me. I sweated, shifted my weight and lowered my gaze farther to the floor.

The mongoose laid out the terms. It came down to how we wanted to be transported across. By car or van, straight across the border checkpoint was the most expensive and the least hassle, though the risk was still high. That was first class. Second class involved travel on foot through the drain pipes on the other side of the Tijuana River levee—the area directly outside the hotel window; a shorter distance, but it involved lying low and maybe sweating it out in several inches of sewage for as long as twenty-four hours until the area was clear of border police. Third class was running the canyons of Otay Mesa from Colonia Libertad to San Ysidro, Chula Vista or the vacant mileage around Brown's Field in South San Diego. A run of about three miles, tough on us *pollos*, of course, but even harder on *La Migra*. If we decided to go that route, he said, we could arrange for temporary housing and transportation from certain farmhouses, garages, barns, etc., either to downtown San Diego or on to San Clemente and Los Angeles. Herman Villez had three hundred dollars, the price of a third-class ticket, so that was what I was interested in.

"I go to L.A. and my friend wants only to go to San Diego," Pedro said.

"Do you have someone who will pay?" the mongoose asked Pedro.

"I can pay." Pedro brought out his money.

"It is eighty thousand pesos to Los Angeles. Only twenty thousand more than San Diego. Is your friend sure he does not want to go with you? It is a bargain." The mongoose's voice was thin and whining. "Perhaps you have a friend or a relative somewhere who will pay the extra money?" He was talking to me.

I shook my head and produced sixty thousand pesos from the denim pants pocket beneath my outer pants. The money was folded and filthy and I handled it lovingly as if it were more than I had ever seen, much less possessed.

"Is he a mute?" the mongoose whined.

"No." Pedro laughed and clapped me on the back. "Say something, José. Callado, that's what I call him."

I cleared my throat and put a nervous tremor in my voice that wasn't all that hard to come up with. "I wish only to go to San Diego. I don't have enough money to go farther and I am told I can work in the strawberry fields there."

"You're too late for the strawberries. Don't you know that?" the mongoose asked me.

I shook my head, still looking at the floor.

Pedro again came to my rescue. "That's no sweat, he's a first-class mechanic."

"Your friend," he wheezed, "he is very timid for such a large man. He is no Mexicano, I think."

"He's from what-you-call-it, Nicaragua."

"Your friend can answer for himself."

"Yes, I'm from Managua," I said.

"What does the flag of Nicaragua look like?" he asked me.

I had to meet his eyes now. Putting on a puzzled expression, I said, "It is blue and white. Two blue stripes and one white stripe in the middle. In the white stripe there is a triangle. Why?" I was picturing a photograph and map I had seen in *Time* magazine six months ago and I hoped I wasn't confusing Nicaragua with El Salvador, but I assumed the mongoose didn't know the difference between either of those flags and that of Luxembourg. It was an assumption that was probably naïve and might kill me. The thing is, he just didn't look that goddamned smart and it was the only answer I had.

He ignored my question and said, "You know, sometimes *La Migra* sends agents to pretend they are Mexicano or maybe even from Nicaragua or someplace. We always find them out and we leave them on the mesa. We don't kill them, but sometimes we pull all their teeth."

The silence that followed grew for several moments.

"Hey," Pedro said, laughing, "this guy's a fucking banana farmer or something. He doesn't know anything. How could he be *La Migra?*"

The mongoose studied my face. After a while he said, "How could he? He can't even speak Spanish well. *La Migra* wouldn't send someone who talks like a monkey." He grinned at me and I grinned back.

"You look like a North American," he said, and his grin disappeared.

"Are you kidding?" Pedro looked me up and down.

I straightened and shrugged, smiling stupidly. "Well, that's good."

The mongoose held out his hand for my money and I gave it to him. He wrote in his ledger and then poised his pen over the clipboard. He asked my last name and Pedro's, entered them on the paper and said, "You are lucky to come tonight for our party. Do you know what we are celebrating?"

I shook my head. Pedro didn't say anything.

The mongoose grinned once again and winked. "No moon," he said, and waved us out of the room. The smelly old man from the Copa entered as we left.

Jesus directed us to a bus on the street. We paid the driver his two thousand pesos and found seats. While we waited for the bus to fill up, I tried what little yoga breathing I remembered and attempted to relax the knots that had formed in every muscle I was aware of. I wanted a drink badly, but this wasn't the time.

"Are you okay?" Pedro asked me. "Did that fucker scare you, José? I told you, relax. You're with the *chilango* here, man. The original *Chilango Chingon.*"

He was trying to make me laugh and it worked. He was telling me literally that he was the street-savvy dude that fucked all the other street-savvy dudes' wives, sisters and mothers and got away with it. Maybe I shouldn't have laughed because someone from Nicaragua probably wouldn't have gotten it. Laughing helped though.

It must have been close to midnight when the bus, with a

complement of some fifty men and women, and three children counting the fifteen-year-old, pulled out from the Hotel Londres side entrance and ground its way across town toward Colonia Libertad. When we got out of range of the mosquito whining of the band's Farfisa organ drone, my headache left and I began to feel excited. I'd gotten away with it all so far and I figured the worst was behind me.

As it turned out, I was batting a thousand over the summer for figuring dead, cold, bloody fucking wrong.

Pedro gave up talking to me and comforted the old Indian and his daughter by telling them how lucky we were to arrive on a night with no moon. Pedro had personally planned it that way, of course, he said with a straight face, and it was a measure of their good fortune to be with him. "I am so lucky, it's incredible," he said, and seemed to genuinely comfort the old man, his daughter and those who were eavesdropping while pretending not to. In that moment as the bus bucked and swayed toward Colonia Libertad and North America, Pedro had become our good luck charm, a cocky talisman against the thousand things that could go wrong. As for myself, I almost felt the same way—Pedro's charm and optimism were that infectious—but I was also experiencing a sense of déjà vu that had to do with a lot of "immortal" and lucky grunts in Nam that never made it home. I knew what it felt like to be invulnerable and lucky, and when I caught a large piece of shrapnel one afternoon just above my stomach that chewed away a piece of my lung, I never quite understood what had gone wrong. Ever.

The bus moved through downtown T.J. like some belching, lurching old hippo with emphysema. Soon we were climbing the steep cobblestone side streets of the city's east side. It was a very picturesque area of town during the daytime: one- and two- story adobe houses sagging and leaning toward each other over narrow streets where women still carried things on their heads and men in sombreros would siesta in the shade. Exotic pastel poverty. But at night, in a fuming bus laboring up the tortured streets that led to the bluff overlooking the imaginary line that separated the known from the unknown, it was frightening.

At the top of the hill, we drove along the new road to the airport until I could make out small fires burning in trash barrels and the sounds of a guitar and an accordion. The driver turned into a huge vacant lot that was used for baseball and soccer and, when the sun went down, as a "staging area" for the transportation of armies of illicit international traffic. There were at least a hundred people gathered on the field and three other buses, several cars and vans arriving, dropping off hopeful immigrants.

As we stepped off the bus, I could see more vendors selling sodas and *tortas* and goat's head tacos. Pedro and I stuck close to the driver, who gathered our group together and told us to wait for our *pollero*. It was the taco vendor and another man who were playing the guitar and accordion in between sales. The song they were singing told of a man who was afraid of dying in the North. In the song he asked that his friends tell *La Migra* that he was only sleeping so that his body would be brought back to Mexico for burial.

Pedro wasn't interested in huddling around with the frightened group we had come with. The old chain-smoking man who smelled like cabbage and piss had attached himself to us and he bothered Pedro as much as he bothered me.

"Stay here, old man," he said. "I'm going to check things out, make sure these *cabróns* know what they're doing."

The man nodded and grinned, turned to the others and announced, "Pedro will make sure it is safe."

"C'mon, José." We walked across the field and looked out over the dry river valley and the absolute blackness that lay beyond. I knew what was there, Brown's Field airport, the city dump at Otay, a string of automobile junkyards, a few truck stops and mini–shopping malls, but none of them were visible from where we stood. It was as black as a murderer's heart out there; worse, it looked for all the world like some hostile, uninhabited planet. The ground dropped away into shadow like a colossal wound in the night; beyond that were the canyons running through Otay Mesa for a mile or two before the sparse, feeble lighting along Route 75. The sky was pocked with cold starlight and the occasional winking of a small aircraft from Brown's Field. The Promised Land, the United States, Sweet Land of Liberty. It looked as inviting as an open grave.

"Reno is out there somewhere, man," Pedro said.

"Steaks and Chivas," I mumbled.

"That's right." He paused. "It *is*. I know."

In the starlight his face looked awed and afraid, the face of a boy.

When we got back to the bus, the old man seemed relieved. "The *pollero* is here. We were waiting for you," he said to Pedro.

Our *pollero* was a large man, as tall as I am. He wore a navy blue stocking cap from which a pony tail appeared and then disappeared into a dark sweatshirt. He held an old World War II infrared scope in one hand and two stones in the other. I couldn't see his face entirely, but I saw enough of it to know that I had never seen him before. He tucked the scope into the belt at his waist and held the two stones over his head.

"Silence," he said in a hoarse voice as if he was used to shouting, or unused to speaking. "Everyone must remain silent. Silent as death. Silent as these stones." He paused for effect and held the stones so we could all see them. I noticed other groups moving off in the background, beginning their trek north by descending the well-worn cliff face. "There will be no talk." He waited for the words to sink in. "No sound. No sneezes, no curses, no crying." He directed this last to the daughter of the old Indian, who had begun sniffling again. "The only sound will be this." He clicked the stones together three times. "You hear?" He clicked them again. "This sound will guide you. It is the only thing you will hear out there. Stay together"—he paused again— "and listen." He snapped his fingers twice. "Stop," he said. He clicked the stones yet again. "And follow." With that he turned and motioned us forward.

We traversed the length of the field and then started down the steep path into darkness. Pedro first, then myself. The old man was behind me and tried to fumble a cigarette out of his coat and into his hands; the *pollero* reached past Pedro and me and slapped it away from him. "No," he said, as if to a child. And then, hoarsely, "You stink, old man." Behind me was a couple, a man and a woman I hadn't noticed before. Behind them were some dim figures I vaguely recognized from the bus and the hotel.

Silhouetted against a trash fire were the old Indian and his daughter, who brought up the rear. All in all there were fifteen of us. Sixteen counting the man who followed the Indian. I don't know where he came from. He hadn't been with us on the bus.

It took several minutes, fifteen or twenty, to get to the bottom of the incline. A sewer pipe lay across our path and beyond that a trampled cyclone fence. It was the border.

Our nameless *pollero* stepped over the mashed chain-link wire and clicked his stones. We followed him into perfect darkness. Into the United States.

No one stumbled or cried out; the way was as smooth as a child's cheek. The clacking of the stones came at intervals of two every minute or so. After some time they echoed to either side of me and I knew that we were in a canyon. Once the clicking of the stones gave way to a muted finger-snapping sound and our parade was brought to a halt. Several of us piled into each other without a sound. The man behind me stepped on my foot and apologized with a hand patting my shoulder. I could hear soft footfalls and the sound of sifting dirt. Our guide was climbing the wall of the canyon.

I saw him standing out against the faint starlight above me and to my left. He held the nightscope to his eye and scanned the mesa ahead of us. Satisfied, he lowered himself down again with a whispering of falling dust. In a moment we were moving again.

My hand was on Pedro's shoulder in front of me. The man behind me held on to my waist. Someone to our rear stumbled on a root or cactus and hissed in pain. We climbed, descended, climbed, paused, drank from a carton of orange juice someone passed, continued. A rattlesnake wound its way above our heads through a chiaroscuro of broken rock. Each of us pressed the one behind us away from the wall where the snake, just as eager to avoid us, slithered upward. I remember feeling a warmth toward all the faceless strangers behind me, a sense of protectiveness toward them, a feeling of dissolution into a greater whole, a sense of *us*, though I didn't know any of their names, where they came from or what their dreams were. I no longer felt like an actor, a poser, a fraud. They were me and I was them. Our reasons for being there in that canyon in the dark were irrelevant, homogenized. We all had the same set of ears and eyes, adjusting now to the pitch blackness. We all strained for the muted clacking of the guide's stones or the snapping of his fingers. We were a single entity bound together by the night, the unknown and mortal fear. It was very much like being on a night patrol in some bum-fuck boondock north of An Hoa with men you hardly knew but loved somehow nonetheless.

Maybe if I hadn't started thinking about that, I wouldn't have spaced out, gone blank, drawn a big scary zero the way I had in that gun shop on El Cajon Boulevard. I'll never know, but the fact is that I did. Somewhere in those canyons that night, before the shooting started, it occurred to me that I didn't know what was going on. I didn't know where I was or why I might have been there. Nathaniel York, José Gato, Herbert Hoover, Peter Pan, Ishmael, Ringo Starr, Napoleon—whoever; I didn't know who I was or might have been, much less who I was pretending to be. It was all a mystery, a dream or nightmare maybe, except that a certain calm crept over me. It was all vaguely interesting. Who am I and what am I doing here in the dark with all these quiet people walking very quickly? Why all these paranoid vibes? Why is there no sky? Shouldn't it be blue? Why is the sky blue anyway—when it is blue, that is?

Why is a duck?

And then there were gunshots.

17

IT WAS IMPOSSIBLE to tell who was shooting at who. Even if I had had the vaguest idea where I was or what I might have been doing there, it still would have been impossible in that pitch blackness. Several sharp pops and two or three flashes from gun muzzles up ahead were followed by screams, echoes from the gunfire, the clicking of spent cartridges hitting rocks and someone shouting in hysterical Spanish. A pair of arms grabbed me from behind and threw me into a bush. Without thinking, I brought my knees up to my face, my heels protecting my balls. I tucked my chin into my chest and covered my head with my arms, mashing my hat over my ears. Vaguely aware that I was wearing glasses, I wondered why. They seemed unfamiliar.

People seemed to be running everywhere. A man next to me was saying *Madre de Dios* over and over again.

Return gunfire sounded very close up ahead, a medium-caliber pistol.

The sound of scrambling feet and a body hitting the dirt next to mine caused me to look up. Someone was kneeling over me, his shape blotting out a few stars. "C'mon, José. Follow me." He tugged at my shirt and I rose to follow him though I didn't know why. It occurred to me that he had spoken in Spanish and that I understood him.

We ran several yards in the direction of the gunshots, which I didn't think was such a good idea. Whoever it was who had called me José was still clutching the front of my shirt. I stopped and grabbed his wrist and squeezed it until he removed his hand. He whispered something at me in Spanish that danced just at the edges of my hearing or maybe my comprehension. I sensed him climbing an embankment to our right. I could just make out that he was waving me up after him.

From behind us a new gun entered the chorus. It sounded like a cannon and echoed everywhere. This was some sort of nightmare, but I knew I wasn't sleeping. People were shouting again. A woman screamed. It wasn't fair. I was involved in some kind of battle in some war somewhere and I didn't know where or why. On the heels of that thought came a sense of déjà vu.

Two shotguns opened up to the left and in the brief glare from the muzzles I could see that I was in the bottom of a canyon. A piece of earth exploded a foot away from me and I clambered upward without thinking.

The next moment I was running over flat terrain, following the man ahead of me. A pair of headlights appeared over the top of a rise about a hundred yards in front of us. *"La Migra!"* the man ahead of me said. "Get down." He threw himself into a copse of stunted bushes and I followed him. Sharp cactus dug into my legs and arms. I tried to draw myself up into as small a target as possible. As I was doing this I felt the gun strapped above my ankle. My fingers closed over it and I started to remember what it was there for. It came back slowly, but not all of it. Before I could piece it together, I could hear the sharp/dull hacking of helicopter blades approaching very fast from the same direction the headlights were coming from.

Suddenly the mesa was bathed in the harsh sweeping light of a search beam on the chopper.

"C'mon, José. Back down." The man, who sounded more like a

boy, got up and sprinted for the canyon once again. Gunshots were still coming from below, illuminating the pitch walls like flashes of subterranean lightning. He disappeared over the edge just as the searchlight caught him. I could see that he held a knife in his hands and I remembered his name was Pedro. Everything was coming back to me, but too slowly. I still didn't know what the hell had happened and was still happening down there. For a minute I entertained the idea of just sitting where I was. Maybe the Border Patrol would take me and I'd be charged with aiding and abetting. Then again maybe they'd miss me. In either case the border cops weren't the bad guys. The bad guys were the ones shooting at people down in the canyon and I didn't want to go back there.

More muffled shots echoed up and down the length of the sunken ambush gallery. The chopper played its light directly over me, then passed. The pair of headlights had become four. The first vehicle was an aqua sedan that rocked to a halt in the light of a Ram Charger's floodlamp. A driver emerged from the first vehicle and pulled a shotgun from the dash. He tucked his leg under the car and used the door for cover, playing the muzzle back and forth in my general direction. The guy on the passenger side ran from the car and pulled a pistol from the holster on his belt. He ran to the lip of the canyon and launched himself down as if he had a parachute.

Two men from the Ram Charger followed the first agent down into the canyon. Another man crouched at the edge with a loud hailer. Only two border cops remained on the mesa, the drivers of the vehicles. The Ram Charger swung around and aimed its headlights down into the blackness just as the chopper swung by, much lower this time, and played its beam up and down the floor of the small gorge. I was back in darkness now.

The gunfire had stopped momentarily. The guy with the loud hailer began to say something which echoed incomprehensibly and was further garbled by another loud hailer on the chopper saying something else. Faintly, I could hear, *"Alto, por favor. No les haremos dano!"*

This was answered by three or four gunshots that sounded just the way they do in movies because they were echoing and ricocheting all over the place.

,Pedro screamed, "José! I'm shot. José! Oh *chingado!*"

Without thinking about it as much as I should have, I scrambled out of my bed of cholla cactus and broke into a crouching run in the direction of his voice. I held my .32 too tightly and forced myself to relax my grip. I thumbed off the safety. No one seemed to notice me.

I half slid and half climbed my way down.

Silence. The silence of a summer night in no man's land.

A groan several yards ahead of me gave me a bearing.

"José." He sounded hoarse.

A gun roared from behind. I heard the bullet whine past me, strike rock and spin off into the blackness.

From the loud hailer came the metallic voice of authority. In Spanish, it said, "Lay down your weapons. There is nowhere for you to go. The canyon is sealed ahead of you and behind you."

Another voice in English called, "Richie! Steve! I'm pinned down here. What the hell are you doing?"

"We'll get you out. Take it easy," came the reply above me and to the right. "How many?"

As if to oblige, two shotgun reports deafened me. By the flare from the muzzles I could tell that they were directly beneath me and concealed behind a makeshift grave of piled rocks under a crude crucifix. They were firing in the direction of the pinned agent's voice and that of Pedro Luna.

Everything happened very fast. The pinned agent crouched over his boulder; guessing that a pair of shotguns, or maybe one double-barreled one, needed a few seconds to reload, he got off four rounds from his .357. I wished he hadn't done that because two of his bullets ricocheted much too near me, one of them biting into the dirt just beneath my boot heel. The helicopter put in another appearance and bathed the whole scene in garish white light. The chopper hovered and skewered the two men behind the man-made rock break with a few thousand watts of brilliance. They were about ten feet from where I was.

One of them saw me.

The other one was aiming at the chopper. I pulled back the breach on my pistol and shot the guy who was about to shoot me. The gun jumped in my hand. I brought it back down, held it a little more firmly and shot him again. He collapsed and rolled downhill a few feet. The agent behind the boulder jumped out and got off two rounds that didn't hit anything. It would have been hard.

In the light now, I could see that the guys with the shotguns had a perfect field of fire in either direction, but were protected by two rocky abutments. You would have to be directly across from them to do any good. I was directly across from them more or less. The other shotgun wavered, trying to decide whether he should hit me, the chopper or the agent. Before he could make up his mind, I shot him too. I emptied the clip into him. It looked like he was doing some epileptic break dance for a while and then he didn't move at all.

For my trouble, I got a .357 round singing over my head from the agent whose life I had just saved. He called out to me in Spanish to throw down my gun and lie on the floor of the canyon. I threw my pistol where he could see it. In English I said, "Don't shoot. Your rounds are going all over the fucking place here and you might hurt yourself."

He advanced toward me slowly, his gun leveled at my face more or less. The two other agents I took to be Richie and Steve clambered down after him and stepped into the light from the hovering chopper. "You speak English."

"Sort of," I said. "I picked it up on the streets of Manhattan as a kid."

I felt deranged and wired and scared. I said some more things, but I don't remember what they were. Whatever I said, it didn't impress anybody. "I said lay down on the dirt," someone repeated. I looked at his gun, but didn't lie down. In a minute I was looking at three guns.

"Fuck you," I said. "I've been lying in the dirt all night."

None of this was supposed to happen. Hundreds of wirecutters come through these canyons every night of the goddamned week without getting shot at or busted. Why me? I'd learned to stop asking that question a long time ago, but it occurred to me again. Sue me.

"I've got a friend," I said. "Over there. He's shot." I pointed toward where I'd heard Pedro's voice.

And then I recognized the agent who'd done the John Wayne flying leap into the canyon. The guy who was pinned. The guy whose ass I had just saved. He was the same pleasant-looking, short, muscled agent who had shown me around the detention center in San Ysidro earlier this summer. I couldn't remember his name.

He spoke first as Richie and Steve patted me down for more guns. "I know you from somewhere," he said.

"Yes," I nodded. I realized that I had lost my glasses and my hat at some point. "I'm a reporter. I talked to you a few months ago about catered dinners for busted illegals."

"Right." He was smiling now. "The bogus reporter. Who the hell are you, man? And what are you doing out here?"

We started walking back up the embankment. I found my hat in a bush and put it back on. The chopper had landed on the mesa and a female agent was arguing with the pilot about what should have been done and what should be done now and who was in charge and who was hurt and how the report should read. Another helicopter was coming in from the north. Radios squawked and burst into static. People ran in different directions over the mesa.

"You were looking for someone, right? Wasn't that it?" His name was Ybarra, I remembered that now.

"Yes," I said. "I still am. What about my friend down there? He's just a kid."

"Everybody's dead down there. At least five bodies."

I was being bent over the rear of the Ram Charger and handcuffed. "You were almost one of them," I pointed out.

He looked away and then back at me. "I know. Thanks."

I sat on the edge of the van and watched border cops haul bodies up the slope and put them in bags. They tied the bags to runners on the second chopper. "What happened down there?" I asked.

"Christ! I thought you were going to tell *me* about it."

"I don't know. I was coming through with a bunch of *pollos* and all hell broke loose."

"You wanna tell me why you were entering the U.S. dressed like a taco bender?" It seemed to me Ybarra wasn't expecting a straight answer, but I gave him one—as far as it went—anyway.

"I'm still trying to find out what happened to a friend of mine who disappeared."

"You know I'm going to have to bust you. As far as I know you were smuggling aliens. Even if you weren't, you were aiding illegal entry."

He wouldn't meet my eyes. I said, "You know what's going on in T.J. and up and down your turf, don't you? Kaliman? Morelos? aka Nabor, the acne-faced Lee Iaccoca of *coyotes?*"

"We know what's going on and we're trying to do something about it, but . . ." He trailed off.

"Yeah, well I was right in the middle of it and I figured that tomorrow or next week at this time I would know a hell of a lot more. I could fill you in, Ybarra, if you let me walk. I might have time to catch up to my *pollero.* If he's not in one of those bags. He was leading about fifty of us."

The agent who had handcuffed me heard what I had said and didn't like it. He started to push me into the wire cage in back of the van. "Shut up, asshole," he said. "You're not going anywhere."

"Leave him alone." Ybarra helped me back down. "I want him to take a look at the bodies." As we walked he asked me, "Were you at the head of the line?"

"Yeah, just about."

"Then most of the rest of them must have turned tail and run south when the shooting started." That made sense.

He led me over to the second chopper. Two men and another woman agent had just finished dragging a fifth corpse from the shadowed bracken of the canyon. It was Pedro Luna. He had been shot in the stomach.

"What happened, Ybarra? What the fuck happened down there?" Pedro's eyes were open and I wanted to close them. "Take these off for a minute." I gestured at my handcuffs.

"Why?"

"I want to close his eyes."

"I'll do it."

"No. I want to do it. No offense, but he wouldn't want *La Migra* to close his eyes. You know? Can you dig that?"

"All right." First he took the switchblade out of Pedro's hands, then he opened my cuffs. I placed my fingers over his eyes and gently moved them down. "Who was he?" Ybarra asked.

"A kid who wanted a job."

"I want you to come over here and see if you recognize any of the others."

At the chopper, Ybarra began to pull the plastic garbage bags away from faces. The smelly old man was lying there dead. He still smelled bad. "An old *pollo*. He was with us," I said. The next body was that of the young girl's father, the Indian. "Him too." The fourth body was one of the guys with the shotguns who I had killed. "Never saw him before," I pronounced, and threw the plastic back over his face, reminding myself that he really was going to shoot me if I hadn't done him first. The fifth body belonged to the other guy with the shotgun. I knew him. "This was the guy who was about to blow you away down there." I pulled back the plastic far enough to show his pudgy face and the Tijuana *policia* uniform he was wearing under a brown poncho. "He's a Tijuana motorcycle cop, his name is Manosa." I remembered him standing in front of the Azteca de Oro Hotel telling everyone to stand back. "I don't know what the hell he was doing here."

"He was going to rob you and your friends at gunpoint. It's a popular hobby with certain T.J. cops, or anybody who gets himself a uniform—it's not hard to do. Usually, the uniform is enough and they don't have to fire a shot."

"That doesn't make sense," I said. "He was Bevilaqua's sidekick. Bevilaqua is a *judiciale* detective down there on Morelos's payroll."

"I know who Bevilaqua is."

"Well then, what's the deal?"

"The deal is, maybe his boss wasn't paying him enough. Figured he could pick up a few extra pesos out in the canyons. He probably knew about movements of large parties like yours and could just sit and wait, show his badge and clean up without firing a shot. Maybe he had things worked out with a few *coyotes* to split the proceeds. Looks like something went wrong, somebody got nervous or confused in the dark. Couldn't have been you, could it? You and your little gun?"

"No. I didn't start shooting. I don't know what happened."

"Neither do I, my friend."

"I could find out, Ybarra. None of these guys is my *coyote*. And there was another guy down there shooting. He came up the rear trailing our party. He had a .45 or something. Some kind of automatic cannon. They can't be far."

"We'll pick 'em up. They've got to come out somewhere in Spring or Moody's Canyon and we'll get 'em."

"Don't," I said.

"Whattya mean, *don't?*"

"I mean, let 'em through and let me catch up to them. There's some connection to Morelos in North County and I can place it for you if you give me a chance. Clear the fuckin' canyons, give me a shot. I'll put the whole thing in your lap with a little luck."

Ybarra laughed. "You're crazy."

"So what?"

He looked at me a minute. "Maybe you're lucky too."

"Maybe."

"Come here."

I followed him into the shadows behind more arriving vans. He handed me my glasses. One of the lenses was shattered. He also handed me my gun. "It's empty," he pointed out, "but it looks mean. Maybe it will do you some good." I didn't say anything. I had another clip taped to my leg. "You call me. *Me.* If you get anything. Anything at all. What's left of your party will be running north along this canyon here, it's called Deadman's Canyon." He paused. "Then they'll either take the fork into Spring or Moody's or try to come out by the Travel Lodge. I doubt if they'll do that, there's too many of us around there and they know it. We'll block off Spring, make a show of it. They'll have to take Moody's and come up around Route 75 by the dump. You do the same."

"They said something about putting us up in some garages or motels or something." I tried to remember.

"Yeah, Moody's." We were in complete shadow now. "Go on. If we pick you up in the morning, lost, we'll bust you. You've got two miles, bear to your right. Always go to the right. The minute you've got something solid, and I mean con-fucking-crete, you call me, Border Patrol, Brown's Field sector, Ybarra. I'll be there like white on rice."

"Okay." I turned to go.

"A name," he said.

"José Gato."

"Original."

I ran down and away from the clamoring of radios, into the darker patch of night that was Deadman's Canyon. I seemed to be sliding into Hades. On the warm breeze I thought I heard Ybarra thank me again.

After I had run a hundred yards up the canyon, I stopped and removed the other clip from my leg. I jacked it into place and closed my hand over it. There was still enough adrenaline pumping through me to jump-start a 747. I stumbled a few times over rocks, cactus and junk. The floor of the canyon was littered with the debris of moving armies. I had to catch up with what was left of our party. The possibility that they had all turned back to Mexico occurred to me, but I dismissed it. I had a recollection of people rushing past me in the darkness, both ways. Some running toward the firefight and others away from it. The guy with the cannon had rushed up from the rear. *He* at least had to be out here somewhere. He couldn't have made his way back without being picked up by Ybarra and his Rough Riders. Not now.

Trying to pace myself so I wouldn't create a racket wheezing and panting, I tried to come up with a scenario for what had happened back there. I might never know for sure, but it probably went something like the way Ybarra had it figured. Manosa and at least one other guy were waiting to ambush the party, take any cash or valuables and probably divide it up later with our *coyote*. It had to be that way because Manosa would have been meat on the streets of T.J. if he wasn't kicking back to Morelos's people. Something had gone wrong though. I couldn't get the idea out of my head that it had something to do with Pedro. Pedro and his knife. If he had pulled a knife on Manosa or his friend, one of them might have panicked and fired at him. Our *coyote* would have been close enough to think they were actually shooting at him too and might have freaked, returning fire. Once guns start going off, you never know how people will react. I've seen men run straight at enemy positions under fire, not out of heroism, but mindlessness. One guy even got decorated for valor after he charged a V.C. rabbit hole and scared the shit out of them. His gun was empty and I knew for a fact he was strung out on smack, hadn't had any in three days. He was just flipping out. The V.C. ducked back into their tunnel and disappeared so our outfit could move on. The guy, whose only name was Midnight as far as I knew, kept on running. I saw him throw his gun away and just keep on charging through the trees. I never saw him again until his picture was in the paper receiving a medal from a VA hospital bed. That was a year later.

I don't know why I was thinking about Midnight. Maybe I was trying not to think about Pedro Luna. Maybe Pedro had nothing to do with what had happened. Maybe I just wanted to be mad at him.

The canyon split in half and I followed the right fork. I had to rest for a minute. I think I had just jogged a mile and my knee was throbbing. As I was staring up at the stars and wiping sweat from the palms of my hands onto my shirt, I heard the clicking of stones ahead of me. I listened again and heard muted finger snapping. Hugging the side of the trail, I moved cautiously in the direction of the sound. After another thirty yards or so, I could make out figures moving hurriedly and quietly away from me. I ran after them.

The man closest to me pivoted when he heard me and drew a large, boxy pistol from his jacket. He held it with two hands and pointed it at me. I raised my hands in the air. I was still palming the automatic. "Señor," I said, "señor, please don't shoot. Mother of God, everyone is shooting guns! Please. I was being guided through these *arroyos* of hell when someone shot my friend. *Ratteros* maybe. I escaped. I am lost. Don't shoot."

"Be quiet. Follow, quickly." He waved me forward with the gun and I shuffled past him. There was no light of any kind, yet my eyes were completely adjusted and I could make out his face: bony and dark, eyes scanning behind him, having dismissed me. He replaced his .45 and I thought I could hear him curse as he ran to catch up with the column of *pollos*. He pushed me forward harshly when I paused to put my gun in my pants and replace my glasses with the shattered lens. *"Hijo de la gran puta,"* he repeated. "What a night!" He gave me a bony smile full of bad teeth.

I smiled back at him tentatively. "Terrible," I said. It was him, the guy with the cannon back there. The guy who had attached himself to the rear of our column way back on the soccer field. He

didn't have his white cowboy hat but I knew him from somewhere
else too.

Wild Bill Tooth Decay.

I was real happy to see him.

18

MY GUESS WAS that there were at least thirty of us in Spring Canyon. I edged my way to the front of the column and saw that there were two *coyotes* leading the group. Everyone was moving much faster than our original party had. One of the *coyotes* was my own, original, fearless leader with the pony tail and the stocking cap. He had obviously hooked up with another group—moving through a parallel canyon that joined either Spring or Moody's— after the fiasco in Deadman's. He was playing his old WWII nightscope frantically ahead of him, running up the sides of the slope and clicking his stones like a flamenco dancer on Dexamyl. The idea seemed to be to get us to a rendezvous point somewhere along Route 75. We weren't far. I could hear the sound of an occasional car passing up ahead.

Taking a quick inventory, I recognized a couple of faces that had been with us on the bus. One of them was the daughter of the old Indian who had been shot. She had a glazed, dreamy look about her as she shuffled ahead. Another woman with a serape had taken the younger girl under her wing—almost literally as she was sharing the serape with her, though the night wasn't even cool.

We walked for another fifteen minutes and were brought to a halt again by snapping fingers. Wild Bill came jogging up from the rear and conferred with the point *coyote*. Word was passed down the ranks that we were to wait here for cars that would take us to a place to sleep during the day. No conversation would be permitted.

We sat at the bottom of a drainage gully beneath a chain-link fence, which meant to me that we were on someone's private property. I counted two trucks and six cars that passed above us during a ten- or fifteen-minute period. Someone near me was rattling rosary beads and praying under his breath.

Another truck. Three more cars. I had no idea what time it was. It must have been two or three in the morning, but I couldn't have said for sure.

I must have been right about our *coyote* linking up with another group because I could hear a small child's cries being muffled.

The next car slowed to a halt above us nearby. There was movement ahead of me. Several people were climbing toward the road. The rest of us were told to wait. After a few minutes I could hear the car driving west again. More traffic passed up ahead and I began to feel sleepy. I might have dozed because it came as a surprise to find myself suddenly waddling up the side of the road with a half dozen others.

At the fence, the *coyote* had folded back a piece of the chain wide enough to admit one body at a time. I could see tall, sodium lights a quarter mile to either side of the hole in the fence, but we were situated in a dark stretch of 75. We were quickly herded down the road several yards toward a station wagon with darkened headlights.

The driver stood at the rear, looking up and down the road. Our pony-tailed *coyote* was peering through his nightscope back through the canyons and over the slate expanse of the mesa we had just crossed. The lights of Colonia Libertad shimmered weakly from very far away. I took one last look around for Wild

Bill but didn't see him, and then I was climbing over a kid lying on the floor of the wagon. Someone else pressed himself almost on top of me. A third body, a woman, wedged me farther into the car. Blankets and boxes were thrown over us and the rear door slammed shut.

At least five of us were packed in together, though I suspected there might have been more. The sour smell of sweat and fear mixed with that of bad breath and mildewed blankets clogged my nostrils. The station wagon took off and we headed west for nearly a mile. Someone's elbow was in my cheek. A foot pressed against the back of my head and someone had folded his arms over my calves to rest his head. The car turned north and headed uphill.

The road twisted and turned, or at least our station wagon did. As we hit potholes, everyone was thrown into each other harder. Men breathed grunts and curses. The woman nearest me kept whispering, "Everything will be all right. This isn't so bad."

At some point we leveled out and hit a flat stretch of road. After five minutes of it, the driver made a right and slowed. I could hear the tires crunching on gravel.

The rear door opened. *"Vamanos! Vamanos!"*

Painfully disengaging from each other, we didn't have time to check out our surroundings. I took in a row of low buildings in pastel, cracked stucco bleached of color by the starlight and then I was pushed through a waiting doorway.

The floor was covered with sleeping bodies. A double bed in the middle of the room held three adults and two children. I stepped on someone, who hissed and shifted his position to clear a path. Looking for a place to sit or even stand, I found myself in the bathroom of a motel room that should have been condemned during Kennedy's administration. For all I knew, it had been.

Someone was sleeping in the shower stall. Someone else was sleeping next to the toilet. A woman with gray streaks in her hair was sleeping on the toilet, her head on the tank. A child lay under the sink. I backed out of the bathroom and leaned against a vinyl plastic wall that gave way to my weight. I fell into a closet the size of a phone booth. Bingo. Bedtime.

My eyelids fluttered and I began to sleep as soon as my back felt the wall. Someone was standing in front of me, her arms clutching her waist, shivering, though the heat was something you could have cut with an oar. It was the Indian's daughter. She swayed and tried to lean against something, but she couldn't without disturbing either me or the body sleeping behind her. I got to my feet, feeling as if I were climbing up from a tar pit. I put my hands on her shoulders and guided her into my former position in the closet. She didn't say anything, but let me do it. She sat stiffly, still holding herself as if to let go meant coming apart.

When her eyes closed, I squatted on my haunches and let my arms hang between my thighs, touching the floor. I wondered if I could still sleep that way.

I could.

When I woke up, I was stretched out, my feet in the closet. People were stepping over me to get in and out of the bathroom. The girl was still slumped uncomfortably in the closet. By the light, I figured it was very early morning. *"Que hora es?"* I asked no one in particular.

A cheerful man in a stained, polyester blue suit jacket who was waiting in line for the john pointed at his digital watch and announced that it was 9:17. "You sleep late, my friend."

"Yes, I'm tired."

"You missed breakfast," he informed me. "Steak, eggs, coffee, beans . . . a little Sangrita."

"I did?" I ran my hand over my face and disengaged my feet from the closet. Everyone in line for the toilet laughed, slapping at each other.

"Delicioso!" Someone said.

"Too bad, there was plenty for everyone, but we were too greedy. It's gone now." This brought more yuks.

"Very funny." I laughed. *"Que paso?"*

"Not much, *amigo.* I have been here for two days. Villapando here has been here a week."

I got to my feet and checked on the girl in the closet. She was as okay as she was going to be.

"When do we leave?" I risked another round of guffaws.

"Some went last night," Villapando, in the blue suit, said. "More are sure to go tonight. No moon again."

The man behind him said. "I don't know if it makes any difference. People are moved out every night, but more come every
night."

"Where are we?" I asked, trying to cut ahead in line. I had to
piss myself.

"North America, *cabron.*"

"San Diego?"

"I think so. I saw pictures of Chicago and New York and it don't
look like this place, that's for sure." More laughs.

"Can we get something to eat?" I expected everyone to crack
up, but no one did. I noticed a man urinating in the sink next to
another man sitting on the toilet. Someone else was urinating in
the shower. The fact that I was taking note of this seemed to
bother everyone. They were embarrassed. More than that really.
Mortified, angry, but impotent and "putting a face on things" the
way British POWs do in old movies like *Bridge on the River Kwai.*
No one at the yacht club would have been surprised; they were all
Mexicans after all.

I found myself a place in line, near the edge of the bed. Outside
the sun was prying its way over the Imperial Valley and through
the box windows with no screens. The guy behind Villapando
shouted over his shoulder. "You wanna eat? You can get a ham-
burger for five bucks from the motel guy. A Beer? Two bucks.
Milk, a dollar and a half. Coffee? Two bucks. That's 450 pesos, a
cup of coffee. You buying, *cabron?*"

Yeah, I was buying. "How do I talk to the man?"

"Bang on the walls."

I gestured to a boy of fifteen or so, shaking my fist. He pounded
the walls with his fist. The boy said, "Can you get my mother
something to eat? She's sick. We don't have any money left. She
must eat. Something."

In response to the banging, a sleepy-eyed, red-haired man
came to the door. "You people have to be quiet," he said in
English. "*Silencio! Silencio!*" he added with an Okie accent. "*Inmigración* might find you, *La Migra.* Shut up!"

I weaved my way to the door over reclining, resigned postures.
I waved two thousand pesos at him. "Milk," I said in English.
"Coffee. Food." He took the money.

"Gotcha. Milk, coffee, food. Sure thing, Burreeda breath." He made sure the door was locked and walked away. I sat back on the bed.

Eventually I got to take my piss. The toilet was overflowing with paper, feces and water the color of honey. It wouldn't flush anymore.

I talked to Villapando and the other comedian named Frederico. We joked about America and Mexico and Nicaragua; bananas and coffee, hot dogs and tacos, marijuana and cocaine.

After two hours the red-haired guy showed up with a bag of potato chips. He promised more later, but we knew he was full of shit. Villapando told me not to make a fuss. We passed the potato chips among the women and kids. They didn't go far.

By two o'clock in the afternoon the woman on the bed had passed out from the heat and several others were in danger of heat stroke. The windows didn't open. I looked up and down the parking lot outside and couldn't see anybody. No one had answered the banging on the walls all afternoon. Looking for something I could use to break out a window—there wasn't even a lamp in the room—I settled on my boot heel. I climbed on an end table and kicked out one of the panes of glass, then I kicked out the next one. They broke with the muted sound of shattering rock candy. The boy with the sick mother thanked me, but everyone else cursed me for a troublemaking fool.

When I tried to make my way across the room to kick out the other window and get some cross-ventilation, three of the men including Villapando and Frederico, stopped me.

"Get out of my way. We'll all suffocate."

"No. No. If we sit very still, it will be all right." Frederico's hands fluttered in front of my chest in a nervous, restraining manner.

I pointed to the woman on the bed. "Like her?"

Others joined the argument, both pro and con. A few raised their voices.

After a minute of this, the door flew open and Wild Bill Tooth Decay stood in it looking angry and sleepy. We had disturbed his siesta. He had a cowboy hat on again, but not a white one. This one was a stained brown. "What's going on in my chicken coop?" He tried to sound friendly and smile at everyone, but he looked too much like a scarred death's head and his smile only exposed more teeth that were either missing or discolored and looked filed. It was the first time I had seen him full on in daylight. He was one tough Mexican. A killer of old men. Another man appeared behind him. He wore a denim jacket, Levi's and no hat. Brown, wavy hair curled over his ears. He wasn't Mexican and I'd never seen him before. Even if he hadn't been wearing shades, I could tell that he would always have that same expression on his face. The same expression you see on cinder blocks.

Several people began talking at once about food, the heat, the toilet and the sick woman.

Wild Bill raised his hands for silence and announced that as soon as it was dark, some of us would be leaving for the north. The rest would be divided into two rooms. As for food, sandwiches would be distributed shortly, and juice.

I kept waiting for him to notice the broken window, but he didn't.

"What about my mother?" the boy on the bed asked. He was wiping her forehead with a wet bandanna.

"Bring her outside. We have a more comfortable place for her." He looked around the room and selected a young woman. "You too, you help to take care of her." He continued looking and noticed the Indian girl who stared at her hands in her lap as if they were windows into someplace very far away. "And you." He lifted her to her feet and she looked around confused. "You two will be the nurses, eh?" He laughed. I didn't like it.

He took her outside and closed the door behind him.

Five minutes later the door opened again and the overweight, red-haired man who I took to be the motel owner stepped in. He carried two grocery bags. "Here ya go, *amigos*. No tacos today. Heh heh." He handed the bag to Frederico and backed out the door.

Frederico distributed peanut butter sandwiches—no jelly—on white bread and brought out paper cups and a gallon jug of Holiday Punch Fruit-Flavored Drink. It tasted like filet mignon and Rothschild '59.

Along with most everyone else I dozed uneasily through the rest of the day. My eyes kept snapping open when I'd see the two men in the canyon jerk with the impact of my bullets.

It was dark when I heard a scream from one of the other rooms.

Hushed conversation filled the darkened motel room. *What was that? It was the Indian girl. No it was the other one. Be quiet, let us hear.*

But whoever it was didn't scream again. That could mean almost anything. I got to my feet and made my way along the wall to the broken window. A breeze lifted the rag that once served as a curtain. I began to climb out.

"Where are you going, José?" It sounded like Frederico.

"I heard a girl scream, didn't you? What do you think that means, eh? You saw the way that ugly *coyote* looked at the girls."

"What do you think you are going to do about it?" Another voice from farther into the room.

"I think I am not going to sit in the dark like an old woman waiting for her to scream again."

"Don't do it. *La Migra* is all over those hills with the green eyes that see in the dark. They will find us all and then where will we be?"

Someone else said, "You don't know how many men there are."

"No I don't." Removing my glasses and placing them in my shirt pocket, I went through the window feet first and looked around. The motel was situated with its back against a natural wall of earth. I saw a dumpster to my right, stars overhead. It was another hot night, but I breathed in the fresh air greedily. Until then I hadn't realized how foul it was in that room. I put my head into the window again and said, "I see there is a reason we are called *pollos,* eh?"

I crouched and made my way along the wall toward a lighted window some fifteen yards to my left. I drew my gun from my pant leg. Halfway to the window I heard a noise behind me. Spinning on my haunches I aimed the gun toward a shadow. A man's voice cursed and I could see Villapando brushing himself off and standing. I waved at him to get down. He couldn't have seen my smile in the dark.

Standing slowly beneath the lighted window and to one side, I heard Villapando creep up behind me. I touched his shoulder and nodded at him approvingly. He saw the gun in my hand and almost jumped. I put a finger to my lips. Moving my head very slowly toward the window, I could see a room with bullfight posters, ancient motel art and an electric fan sitting on top of a file cabinet. The motel owner sat on a broken couch with springs and stuffing poking through the faded tartan plaid pattern of the upholstery. He held a can of Bud and stared at a black-and-white movie with Charles Boyer in a tuxedo. Across the room was another couch on which the boy sat cradling his mother's head in his lap. There was no sign of the girls. Directly below me was a desk with a phone, an empty Kentucky Fried Chicken bucket, old newspapers, an adding machine and various other junk. Someone was sitting at the desk and speaking on the phone. I could see the back of his head and a pair of huge shoulders draped in a tailored, beige jacket. One hand was visible as it toyed with a pen. The hand was huge and bore two gaudy rings that looked familiar.

Listening, I could only make out that he was speaking in English. I caught two words: "August" and "units."

Nobody had screamed in here.

Villapando followed me to the corner of the building. Here were piles of rotted scrap lumber, a couple of rusted gas pumps, the rounded kind you never see anymore. Farther off to the right was a long, low shed covering a row of vehicles: two panel trucks, another station wagon and a shiny new Olds Cutlass.

The first panel truck was white and bore the words "Vita-Gro Farms."

Beyond the shed of vehicles was an old trailer, an Air Stream up on blocks. There were lights inside and someone moved across the window twice. As we crawled closer, in the shadow of the shed. I could hear voices, Wild Bill's laughter, a girl crying.

I ran the remaining yards to the trailer, feeling exposed in the starlight. I moved around to the rear and Villapando came scuttling after me. I motioned for him to stay where he was and I stood on a pair of tires to peer in through a dusty window.

The Indian girl was stretched out on a low table, her skirt around her waist. Her underwear around her ankles. She lay staring at the ceiling the way she had at her hands earlier, not seeing. The other girl, maybe twenty, was naked and huddled in a chair crying. Blood flowed from her nose and down one leg. Wild Bill was pulling on his pants while his partner, without shades now, kneaded the Indian girl's thighs and breasts. His expression hadn't changed, but his upper lip was curled with what might

have been pleasure. He began to unbuckle his belt. "This one
don't give a shit, Peppy."

"Yeah, she don't give a shit, Ed," he echoed in English. So Wild
Bill's name was Peppy. There is something about knowing someone's name before you kill him.

A shotgun lay against the door directly opposite me.

I handed my .32 to Villapando. "I'm going around to the door.
When it opens, break the window and point that at the *Nort
Americano.* Make a lot of noise. Make sure he sees it. If he moves,
shoot him. Can you do that?"

"Oh *chingado,* I don't know."

"At least make sure he sees it. Maybe that will be enough." He
nodded and swallowed. I gripped his shoulder again in reassur-
ance.

Feeling around under the trailer, I found just the thing in case
that door didn't open on cue—an old tire iron. I gripped it and
crawled out under the front door. Crouching, I slowed my
breathing and tried to distribute all of my adrenaline evenly.

I lifted my free hand and grabbed the doorhandle, pulled down
and away.

It was locked . . . and they heard me.

"Who is it?" Peppy called in Spanish.

In English, I answered. "Hey, Peppy, c'mon," and stepped to
the side of the door, raising the tire iron.

"Who the hell is that?" It was Ed.

The door swung open and Peppy stuck his head out. I brought
the tire iron down and the pulpy, cracking sound of it crushing
his skull was joined by the sound of breaking glass. Wild Bill
Tooth Decay, aka Peppy, the old bartender's murderer, fell out of
the trailer still clutching the shotgun. I reached for it and a shot
from the .32 went over my head and nicked the doorjamb.

I looked up, into the trailer, and pumped a shell into the barrel.
Ed had moved fast. He held the oblivious body of the Indian girl
as a shield and backed into the rear of the trailer. In one hand he
brandished a .38. He waved it back and forth from the door to the
window. If I'd had the .32, I could have got him, but with the
shotgun I would hit the girl too.

"Drop 'em both or I kill this bitch!" He jammed the gun up

against the girl's face. She looked at it, puzzled, and then her eyes darted around the room wildly.

Villapando dropped the gun. I heard it hit the floor of the trailer. "He'll kill her, José!" His voice was shaking.

"He's right, José, your turn. Throw it in here."

There was nothing else to do. I put the safety on and was about to toss it into the trailer, kissing off any hope of surviving the night, when the Indian girl bit Ed's hand and twisted away from him. The other girl, naked and bloody, scrambled for the .32.

Ed pointed the gun at her.

The Indian girl flew out the door of the trailer past me. I was holding the shotgun, with the safety on, by the barrel. Almost useless. I threw it at Ed's arm and hit him at the elbow. His shot went into the floor. I dove for the girl who was fumbling with the .32 and wrenched it away from her as she brought it up to shoot Ed.

Ed and I were pointing live guns at each other. Other guns appeared at the door of the trailer. One of them, a .45, was held in a massive hand full of rings. It belonged to Conan the Barbarian. The motel owner held a revolver. Three guns, all pointed at me.

Behind the motel owner I could see some scurrying going on in the parking lot. A Mexican held Villapando by the collar and someone else was chasing down the Indian girl. Headlights played over gravel.

I dropped my weapon and slid it toward Conan. I was wondering if he recognized me when I sensed Ed moving toward me.

The first thing I did was to cover my head with both arms. I took the blow from the butt of the shotgun on my right forearm— and my face was on the floor. A booted toe tried to punch through one of my kidneys. The world turned red and black and there wasn't anything to breathe. He kicked me again in the other kidney and someone said, "Stop." I tasted blood where I had bit through my lip.

"I'll take him with me." I looked up into Conan's face. "It is my curious little cat friend, no?"

"Mr. Gato to you," I managed to wheeze.

19

EDDY GRABBED ME by the hair and lifted me to my feet. I stepped on my ranchero's hat and my glasses on the way out of the camper. In the parking lot I could see the motel owner pistol-whipping Villapando. Blood and teeth flew through the darkness. The fat, red-haired man was saying, "Somebody's gonna call the cops. The Border cops, you greaseball. They're gonna wanna know what the fuckin' shooting's all about."

Eddy let go of my hair and threw me toward Conan. "Tell 'em you were drunk and shooting rabbits. C'mon, let's get everybody out of here."

"Rabbits? Are you shitting me? Rabbits?"

Villapando had lost consciousness. The motel owner and a Mexican kid of about eighteen lifted him and placed him into the trunk of the Olds Cutlass. The two girls were shoved in after him. The kid tossed in the naked girl's clothes. She was silently hysterical, her shoulders rising and falling. The Indian girl seemed to be aware of her surroundings now. She helped the other girl cover herself.

All the vehicles from the garage were lined up in the lot. People were being herded out of the motel under Conan's supervision. Ed stood behind me resting the muzzle of the shotgun against the base of my neck.

Though none of the vehicles had their headlights on, I could see that people were being stuffed into trunks, vans, station wagons and even a Volkswagon hood. The Vita-Gro Farms truck held at least twenty people, who, once inside, were covered with bags of fertilizer.

Conan approached me and put his face down next to mine. He pointed his forefinger at the corner of his left eye. "You see what you did to me?" I couldn't see anything. There might have been a scar there. "You remember?" He waited for me to say something. I didn't. "I remember." His fistful of rings went into my right eye. The whole side of my head went numb, and blood began to flow from a quarter-moon gash from the side of my eye up into my eyebrow.

In the next moment I was in the trunk of the Cutlass with the unconscious Villapando, the Indian girl and the other half-naked girl. Blood covered all of us like a greasy coat of paint.

The car began to move and we were jolted against each other painfully for ten minutes until we hit the freeway. "Where are they taking us? What is happening?" The Mexican girl clutched the front of my shirt and tried to wrench an answer out of me.

"It will be all right," I told her. "Don't worry." I said it several times and it sounded just as lame, but she seemed to calm down.

The Indian girl spoke from behind me. "Thank you, Señor Gato," she said. I turned my neck as far as I could, but couldn't see her. "Thank you for what you did."

"It's nothing." It was. Exactly nothing.

Half an hour went by and we began to climb at a steep angle upward. That meant we were heading inland as well as north.

Blood dried on my face and the Mexican girl's forearm, bonding us together like some kind of nightmarish glue.

Villapando came around after we had been traveling for an hour. He cried out and spat and thrashed in the trunk, kicking me

and producing cries from the two girls. I told him to calm down
and let him know where he was.

When his breathing came easier, he spoke. "You killed that
coyote back there, didn't you? The one he called Peppy?"

"Yes."

"They will kill us then."

"Maybe. I'm sorry." I began thinking about my talent for getting other people dead. "I think they'll just kill me."

A long silence—accompanied by tires against freeway and a
humming engine—stretched, became more silence.

Eventually the Indian girl spoke again. "Where do you think
they are taking us?"

"Northeast San Diego. In the mountains," I told her.

"Why?"

"I'm not sure yet. We'll find out."

"Who are you? You are from here, aren't you? You are not
Mexicano. You spoke English back there."

"My name is York, what's yours?"

"Macinta."

Villapando introduced himself and eventually the other girl
was coaxed into informing us her name was Estela. We were
climbing at a steep angle now and were driving slowly over a
gravel road. We had been traveling over an hour, I figured.

The Olds pulled to a stop. The engine was still on.

Voices.

We heard the sounds of other vehicles laboring up the gravel
road behind us.

Conan's voice told Eddy and someone named Mariposa—
probably the kid—to open some doors.

I heard the kid ask, "You gonna put 'em *all* in there, Hector?"

"Just do what I tell you," Conan answered.

After a minute the car pulled forward, maybe twenty yards. The
sound of the engine echoed off walls, then died.

The trunk opened and I was blinking up at Hector with one
eye. He was silhouetted from behind by a bare light bulb hanging
from a wooden ceiling. Eddy appeared next to him, the shotgun
poised lazily across his forearm.

"Hey, Conan," I said.

"Shut up," Hector told me.

"What is this Conan shit?" Eddy asked, looking at the bigger man. "Who is this guy?"

Hector reached down smiling and poked at my swollen eye. He laughed. "You stay here, Mister Gato. You and you"—he pulled at the two girls—"come with me."

I had to sit up to let Estela out of the trunk. In the light I could see that Villapando looked pretty bad. I could also see that we were in the garage beneath the "servants' quarters" on Rachel Cole's estate: the place full of farm machinery I was supposed to guard that night.

A caravan of three Vita-Gro trucks pulled up parallel to one another in the garage. The drivers got out of them and threw sacks of fertilizer onto a pile in the corner. A dozen or more women got out and were herded up a flight of wooden steps. Their questions and protests were silenced by a driver's sharp threats.

Hector grinned once more and slammed the trunk on me and Villapando.

The Olds backed out of the garage and we were driving down the road.

Five minutes later we came to a stop and the trunk opened again. Hector and Eddy pulled me out and threw me on the flagstone driveway behind the estate. Through my one good eye I could see the bell tower above us. I wondered if they were going to string me up there after all.

Mariposa and another guy dragged Villapando off into the darkness toward the outbuildings I hadn't been allowed near on my last visit. Hector and Eddy frog-marched me through the archway and into the courtyard with the swimming pool full of carp. They stopped at an unlighted room with drawn venetian blinds on the ground level along the east wall of the courtyard.

Hector pounded on the door. "Ryder! Ryder! Get up. Are you in there?"

A light came on and the door flew open. Ryder stood in front of us wearing a pair of jockey shorts. He held a Baretta 9mm in his right hand. "What the fuck?" he said.

"Hi, Sandy," I greeted him.

He peered at me with sleepy eyes. "Who the . . . Jesus Christ!"

"Not exactly," I demurred.

Hector shook me by the collar. "He came through with a group last night. He killed Peppy."

"Wait a minute, slow down. He came where? Who the fuck is Peppy?"

Hector explained it all to him.

"You still looking for the girl? Her brother? What?" Ryder asked. Hopelessly confused, he backed into the room and pulled on a pair of Levi's. As he woke up, he began putting it together and started getting mad. "You're dead, you know that? You son of a bitch, you're dead. We're gonna kill you. Wait a minute . . ." He began to pace and ran his fingers through his blond hair. "Okay." He rifled through a trunk at the foot of his bed. His room was full of guns, flags, medals and photographs. One poster was a grainy, black-and-white blowup of a nineteen-year-old, crew-cut kid in fatigues standing in front of a pile of sandbags holding two human ears in each hand. Dark streaks ran from the ears down his arms. In the foreground of the picture someone was holding up a sign that read, "Tiger Ryder, Tet '67."

Ryder produced a pair of handcuffs and tossed them to Eddy. Eddy pulled my arms down behind me and cuffed me.

"C'mon." Ryder grabbed a ring of keys and led us across the courtyard. "We stick him in here." He walked down a flight of stone steps and fit a key into a stout wooden door with wrought iron hinges. "Walters is gonna wanna see you, dead man." He threw me into darkness and I tripped over something. The door swung closed behind me; the wood booming against stone echoed for several seconds.

"Say hi to Rachel," I said, but he couldn't have heard me by the time I got it out.

I lay where I had fallen, shaking and sweating. After a while I slept only to wake up and sweat and shake some more. The night went on that way.

Just before dawn I heard the same minor key chanting and droning that I thought I had heard only two weeks ago. It wasn't the cocaine. It sounded like the Vincent Price Chorale, only much closer than it had been from Rachel's room.

It seemed to come from beneath me. The floor was hard wood and the walls were stone. When I coughed, the sound was repeated twice.

Crawling on hands and knees I felt for what it was I had tripped over. It was a cardboard box. I felt inside and came up with a handful of cheap jewelry, items of clothing, rosaries. Another handful produced wallets, photographs, eyeglasses and shoes. I felt my way around the room, my eyes adjusting to the dark, to pace off the dimensions of my suite. I found more boxes full of the same kind of stuff stacked against walls.

My eye throbbed. My arm, where Eddy had clubbed me with the shotgun, wasn't broken, but it wasn't very useful either. My back felt like the road to Stalingrad. Still I crawled around the room and examined the artifacts of people's lives. What the hell had happened to them all? Whatever it was, apparently they didn't need their shoes or their glasses anymore.

Eventually some light leaked in through the crack beneath the door and where the wood had warped away from the stone along the hinges. I went through the wallets. No money, no credit cards, just a lot of family pictures and scraps of paper with phone numbers, names, addresses. All of it belonged to people with names like Rodriguez, Velasquez, Sanchez, Padero. I found Mexican driver's licenses, business cards, government health IDs and a few old *Bracero* cards.

I spent most of the morning going through all the stuff until I found something I didn't know I was looking for. I hobbled closer to the light to make sure. It was a duplicate of the photograph that Juana Villez had given me; there was the dapper old man, the dour old woman, Herman and Juana Villez.

I went back to the box and rifled through more of it. Belts and wristwatches, rings, necklaces, two men's wallets. One belonged to a Carmen DeCordoba, the other to Herman Guillermo DeFelipe Villez. He had a driver's license and several scraps of paper. On one of the scraps was the name "Morelos" and the word "Coahuila"; on another were the words "Case del Sol Chula Vista." The only other thing of interest was a page from a letter he hadn't finished. The first page was missing and all that appeared at the top of the paper I held was one paragraph. It read:

". . . together again soon. If the mules don't come to drive us tonight, then certainly tomorrow night I am told. Your job in the San Diego cantina sounds better than cleaning after North American tourists in the hotel, and you have made so much money. I am ashamed. Soon, though, I will make even more money than that when I get a job with a North American rodeo. Be careful, let no one take advantage of you, trust no one until I can be with . . ."

Three quarters of the page were blank. He had been interrupted, possibly by the "mules" to drive him here. I still didn't know what happened to Herman Villez, but Walters was right about one thing—he was dead. Only he wasn't dead from knife wounds inflicted in a Tijuana bar.

The door flew open and woke me from a bad sleep. Ryder stood against the light in full Army surplus regalia.

He showed a flashlight into my eyes. I blinked and sat up. "C'mon, dead man. Time to say hello to the hosts."

Shielding my eyes, I got to my feet. I blinked into the sunlight and could see that I was being escorted by Manny of the many chins. He still had his pearl-handled .45 and it was pointed at my back. I noticed he walked with a limp now.

"The last time I saw you boys, we were playing tag in the rain down the road."

"You were lucky." Manny jabbed the gun into my ribs.

"I wasn't lucky. You guys fucked up. You guys could fuck up a wet dream."

They marched me up the stairs and I gestured at Manny's limp. "Tennis knee?" I asked.

"Fuck you. Shut up. Shut up or I'll kill you here."

Ryder restrained him. "Later," was all he said.

We entered a corridor I vaguely remembered being drunk and lost in several days ago. Ian Broctor passed us in the hallway. He was wearing the kind of thing the Ayatollah Khomeini favors for leisure wear. He paused and Ryder halted the procession. Broctor studied me with his holy, penetrating sniper-on-a-rooftop look. He clasped his hands in front of him and remained silent for a moment. He was supposed to be withering me with his psychic emanations. Finally, he said, "You are a self-destructive soul. Marred by the beast's illusions. I saw your death in a vision. Your death on a battlefield, your body brought to the temple before me. I would have told you, but you would not have listened."

I cleared my throat and whispered piously, "Shove it, Broctor."

Everyone tensed. For a moment he looked like a man who just discovered he had crabs and then he moved down the hallway in a flurry of robes. Obviously someone wanted me alive, at least for a little while.

Ryder and Manny showed me into Rachel's living room. They seated themselves on two chairs, their guns trained on me—I saw that Ryder was sporting a Mauser machine pistol today—and left me standing in front of the piano, handcuffed, bloody, bruised and stinking.

Rachel came down the curving stairs dressed in an emerald green pantsuit. Her hair was tied back the way it had been when I first saw her and she wore the same gold hoop earrings. She paused on the stairs when she saw me. I had two or three days' growth of beard beneath my probably discolored eye so she didn't take that long to recognize me.

She looked me up and down, started to say something, decided against it. All she said was, "I called Gene. He's coming. He'll be here tonight."

"Well, what does he want us to do with him?" Ryder spoke up.

"Nothing," she said. "Keep him locked up, but feed him. Don't hurt him." She paused for emphasis and crossed the room toward me. She touched my swollen eye with all the delicacy of a wanton child intrigued with pain and bashed flesh. "He wants to kill him himself."

"After all we meant to each other," I got out and then she slapped me hard up against my punched-out eye. I staggered back a few paces. Both my eyes teared. She ate that up.

"What did you hope to gain?" She lit a cigarette from the Russian box. "I thought you were . . . well, I didn't think you were . . . *such a fool.*"

"The Border Patrol knows where I am. Exactly," I lied.

Rachel tossed her head back and laughed. "Get him out of

here." She waved me away, still laughing. I'd never seen her laugh that way. It was real. I had said something funny.

I was taken back to the wood and stone room full of the personal effects of ghosts. Ryder threw me a bucket to use as a toilet and later someone I didn't recognize, carrying a gun, brought a cheese sandwich and an orange. I wondered if the orange was compliments of Broctor. Light came and went around the door twice so I figured I had been there two days and two nights. Every night I heard the chorus of chanting coming from a room nearby.

Walters never showed.

On the morning of the third day Manny appeared, handed me an avacado and told me to eat it quickly. I did and then he instructed me to carry the bucket outside. He led me around the rear of the south wing and told me to throw the contents onto a compost heap. After that I washed out the bucket with a hose and left it with some garden tools. Manny walked me nearly a half mile toward the outbuilding where Villapando had been taken when we arrived. Neither of us spoke.

The outbuilding was a long, low, ranch-style structure. Armed men, I counted six, milled around talking, smoking and pacing the quarter acre around the building. Half of it was used as stables for three or four horses and the other half housed a dozen men with no more amenities than a single toilet, some straw and a few horse blankets.

My eyes were still unused to the daylight so Villapando recognized me first. "José!" He approached me and clasped my arm.

"York," I said. I could see that his jaw was broken, swollen and at a bad angle to the top of his face. Blood had congealed at the corners of his mouth and around some wounds at his temples.

"Yes, York." He looked me up and down and said, "What is happening here?"

"I don't know." I looked at the other men in the room. All of them, except myself and Villapando, were very young, none of them older than thirty and most much younger. Everyone seemed reasonably well fed and uninjured.

Villapando told me that every night more men would arrive and every morning, some would be taken away in the backs of the fertilizer trucks. Only the youngest and strongest were left here. "As you know, the women are taken to the other place." He gestured up the road with his ruined chin. "What can they have in mind for us in here?"

"I don't know," I repeated. "We'll find out soon, I think."

It wasn't all that soon. We were kept for another ten days. I ate better than I had in my private room and slept easier. Villapando was right. Every night a shipment of men would be brought in and every morning they would be shipped out except for a few additions to our group, mostly boys of eighteen to twenty. My insistence on medical attention for Villapando was met with all the interest a lizard might take in the stock market.

On the fourth or fifth day, Walters showed up. He was wearing a brushed suede hunting jacket and a pair of desert boots. He arrived in Ryder's Renegade, Ryder behind the wheel, Carlos in the backseat. They approached the stables and peered in through the dusty glass.

Walters smiled at me and shook his head. I gave him the finger. He laughed and disappeared again. Carlos approached and wrote on the dust on the window. He wrote backward so I could read it, SHITHEAP.

One afternoon as Villapando and I were pitching pennies—*centavos* actually—for pieces of straw representing five dollars each, we heard gunfire from the tree line above the stables. Other sounds. A helicopter and several car engines. Our number had grown to twenty-three men and we all jockeyed for position at the windows. Land Rovers and Jeeps drove past the stables full of men. Very few of them were Mexican.

It was an odd sight. A convoy of four-wheel-drive vehicles carrying what looked to be eight or nine overweight, balding businessmen dressed in hunting gear and armed to the teeth with automatic rifles, Ingram pistols, Uzis, CAR 15s, Weatherbees with scopes, bow and arrows, binoculars, knives and bottles of beer. One of them was the Republican congressman I had seen in Rachel Cole's living room several weeks ago.

The convoy rode past the stablehouse washing the windows with more dust. As the vehicles approached the treeline, the passengers joined in the chorus of gunshots, firing into the air and hollering, *"Yeehah! Ariba!"* and *"La Cucaracha!"*

Ryder pulled his Renegade up to the stable. Manny was next to him, Walters and Carlos were in the back. A private, very small white chopper with a sporty blue stripe took off from the north end of the estate and flew overhead.

I studied Ryder. He was wearing his camouflage fatigues, his face was painted with commando grease, brown, green and black. On his head was a black sweatband. Robert De Niro in *The Deer Hunter*. He carried his Walther P38 and his crossbow. In the Renegade, Walters was dressed for a hunting weekend in a safari jacket and an Indiana Jones hat. Manny wore his Members Only jacket and Carlos wore a tan *Guayabera* shirt.

Ryder instructed the guards to open the doors and file us out on parade in front of him. They opened the doors. We filed out.

When everyone was in position, Ryder said, "You men have been selected as the fittest wirecutters for our game. You have one hour to disperse in any direction you care to go." One of the guards translated this into Spanish. "This estate is one hundred and twenty-eight square acres. It's surrounded by a high-voltage fence. There's water out there, even some food hidden around. Of course there's some fruit, berries, like that too. You will be hunted. Most of you will be killed. Any one of you who survives until sundown tomorrow night will be given a thousand dollars and transportation to anywhere in the United States."

He sounded like a game show host. I wanted to laugh, but I couldn't.

"Clear enough? Okay." He paused, looked over at me. "Jew York," he said without even a sneer, "you're mine. Walters, Manny, Carlos and me each have a bet we'll get you first. They'll lose." He looked at his watch and raised his voice. "Starting . . ." he paused, drew the Walther from his holster, thumbed the safety, drew back the hammer and pointed the barrel at the blue, late August sky. "Now!" He fired into the air.

No one moved.

20

VILLAPANDO LOOKED OVER at me as if to say, "Is he serious?" The other men in the group followed his gaze. I was the gringo, and one of them besides. They wanted me to tell them, "Don't worry, this is just a little Yankee humor, our way of saying welcome to the U.S."

I turned to Ryder. If there was any doubt about what he had said, there wasn't a trace of it in his face. There wasn't a trace of anything there. He was still holding his pistol. He lowered it and pointed it at the ground, lifted it marginally and fired a shot into the thigh of the boy closest to him. The boy's left leg went out from under him, backward. His whole body was lifted off the ground and he went into the dirt face first without a cry. He looked up and the blood had gone from his face. He didn't seem to know what had happened.

Several of the others began to run. Villapando turned one way, then another. I grabbed his arm and said, "C'mon. We've got to help him."

Everyone was running now, in all directions. Ryder walked back to the Renegade and started it. He fired several shots into the air and howled. He drove up the hill toward the tree line and the other vehicles.

Villapando and I lifted the boy by the shoulders and I jerked my chin ahead of us. "This way," I said. The boy was breathing hard and grimacing, but he still made no sound. He leaned against the two of us and allowed himself to be half lifted as we walked north toward high, rocky ground. Villapando was shaking. So was I.

We descended into a gully and then climbed up its other side moving as quickly as possible. The boy began to produce sharp, breathy grunts from high in his chest. "Wait a minute," I said. We set him down on a dead tree stump and I tore the sleeve from my flannel shirt. As I wrapped it above the free-flowing wound on his leg, I looked toward the tree line. Both Ryder and Walters were watching us through binoculars.

"It's okay," I lied to the kid. "You'll be okay. These fuckers are just trying to scare us."

"I'm scared," he said quietly. "They're doing a good job."

"Let's go." We lifted him again and he hobbled a little faster now. In five minutes we were at the top of the first group of boulders. The going was slower now, but we had to get dug in somewhere as high as possible: somewhere they'd have to come for us on foot.

Someone else had had the same idea. As we rounded a high boulder, a rock went whistling inches from my head. "Ese! It's me, York, José, whatever!"

Two of them were crouched at the mouth of a small cave big enough for only one. They had a pile of good-sized missiles stacked in front of them. I recognized "Ojo Blanco" with the cataract in one eye. The other one's name was Juan Garcia—like five or six of the others. I had pitched *centavos* with him a few times and he owed me one hundred and fifteen dollars.

"That's no good in there," I said. "It's a trap. We've got to get higher up." They looked uncertainly at us and then nodded and followed, bringing a rock in each hand.

We climbed steadily for half an hour, always moving north. I figured we had ten or fifteen minutes before they came after us. A well-worn path appeared going east and west. A Jeep could handle it at slow speed. A rocky overhang a few yards away would make a nice place to drop rocks or people from, but Ryder and his party would know that. Villapando pointed it out. I shook my head and said, "Keep going."

It occurred to me that Ryder would know enough to be wary of the highest ground, which was a narrow bluff two hundred yards to the right. We didn't have time to get there and we'd be too exposed anyway. Garcia found a length of stout tree limb to use as a club. He swung it at the top of a cactus and then dug the point into the piece he had hacked off. He now had a crude morning star mace. Clever maybe, but the broken cactus was like a neon sign reading "Kilroy was here."

The wounded kid passed out and we had to drag him the rest of the way toward a promising-looking spot halfway up a fall of boulders twenty yards or so from the path. We found a trenchlike area we could fit in without difficulty. Our backs were against larger rocks and we had a good vantage point looking south. Still, if they came for us over the bluff behind us, we were fish in a barrel. The kid came to and wanted some water. No one had any. He said he was okay and that his name was Alberto.

The helicopter I had seen earlier passed near us and we clung to the sides of the rock. It kept going, heading north.

Gunfire from the tree line announced the beginning of the hunt.

Villapando prayed. Ojo kept pissing every minute or so into some scrub weed. I tried to think, but it was almost impossible while trying to keep my heart from climbing out of my mouth. I studied the rocks around us, looking for something, anything at all that might help.

The engine of one of the vehicles announced itself, getting closer. In a few minutes we could hear voices and laughter. It appeared on the path moving at about ten miles an hour. It was the Renegade, but Ryder wasn't in it. Manny was behind the wheel and Carlos ran alongside carrying a .220 Swift with a scope. In his free hand he held a burning joint. Walters was in the backseat chuckling and drinking something from a thermos that sweat with the day's heat against its coldness. They stopped directly underneath the overhang I had pegged as the first sucker move. The Renegade was bait.

Unless I missed my guess, Ryder would be coming up on foot behind that overhang. Tiger Ryder moving swift and silent like the deer. I motioned to the others to remain quiet. They remained quiet.

Someone burst from the shadow of a stunted California oak. It wasn't Ryder. It was a Mexican kid who had hid in the wrong place, taken the bait. He stumbled and launched himself down the shale. Halfway down he collapsed to his knees and toppled forward onto his face. An arrow protruded from the base of his neck.

A voice carried across to us. "Shit!" Ryder appeared from behind a boulder, a crossbow at his side. "Hey, Jew York! Hey, dead man!" His voice echoed then died. He turned to face the pile of rocks we hid behind, thought again and turned to the higher bluff behind him. He howled at nothing and disappeared behind the boulder again. He might have been moving toward us or the other promontory.

"Stay here," I said to the others, and edged my way past them. When I reached the west side of the rocks, out of sight of the Renegade, I climbed. At the top I peered out at a shallow canyon that had been carved by spring runoff over the years and dammed up at its narrowest point by a season's worth of tumbleweed and dried flotsam. I picked up a rock that weighed maybe ten or twelve pounds and lay flat across an uncomfortably jagged fault. A twisted force of a pine bush and some cassia grass rustled in front of me, affording me some cover. I lay there for a very long time, it seemed, breathing evenly, tasting dry metal in the back of my mouth, remembering how tired fear can make you—and trying not to let it do that.

A sound behind me startled me and I spun onto my back, the rock poised beyond my head to launch it at whoever had made the sound. It was Villapando scrambling up the way I had come. He stood and as I hissed at him to get down. Something else hissed through the air and Villapando staggered backward. A feathered bolt protruded from his forehead. At first I thought it was a dart of some kind because it looked so small and there was no blood where it had entered just above his right eye. He leaned backward and fell. For a second he seemed gracefully poised, motionless at an impossible angle to the earth below him. As he went down I saw the arrow, slick with blood and gray, pink matter that had emerged from the back of his skull. He went down quietly and after a second I heard his body hitting the rocks.

I turned and saw Ryder at the bottom of the gully. He was crouched, knocking another bolt onto the bow. He didn't see me. I launched the rock toward him and it sailed down too slowly. It cast a shadow over him as it fell and he looked up, dodging the thing at the last minute. He tossed the crossbow and grinned, climbing toward me. I found myself flying through the air. In the next moment I was on him, my hands around his neck.

He brought both arms up between mine and flailed outward, quickly breaking my grip. My roundhouse right caught him along the side of his face and he went down.

He came up with a bowie knife in his right hand. He shifted it to his left, back to his right, back again. I launched my foot at him and caught his arm. He grunted and the arm hung for a moment, useless. The knife was in his other hand. He poked it at me and I danced back. He swung it in a wide arc back and forth, and I found myself moving away until my back was up against a rock. He said, "I'm really gonna like this," and lunged at my crotch with the blade. I turned to the side and heard it strike stone. I brought my elbow down onto the base of his neck as I turned. He went to his knees. I kicked him in the ribs and he doubled over. I kicked him again along the side of his head.

Ryder was sprawled on the floor of the canyon. I saw the knife where he had dropped it a foot away. I didn't see the tiny Walther PPK in his hand, but I heard it. The first bullet whistled past my chest, the second went wide somewhere and I was on him. My left hand pinned his wrist, the one with the gun. My right hand was on his throat choking him. His left hand dug into the pressure point on my arm, the soft place between the biceps. My arm went numb, I couldn't feel my hand on his throat, but I willed it to close, tighten.

We remained, locked that way while the sun stood still and the only sound was a roaring in my ears. I stared into his eyes above the commando greasepaint which seemed to stand out in relief as

the blood left his face. At the last moment I noticed that he had
worked the pistol around in his hand. It was pointing at my
forearm, just above the wrist.

I let go of him and the gun went off. The round went between
us as I leaned back as far as I could. I locked my hands together
and brought both fists down into his face as he tried to choke air
back into himself. I did it again, several times until he wasn't
moving anymore.

The gun lay in his open palm. I picked it up and held it to the
side of his head while I felt for a pulse on his neck. He was still
alive. One of his legs bucked, probably involuntarily, beneath me
and I pulled the trigger. The bullet entered neatly and exited
messily. After a second or two, blood spouted in a small stream
from the entrance wound and covered the gun and my hand
before I pulled it away.

I got up and my knees folded. Kneeling, I vomited some watery
stuff, shook, felt the sweat cool everywhere on me. With detach-
ment I watched myself scrape my hand and the gun into the dirt
to clean the blood from them.

There is no way to know how long I knelt there scraping my
knuckles in the dust, retching, but eventually I became aware of
more gunshots ricocheting off stone. I got to my feet, and instead
of climbing back up, I retraced Ryder's steps through the tumbleweed break and around the side of the boulder fall.

I saw the Renegade. No one was in it.

I couldn't tell where the shots were coming from but they were
striking the rock face where I had left the wounded kid, Garcia
and Ojo Blanco. They were being pinned down by three different
guns. One was the .220 Swift judging by the keening whine of the
high-velocity bullets flying from rock to rock. The other made an
innocuous burping sound that stitched the air and could only be a
machine pistol, an Ingram, Uzi, CAR 15, something like that. The
barking of Manny's .45 was unmistakable and I got a fix on that
first.

He was just ahead of me and below me. A stand of high pampas
grass concealed him as he jacked another clip into the pearl
handle. His shoulders shook with laughter. He stood out in his
burgundy Members Only jacket like a fire hydrant, though no one

would have been able to make him out from above. I pointed the
Walther at his back, pulled the hammer and said, "Manny."

He turned and I shot him twice. He looked very surprised, then
angry. He lifted his gun at me and I shot him again. His face took
on a philosophical expression and he relaxed, slumping like a
narcoleptic catching a few Z's with his eyes still open, but lidded.
Three black holes, the size of nickels, studded his jacket. You
couldn't tell he was bleeding unless you looked at the grass
beyond him. He was dead, but he looked like he was just thinking
everything over.

The machine pistol sprayed bullets everywhere. Some of them
sang off the rocks near me and I kept down. When it let up for a
moment, I stopped eating dust and squinted into the sun, wiping
dirt from my face. Walters was in the Renegade and starting it up.
He drove in reverse spinning gravel and raising clouds of exhaust
and dust. My gun was empty. Walters was gone.

The .220 Swift that Carlos was using had a fix on me now and
the rounds were coming uncomfortably close. I scrambled back
the way I had come, stepped over Ryder's body and scrambled
upward toward the place I had left the three Mexicans.

Juan Garcia was still alive. White Eye was dead with three
bullets in his brain. The kid, Alberto, was dead too. He hadn't
been hit, he had just died from blood loss and terror. His pants
were fouled. Juan was praying like an old woman, hugging the
rocks like a long lost lover. He didn't look at me as I stood over
him. He was waiting to die.

"Juan!" I said, and then again, louder, "Juan!"

When he still didn't respond, I took the collar of his shirt in my
fist and shook him. He cried out with his eyes closed, "Please, no!
Please."

"Shut up! Look at me." Tears streaked his dusty face. I realized
he was probably nineteen or twenty years old. "We've got to go
down. There's a knife, a crossbow and a pistol down there. We
need them." He hugged my knees and I hit him alongside the
face with an open palm. "Stop it, Godammit!"

A bullet struck a clump of bottle brush and severed a handful of
stalks. Carlos was still out there with the .220. I got down again
and took hold of Juan's shoulder. He got himself together
enough to hear me. "Stay down and follow me. Don't make any

noise." I put the empty Walther in my belt and crawled on all fours back down the way I had come. Juan stuck close behind me.

We loosened gravel and rocks as we leaped from cover to cover. Carlos had no trouble tracking us. He fired playful shots just ahead, behind and above us.

In the gully, I worked as quickly as possible frisking Ryder's body. Carlos could appear above us at any minute. I produced another clip for the Walther, the Bowie knife and another, smaller knife taped to his leg. Ryder had fallen on the remaining two bolts for the crossbow. I didn't want to waste time moving him and I didn't know where the bow had fallen. I wasn't sure I'd know how to use it anyway.

Motioning for Juan to follow, I scrambled back to where Manny sat mulling over his death. The gun lay in his lap pointed at the ground and hanging from his forefinger. I reached for it and the high pampas grass around me swayed with the motion. Carlos fired at the movement. My hand closed over the barrel and I had the gun. A bullet kicked a clump of dirt three feet in the air to my right. I ducked back around the rocks and looked in the direction the gunshot had come from.

Across the road and up the escarpment on the other side I caught a movement and a glint of sunlight on steel. As soon as it registered, it disappeared.

Checking the .45, I saw that it had a full clip. I handed it to Juan and asked him if he could use it. He looked at it as if it were a microwave oven. I handed him the Walther instead and took the safety off.

"You see the big shadow on those rocks over there?" I pointed to where I had seen Carlos's rifle barrel. He nodded. "When I say 'now,' I want you to fire one bullet at the bottom of the shadow, count to three, fire another, count to three again, fire until the gun is empty. Can you do that? I'm going to run across the clearing and try to climb up there, but you have to cover me. Now don't hold down the trigger. Squeeze it, let it go, count to three, squeeze it again, count. You understand?"

"Yes, yes." The gun shook in his hand and I closed his other hand over his wrist to steady it. While I did that, I saw my own hand shaking. He noticed it and smiled. "You are afraid too."

"You got that right." I didn't bother to smile reassuringly, my lips were stuck to my teeth with some sort of paste. "I'm going up there to kill him. We'll be okay then."

"Good luck. Remember, I owe you a hundred dollars."

"One hundred and fifteen, *you* remember."

I edged my way along some felled tree trunk that had been rotting for ten years and then crawled through some grass that wouldn't have come to my knees if I were standing.

Carlos tracked me. He stood in the shadow, his rifle barrel catching the sun again and fired. Dirt and grass flew in my face. I rose to a crouch and ran across the clearing, pointing at Carlos and shouting, "Now! See him?"

Juan responded by holding down the trigger long enough to fire five rounds one after the other. It wasn't the plan, but he'd probably never fired a gun before. As I ran, I shot blindly in Carlos's general direction. I probably didn't miss him by more than a quarter mile.

Carlos had ducked and that bought me ten yards. The nearest cover was just the sheer wall of the escarpment Carlos sat on; I figured it to be another twenty yards.

The .220 went off again and the bullet ripped a small flower pot–sized hole in the ground in front of my right boot. I rolled forward, came up running and zigzagged toward the shadows ahead.

I was waiting for Juan to let off another few rounds. Nothing. I fired up at Carlos's position. A piece of stone erupted about six feet from where he was crouched. What the fuck was Juan doing?

Carlos leaned over his rock and fired at me again. I darted left and the round slammed harmlessly into the earth where I had been a second ago. Carlos fired again. I darted right. "Juan!" I screamed.

Ten yards to go. I lifted Manny's cannon and fired again into the shadows above me. I didn't see how close or far off my shot was.

I closed the distance to the cool, sheer rock face and spread myself against it panting. Maybe Walters had circled back the way Ryder had, maybe he'd come up behind Juan. Maybe the gun had just jammed, I don't know how long I had scraped it into the dust and sand to clean the blood from it. Something had happened though.

The idea of just staying put and waiting for Carlos to make a move occurred to me, but only for a minute. My cover was only relative. I had to get up behind him or alongside and it had to be pretty close; I'm not that good with a pistol, especially a .45. Even when my hands aren't shaking I'm a bad shot.

Edging along the sandstone, away from Carlos, I searched for a way up. I found one, took a handhold on some roots and pulled myself up. If anyone came down that road I would be an easy target. It was twenty feet or so to a ledge that ran the full length of the bluff; when I got to it, I could see that the only way I was going to get at Carlos was to come up right under him. He had climbed up into his niche, not down into it. As I ran, hugging the last of the morning shadows, I wondered if he was still there. He was. I saw the rifle barrel poke up again, the stock, the scope, the strap, his arm. He looked right at me and brought the rifle around. I had nowhere to go.

"Shitheap!" he said, happy to see me. "Drop the cannon."

Two flat, popping sounds echoed and chips of stone flew out of the cliff between Carlos and me. That was Juan. Those were his last two shots. Carlos turned his head fractionally to the side long enough for me to bring up my gun with both hands. He turned back to face me. We fired at the same time.

Carlos got off only one shot. He didn't have time to work the bolt while I fired three times. I got him in the shoulder. The bullet lifted him off his feet and threw him back. Blood spattered the rocks. The rifle slid down the cliff and clattered to a rest at the base.

I covered the distance between us and lifted myself up to where he lay. He was trying to close the wound with his hand. A piece of bone poked through his fingers. His *Guayabera* shirt was rapidly turning red, his face took on the color of the rock around him. "You gotta help me," he said.

The first thing I did was to make sure there were no more weapons on him or nearby. There weren't. What I found was a box of cartridges for the .220, a canteen full of water, a hand radio transceiver like the one Ryder had given me that night of the party and two empty beer cans. I drank from the canteen, still keeping the gun on him, stuffed the radio into my shirt, and grabbed the cartridges.

"Hey," he said. "Hey man . . . c'mon, you can't leave me here. I can get you outta here."

"Maybe," I said. I handed him the radio. "Get Walters on this thing. Tell him you killed me. Yuk it up like you won the bet, you know. Tell him to bring the Jeep down here."

"Okay. Give me some water." He was losing blood fast.

"First get Walters."

He pressed the side of the thing and breathed heavily. "Come in, Red Hunter, this is Blue Hunter to Red Hunter, come in, Mr. Walters." There was static while we waited. I stood and waved across the clearing to where I had left Juan. He emerged hesitantly from cover and ran across the trail. I called for him to pick up the rifle and come around the way I had come up. Carlos tried again. On the third try Walters answered.

"Carlos! You okay? That son of a bitch got hold of Ryder's gun. He got Manny and I think he must have got Ryder. Over."

My .45 was at Carlos's temple. I nodded. "Yeah, he got 'em both. . . ." I jammed the gun into his head. "I killed him though. Put one through his head. Over."

"Are you sure? Are you looking at his body? Over."

"Yeah, I told you, I got him. I'm hit though, real bad. You gotta get me out of here. Over."

"Yeah, you don't sound too good. We're coming in. Over."

"Hurry."

Juan came up the path carrying the rifle. I handed him the canteen and he drank greedily.

"Gun didn't work," he said. "It was full of dirt, I think. I cleaned it out though."

"Thanks, Juan. I owe you my life." He nodded without any false modesty. He tried to hand me back the Walther, but I told him to keep it. It was empty, but only we knew that.

I took the radio from Carlos and gave him a little water. With the gun still on him I said, "Talk, fast. What the fuck is this?"

"What do you mean? What do you think it is?"

"Why are you and Walters and all those fat-ass business types massacring unarmed people? Are you all completely fucking insane?"

"They pay. It's fun."

I repeated what he said as if the words registered but didn't mean anything.

"We do it two or three times a year. There's a lot of guys that will pay ten grand for a weekend of game like this. That's a lot of money. Give me some more water, I'm dying."

"You're not dying yet. Let me get this right. This hunting party is a little service Walters and Cole run for the amusement of their business acquaintances?"

"Something like that."

"What is he saying?" Juan wanted to know.

"Wait a minute." I thought. None of it made sense except in the simplest, most horrifying terms. Kicks. Jollies for bored, twisted people who could afford it. It probably grossed Walters and Cole a couple of million a year, but that wasn't anything to them. The hunt generated other business, and once an associate or a potential associate had taken part, they could blackmail him into whatever deals they wanted made. That thought led me to the next question. "What's that chopper doing up there?"

"Refreshments and shit."

"What?"

"You know, it flies in champagne and gourmet shit to a spot up in the mountains where everybody camps at night. You can't get at it except in four-wheel drives or on foot." I thought I was going to be sick. The sun was directly overhead and we were no longer in shadow. "What else is in that chopper? Guns?"

"No, no guns. Against the rules."

"Sporting. Cameras then?"

Carlos looked at me for a moment then nodded. "Yeah cameras, you got it."

Telephoto lenses recording bank presidents butchering running men. "Blackmail," I said.

"If it comes down to that. I told you, you got it. You'd be surprised though. I think they only had to threaten a couple of guys."

"Wouldn't Rachel Cole go down the toilet with whoever they tried to blackmail?"

Carlos chuckled, then grimaced. "Give me some water."

"Answer me."

"It's a good question. I don't think so though. You'd be surprised whose been out here on these rides: judges, congressmen, a lieutenant governor. Besides you can't identify the terrain that easily. It could be anywhere. Walters holds it over her though, just in case."

There were a lot more questions, but there was no time. I heard two vehicles coming up the road. I took the .220 from Juan and stuffed it with ammunition. I told him to climb back down. I gave him the .45.

"Find a place where you're covered, but they can see you're armed. Hold both guns on them. Don't shoot unless you have to."

When he was in place, I waved to him. The vehicles were coming closer. I looked over at Carlos. He was still losing blood at a fast rate. He would be dead inside an hour.

The first Jeep was the Renegade. Walters rode shotgun with the Uzi pointed ahead of him. A Mexican I didn't know drove with one hand, in his other he held an M16. The Jeep behind them had two more men in it. Another Mexican and a fat man in a baseball cap with a sunburned nose. He played a Weatherbee nervously around him.

I aimed for the dirt in front of the Renegade. Rock and dust flew into the radiator grill. The driver jammed on the brakes. The Jeep behind them almost rear-ended the Renegade.

There was a silence broken only by the echo from my gunshot. "Stay very still, all of you!" I called down. "Slowly throw your weapons as far as you can from you. You're covered from three directions. Behind you and to your left are two automatic pistols." They turned slowly and Juan brandished the guns at them. "On your right, at the top of that rock is the guy Ryder shot in the leg. He's okay though and he's holding Ryder's crossbow on you. He has three bolts. You can't see him, but he's there. Take my word for it."

The Mexican driver in the second Jeep made a move that was too quick. He tried to get under his dashboard. I fired into the windshield, worked the bolt and fired again. He screamed. The fat man in the backseat threw his Weatherbee into the air and waved his empty hands at the sky. Juan's nerves snapped; he fired and hit the fat man twice. It looked as if someone had shoved him from behind. As he hit the ground, he tried to reach for the wounds in his back. His hands fluttered then stilled.

Walters and his driver responded by immediately tossing their guns and sitting stock still in the Jecp.

I climbed out onto the rocks in full view. From behind me Carlos croaked, "You're going to let me die." It wasn't a question.

Without saying anything, I began to make my way down slowly, the rifle barrel leveled at Walters's chest.

Juan emerged from his hiding place and began to scream, "Fuckers! Motherfuckers! I'll kill all of you!" He laughed, then started crying, laughed some more.

When I was close enough, I told Walters and the driver to get out. They did. Walters turned to face me and smiled. "What do you think you're going to do, York? There are over forty armed men on this estate. Even if you could get off it, you wouldn't get very *far* off it."

I reached over and picked up the Uzi, slung the .220 over my shoulder then picked up the M16. I motioned for Juan, who had settled down, but stood staring at the man he had shot, to come over. I explained very briefly how the M16 worked and handed it to him then I searched Walters and the driver. I found two clips for the Uzi and another three for the M16.

"Cover him." I pointed at Walters. "Sit in the dirt with your hands over your head, Gene." Walters did what he was told. Then I instructed the driver to turn his back to me. When he did that, I set the Uzi on the front seat of the Renegade, unslung the .220 and brought the butt of it down against the back of the driver's head. He went to his knees then fell on his face.

"Okay," I said to Walters, "get up. You drive."

Walters got to his feet and into the Renegade. I took the driver's jacket and his cowboy hat, put them on. I told Juan to do the same with the other driver's shirt and hat and to get in the back. "Don't get crazy with that thing," I said, gesturing at the M16.

"No," he said. "I'm sorry."

Turning to Walters, I told him to get on the radio. "I want you to order everybody up to the rendezvous point in the mountains. Tell them there's a slight problem; you know, a few beaners picked up some guns, and until your staff can get the situation under control, you don't want to risk any of the guests. Tell them the champagne is cold, the barbecue fires are burning, you know, just get everyone out of my way. The first guy I see with a gun, I'll blow your head all over the road. Is that clear, Gene?"

"My friend, you're hopeless. If you think—"

"Do it. And if you say 'my friend' one more time I'm going to severe the muscles in the back of your right knee with Ryder's bowie knife."

He picked up the radio and called "White Hunter." He did a good job. He sounded like an airline pilot telling everyone to have another drink on him while the plane circled the landing field for a while. White Hunter wanted to know what the problem was and if he requested assistance. "No, no . . ." Walters reassured him in his airline pilot/disc jockey voice. "Nothing we can't handle from here. Just taking precautions."

"Very good," I told him. "How long will it take to clear the estate of your buddies?"

"It will take them at least an hour to get up the trails."

"Okay, move this thing under that Juniper tree." He put the Renegade in first gear and did it. To Juan I said, "Keep that rifle right here." I placed the muzzle at the base of Walters's neck then got out and dragged the unconscious driver off to the side. Then I went over and tried to move the dead fat man. I almost passed out with the effort, but I got him out of sight, at least from the air. If that helicopter came by again, I didn't want anyone in it getting upset. After moving the other driver's body onto the passenger seat—which took nearly as long as dragging the fat man—I started up the second Jeep and drove it into a ditch. I covered it with dried branches and grass.

I walked back to the Renegade and found Juan drinking from Walters's thermos, which proved to be half full of good bourbon and ice. He handed it to me, I took a long pull and choked on it. The next one was easier, a low flame seemed to spread through my stomach and chest and up through my neck.

"What are we going to do?" Juan asked.

"We're going to wait an hour," I said.

* * *

We spent the time chatting. Walters was surprisingly talkative and helpful. He didn't entertain the idea for a moment that I could hurt him no matter what I knew. I would never live long enough, and according to him, even if I did, no one would believe me—or if they did, it wouldn't matter. Yes, he agreed with some pride, he and Rachel financed the largest alien-smuggling ring in border history. They supplied what amounted to slave labor to California industry and agriculture. "So very cheap," he said. "You can't imagine. Negligible overhead. A vast market out there and we're locked into the ones that matter. Factories, mines, restaurants . . . oh, it goes on. And of course no one would have it any other way. The economy of this state and several others would collapse without us. Quite literally, I'm not boasting. Take your Juana Villez. *She* wouldn't have it any other way. She's making movies, you know? Very very happy now. She has money, glitz, glamour . . . romance, you'll forgive me, I hope. If you suppose she thinks of you fondly even now and then, well, it's possible, she *is* a woman after all . . . who can say?" He even gave me her address in Beverly Hills. I forgot what it was. I didn't care. "She's an investment of sorts, a pet project. You didn't think I'd waste her on artichoke harvesting or something. Give me some credit. . . ."

After a while, I told him to shut up. He did.

When it was time, Walters pointed the Jeep back down the trail. He drove slowly. He asked for the thermos, "I'm an alcoholic, I suppose, but I really do need a drink, York."

"Save the testimonials for the meetings," I said, and scoured the trail for evidence of more Jeeps, men or guns. Halfway back to the estate, the radio crackled and White Hunter announced that the whole party was at the campsite and that everyone wanted to know what was going on. The chopper came into view over the tree line and the signal became stronger. White Hunter must have been the pilot or the photographer. "Tell him everything's wonderful, but to keep clear of the house."

Walters did and White Hunter acknowledged. The helicopter sheered off to the west.

As we wound our way very slowly down the trail, I peered into every bush and tree in my line of sight for signs of snipers. I remembered how to do it very well, though I hadn't in years. Kind of like riding a bicycle. You relax your eyes and don't look at the leaves or branches, but the spaces in between. Shadows, shapes, things that don't belong. I didn't see anything.

Walters went on about his men, all Wolf Security trainees of a particularly hard cast. These were the men he had initiated into his "covert project." "You know," he said, "not the authority complex profiles, but the mean ones, the men who really like violence. Like Carlos. He's dead, isn't he?"

"Probably" was all I said.

"I don't suppose you'd let me radio the helicopter to get him out? I have an investment in him, as it were."

There was no serious answer to that question and we were crossing the dry levy Villapando and I had carried Alberto through a couple of hours ago. On the upward side as we mounted the crest, the bell tower came into view. I saw something metallic and winking up there that may or may not have been the bell.

"You got a line to the guy in the bell tower?" I asked.

He looked surprised. Surprised enough to tell me I was right.

A second and a half too late he said, "There's no one up there, for Chrissakes, you *are* scared aren't you?"

I told him to stop the Jeep. I picked up the radio and said, "This is Blue Hunter to the bell tower. I've got Walters. Come down out of there and throw your gun and yourself on the dirt where I can see you. You have sixty seconds or I kill Walters."

"There's no one there, I swear it." Walters looked a little frightened. Maybe just enough to convince me I was being paranoid myself. I waited sixty seconds and fired a burst from the Uzi past Gene. He turned pale and I liked that a lot. No one appeared at the base of the tower.

"Okay, drive . . . wait a minute."

Two figures scurried from some undergrowth and broke for the terrain behind us. I sensed Juan taking aim. I took hold of the barrel of his gun and brought it down. Four shots went into the floorboards of the backseat. "Goddammit, take it easy! Those are our people."

They were two Mexican kids who would have been dead if we really were who we pretended to be. Juan recognized them and called out in Spanish, "Hey, stop, man. We've got some guns. We need your help."

They stopped and threw their arms up. One of them called out with existential machismo, "Fuck you! Fuck you, man! Kill us. Okay? Kill us. Fuck you!"

"Shut up!" I shouted. "You gotta help us." Both of them had thin beards from being kept in the stables for weeks. I recognized them, though I couldn't remember their names. They recognized Juan and me and began to run toward us. When they got to the Jeep, they panted, "Give us some guns, man."

"You know how to use a rifle?"

The shorter one said, "Yeah, yeah give that to me." I gave him the .220. "Run alongside us, watch that tower, you see anything, shoot at it."

We went on in. As we approached the estate, there were too many shadows and corners, too many plants, archways and corridors. I looked hard everywhere. Too hard because there *was* a guy in the tower and he fired a burst from an automatic into the hood of the Renegade and into the arm of one of the boys. It wasn't the kid with the rifle.

The .220 came up and the kid who had shouted for us to kill him stood in plain sight beneath the tower while we, Walters included, scrambled out of the Jeep for cover. He fired, worked the bolt, fired again. His shots came within inches of the gunman's position and I wondered where this kid had learned to shoot like that. As if in answer to my unvoiced question, his wounded companion said, "He can shoot the eye out of a quail at two kilometers. His father is a marksman in the *Federalis.* He had to learn."

"That's great," I said, "but quail don't shoot back." I got up to pull the kid into cover but automatic rifle fire sent me clambering back behind the Jeep. A bullet tore through the kid's shirtsleeve, but he was otherwise untouched. I had the feeling he was using up all of our luck. He must have decided the same thing. Unhurriedly, he moved around the Jeep and squatted next to me, wrapping the rifle strap around his forearm and resting the barrel on the hood. He let off one shot after another at about five-second intervals. Each shot disappeared into the shadow of the tower and twice his bullets found the bell. He winced and crouched when a burst of return fire tore up the windshield and chewed up pieces of metal on the right front quarter panel. This pissed him off. He squinted against the flying metal and glass and took aim once more. I sensed him holding his breath and didn't see him squeeze the trigger.

An M16 sailed down and clattered on the tiled roof to get caught in the drainpipe. A moment later the sniper, wearing only half his face, followed it. He rolled down the roof, fell three stories and back flopped into the pool of carp. A small tidal wave washed the courtyard.

I poked Walters with the Uzi and told him to get up and walk ahead of us with his hands in the air. The four of us followed him across the crushed stone driveway and into the courtyard.

The kid who had been hit was bleeding from his forearm. The bullet seemed to have gone clear through. He held his arm up and clutched his elbow, indicating to me that he would be all right.

"Nice shooting," I said with genuine admiration to the short marksman.

"Nice gun," was all he said.

From the ground floor, a set of wooden French doors swung open. Rachel Cole came running out onto the patio wearing a beige caftan and sandals. She was followed by Maria and the old mustached woman, Consuela. First Rachel saw the dead man floating in her carp pond. I saw him now too and recognized him as the guy, Ed, who had attempted to rape the Indian girl in the trailer back in San Ysidro.

Then Rachel looked up.

She saw Walters with his hands in the air followed by a ragged handful of armed Mexicans. It must have been one of her recurring nightmares. Her knees went out from under her and she hit the tiles in stages like a deflating doll. Maria, who had been standing near enough to catch her, just watched her drop. Consuela tried to back her way into the house again.

"Please come over here, Consuela. You too, Maria." I waved them forward. They both seemed shocked that I knew their names. Neither of them recognized me for a moment.

Maria was first. She ran toward me screaming, "Kill them now! Kill him!" She pointed at Walters, then at Rachel. "And her, now!

Please! There are men everywhere with guns, you can't fight
them with these boys. Kill them now while you can. Let me do it if
you have no stomach." That settled any speculation I had about
Maria's feelings about Rachel.

"Take it easy," I said. "Everyone's having so goddamned much
fun killing everyone else around here. . . ." I didn't finish. A
greasy wave of nausea and faintness swelled over me as I looked
at the pool, the dirty blond hair on the dead sniper swayed and
bobbed in a halo of blood. I sat down before I fell down.

Juan rushed over to me. "You okay, man?"

"Yeah, give me that." I pointed at Walters's thermos. There
were still a few shots of watery bourbon in it. I swallowed and got
up.

Rachel began to stir. I told the kid with the rifle to get her to
her feet and follow me. Marching Walters in the lead, I said,
"We're gonna need some keys, Gene. All the goddamned keys to
everything on the estate."

Walters jerked his head. "Ryder's room. He has . . . had keys
to everything."

"Let's go."

I shot out the lock on the door with a short burst, looking over
my shoulder afterward for running men with weapons.

Inside we found more guns than we could carry. I gave the
wounded kid an automatic .22 Browning handgun, stuffed a Colt
Python into my belt and looked for keys. I found a locked gunrack
and shot it open. Inside were ten rifles and a ring of keys. On our
way out, Juan and the two boys stared up at the poster of Ryder in
Nam. "What's he holding?" the sharpshooter kid asked, puzzled.

"C'mon, let's get out of here," I said. I remembered the way to
the basement room where I was held. The storage place for the
personal effects of the dead. I told the sharpshooter and the
winged kid to take Consuela in the Jeep, have her show him
where the old servants' quarters were where they kept the
women. "Get them out of there and down the road. Here, take
this." I handed him the Uzi and the two clips. "Take the women
right out through the front gate. There's gonna be guards down
there, so you'll probably have to kill them. Come up on them
through the trees. Don't wait for them to shoot. Just take them
out. When you get on the road, get rid of the guns. Good luck." I

didn't really know if what I was saying made any sense, I just thought that if we split up, somebody was bound to get out of here.

They both clasped my shoulder and took off.

Rachel was shivering in the afternoon heat, frightened out of her wits. For someone with such a sleek hardness about her, she seemed to come apart in terror when someone pointed a gun at her. I remembered the last time I had done that in her living room that night of the storm. I could use that. Walters seemed too unruffled to be of any help. He was my ace and I had just the hole for him.

"Here we go, Gene." I went through a dozen keys before I got to the one that opened the stout wooden door. Shoving Walters into the dark I said, "There're lots of ghosts in there to keep you from getting lonesome. Every one of them yours."

The key turned and I threw the outside bolt. Walters was a model prisoner.

"Let's go. Rachel, lead the way. First stop, your library. Maria, you show Juan how to get up to the bell tower." I turned to Juan. "Keep a look out. If you see anything that looks bad, there should be a radio like this one up there. Use it. If there's no radio. Fire a few shots and get the hell out of there."

"Okay," he agreed, and started to go.

Maria hesitated. "Kill her now!" She bared her teeth.

"Go on Maria, we need her alive. Meet us in the library. You can help persuade Rachel if she's uncooperative."

"Yes, I can do that." She left with Juan.

As Rachel and I entered the house, she stopped and turned to face me. Her face was blanched and old-looking. She took the front of her thin caftan in both hands and ripped it, exposing her breasts. She sank to her knees and put her hands on the tops of my thighs. "You can still have me. I'll give you anything you want. Money. Women. You wouldn't kill me . . . you couldn't just kill me, I know that, you see. I know that."

"Then you know more than I do." I pulled her to her feet and shoved her ahead of me.

21

WALKING THROUGH the dining room, down the long hallway toward the library, the only sounds were my boots on the carpeting and the ragged, scared breaths coming from Rachel. I thought of the line in a dozen war movies where some guy turns to his buddy in the jungle or a foxhole somewhere and says, "It's quiet, Kowalski . . . too quiet." Eddy in the belltower couldn't have been alone. They wouldn't leave Rachel undefended during the hunt. I wondered where Broctor was, too.

Waving the Colt up and down the corridor, I held out the key ring and told Rachel to point out the one to the library. She did what she was told and the door opened after she used three keys on as many locks.

The room was huge, but it wasn't a library. Bookshelves covered half of one wall. File cabinets the other half. One wall was all windows punctuated by blue velvet drapes with white piping.

Another wall was an exhibit of expensive-looking and bizarre art: erotic paintings, wall hangings from Tibet or Nepal depicting blue demon gods with necklaces of human skulls, flaming swords, huge tongues and hard-ons penetrating eager Indian maidens, primitive sculptures of fertility goddesses, ceremonial knives, stuff like that. There was also a bank of photographs of Rachel with three mayors of San Diego, a former Republican president, a right-wing evangelist and a dozen other people who looked vaguely familiar from parts of the newspaper I rarely read. In the middle of the room was a huge mahogany desk the size of a small aircraft carrier. A computer terminal was set up next to four telephones.

The first thing I did was to walk to the windows and look out. One floor below us was the front of the estate, the cul-de-sac driveway and the dry fountain with the statue of the woman. On the rim of the fountain was the boy Conan/Hector had called Mariposa. He was whittling a piece of wood. A sawed-off shotgun rested next to him.

"How many more guards are around here?"

Rachel hesitated for a moment and then said, too quickly, "The estate is full of Gene's men. You'll never—"

"Shut up. How many are here? Around the house."

"You killed the one in the tower. There's him." She gestured out the window. "Five or six more . . . I don't know . . . around. They should be here any minute. They must have heard the shots."

"All right." I opened the window. "Stick your head out and tell the kid to find the others. Tell him there's trouble out by the stables."

She leaned out and did what I told her to, though her voice shook. That was okay though. She seemed appropriately scared. The kid took off running around the side of the building.

"Now, I want records, documents, proof of what's going on here. We'll start with the files. Open them."

She reached into her desk. I watched her carefully. With a small key she opened the bottom locks on the cabinets. I tore out files and threw them on the floor one after another. None of them had anything to do with what I wanted. When I got to a drawer marked "Personnel Services," I grabbed folders with company

names on them. There were purchase orders for "Unit Deliv-
eries" to Reichenback Laundries in L.A. and San Francisco: 150
Units, $150,000 PAID. They could be for washing machines, but
an investigation could prove Rachel Cole wasn't in the washing
machine supply business. There were similar orders for units
from Mountain Home Mining Co., Surf&Turf Restaurant Associ-
ates, Salinas Harvesters, Highville Valley Fruit Co., all of them
purchasing "units" for $1000 each. Most of them were compa-
nies in California, but some were as far away as North Dakota.

   In another drawer I found hanging files with account sheets
marked PAYROLL MEXICO. There were names and amounts of
money paid to personnel at such and such hotel including two in
Ensenada, condominium maintenance staffs and laborers for
Vita-Gro Farms in some town I'd never heard of in Baja. I bun-
dled several of the papers together with a rubber band and
stuffed them into my shirt. None of it would prove Walters and
Cole were in the slave trade, it was probably all as legal as lemon-
ade, but I was taking them with me anyway. I would need a few
boxes of the junk in the room where Walters was, but most of all I
needed witnesses. I had to get Juan and Maria out and as many of
the others as I could.

   Rachel watched me as I paced the room trying to think of who
to take this to. I could forget the cops in this county; in fact, I
could probably write off any state law enforcement agency at all.
As if she were reading my mind, she started to laugh. "Are you
going to call the police? The FBI?" She picked up the phone.
"Here, call the governor. I'll give you his private number. Tell
him Cherry Cole is calling and wants to turn herself in for smuggling aliens." She held her sides and laughed until tears formed
on her cheeks.

   "Where's the rest of your staff? The houseboys and the other
maids, gardeners, whatever?"

   She composed herself long enough to look up and answer me
levelly. "They're in Barrego for the weekend. I keep a place
there." She was probably telling the truth. She wouldn't want
them underfoot for the big Pepper Belly Shoot and Barbecue. I
continued to pace.

   Absently I noticed the spines of some of the books on the
shelves. *The Tantric Tradition,* books by Arthur Avalon with titles

such as *The Serpent Power, Hymns to the Goddess,* and another one
called *The Cybeline Cults.* One in particular caught my attention—it
was called *The Fifth Yuga* by Ian Broctor. I pulled it down and
looked at the spine. It was heavily bound by some vanity pub-
lisher. Inside were inscrutable diagrams of "world forces," maps
of human "power centers" that all seemed to focus on genitalia. I
read passages at random entitled "Rites of the Chimera" and
"The Transference of the Life Force: The Virgin and the Left-
handed Way." It was a how-to manual of butchery couched in the
language of mysticism. I threw the book at Rachel.

"Where's Broctor?" I shouted.

She flinched as the book hit the desk next to her. "He's here."

"Where?"

"In this room with us."

I looked around.

"You can't see him. He is here astrally."

Reaching into the shelves, I pulled an armload of books onto
the floor. "Cut the shit! Where is he?"

"Physically, he's in his study." I wasn't paying much attention
though, because I noticed in the space I had just cleared on the
shelf, what looked to be a hidden door set into the wall: oak
paneling with seams and an ornate, brass hinge that hadn't been
polished in a long time.

"Sure. Why the fuck not?" I cursed as I tossed more books
from the shelves to expose the door. "Why not have fucking trap
doors in this asylum? This go to his study?"

"No." The voice that answered was not Rachel's. Maria stood
in the doorway. "I'll show you where it goes. Then you can see
why she has to die . . . her and that monster."

Enough of it was exposed so that I could see I didn't have to
remove any more books. The shelves swung out on hinges
tripped by a latch hidden by a volume of Apollonius. "Okay," I
said. "But first I'm making a phone call."

Crossing to the desk, I picked up an old-fashioned ivory cradle
telephone and dialed the operator. "Get me the Border Patrol,
Brown's Field Sector please. This is an emergency."

When it rang, I asked for Agent Ybarra. He was off duty. I
convinced the girl that it was vital I reach him right away. I told

her to call him at home and give him this number. She said she would try and hung up.

"Is Juan in the bell tower?" I asked Maria.

"Yes."

"Is there a radio up there?"

She said there was and I went to pull out my own radio and discovered it was missing. I must have dropped it somewhere during all the fun.

"All right, let's go. Rachel first." I swung the book shelf and the door wide and indicated with my Colt that Rachel step in. She found a light switch and I could see we were in a small anteroom. The only fixture was a small table on which a gold silk gown lay beneath a tierra of beaten silver and a gaudy neck chain with symbols carved into it. None of them meant anything to me. There were more symbols like them on the gown. "Your party dress?" I poked her in the back with the gun and she jumped.

She picked up the neck piece and opened a small compartment in it. From inside the thing she drew a small key and placed it into the lock on another door facing us.

It was dark. Rachel reached for something and I told her to move very slowly.

"It's a candle," she said. She lit it with matches that were apparently lying next to it and we started down a set of heavy wooden stairs. The walls were clammy stone.

"This must be the rehearsal space for the Vincent Price Glee Club," I said. No one seemed amused.

The stairs ended after a single landing and a right-angle turn. Rachel ignited candles and we found ourselves in a space the size of a locker room. In the gathering light I could see that the walls were covered in silk sheets mottled with symbols that seemed vaguely Arabic, Hebrew or Etruscan, for all I knew. In the center of the room was an altar of stone draped with a white linen and bordered by more symbols of the same kind. On the altar lay a long, silver sword with an ornate pommel and hilt; a silk cloth covered part of it. On the floor were diagrams like the ones I had seen in Broctor's book. Part of it was built into the floor and not painted there at all. It was a drain.

Above the altar were wall hangings depicting demons, gods and goddesses. They seemed to be Hindu. I recognized Bajra Dar and what might have been Kali or Shiva or one of those. On a low table behind the altar was a reel-to-reel tape deck flanked by large speakers. I went over to it and turned it on. The room filled with the dissonant chanting I had heard before.

"What is that?" I asked, shutting it off again.

Before Rachel could answer me, a movement to the left behind one of the silk sheets caught my eyes and I turned, leveling the Colt. Broctor emerged wearing white, draw-stringed trousers and a gray sweatshirt. "It is the *bija* of the goddess, recorded in a temple in Nepal ten years ago. It evokes the . . . various aspects of the Blissful Terrible One of which Rachel is an avatar."

Maria moved forward quickly and picked up the sword from the altar. "He killed my sister down here. Ask them how many they have killed here . . . little girls." Maria couldn't wield the sword very well and Broctor easily side-stepped her slow swing. I took the weapon from her.

"That's not a bad question, Broctor. How many have you killed here?"

"You don't seriously expect some sort of number, do you?"

I hit him alongside the face with the Colt. "Why?"

He held his face and stared at me with eyes like embers. "You would never understand."

Maria answered instead. "Because he enjoys it. And she . . ." She circled around Rachel, who stared in horror at her personal god bleeding from the gums. "She believes he is keeping her young forever."

"He has kept me young. Look at me." She opened her caftan again. "You enjoyed me. Do you know how old I really am? I am sixty-one years old. Do I look sixty-one to you, York?"

The bourbon I drank rose into my throat. I suddenly felt the need for more of it. Upstairs, the phone rang. "C'mon, quickly." I held the gun to the back of Broctor's head and motioned for Rachel to climb the steps again. I dropped the sword onto the floor.

Back in the library I picked up the phone. It was Ybarra.

"Remember me, José Gato. Out in the canyons that night. I've got it for you, Ybarra. The north county money behind the Morelos thing. Proof. There's all the proof you need. There's also a small army of armed men up here, so bring help. You've got to do it fast though."

"Wait a minute, slow down. Tell me what's going on."

"I don't have time." I gave him the directions and the names of Rachel Cole and Eugene Walters. "You need choppers, Ram Chargers and a hundred guys if you can get them, all of them armed, you understand. Now is the time, the place is up for grabs. It's me and a couple of kids holding this down. I'm exhausted . . . there's bodies all over the fucking place . . . you'll probably find mass graves . . . there's records . . . witnesses. . . ." I stopped myself before I said, "They're slicing up fucking virgins in the basement too."

"Are you on drugs?"

"No. Look, I know what I sound like, but you won't believe this shit. You've got to get some people up here."

There was a long pause.

"We can't go into some north county estate like the Marines because some guy named José Gato calls up with a story about bodies and guns. Did you call the police?"

"The police are no good. Look, you gave me a chance to turn this up. Well, I'm giving it to you. I'm handing it to you. This is it."

"All right, the best I can do is get up there with as many units as I can round up, but it's going to take a few hours and it's not going to be any army. I'm going to need authorization. If I get it, I'll call El Cajon sector, and Encinitas. I'll come up on my own either way, but it's going to take time, man. That's all I can do."

"All right. All right, but there's people shot up here and there may be more."

"I'll call you back." He hung up and I set the phone down. Rachel smiled at me.

We waited. Maria brought me some food from the kitchen and a bottle of Wild Turkey. She brought Juan some beer and sandwiches. I told her to get the radio from him too. When she returned, I listened for any banter from Walters's people. I picked up a few calls from the mountains, each one asking the other if there was any news from Blue Hunter. Nobody knew anything. The guests were having a good time at the campsite playing poker and drinking.

Someone much closer, much louder, asked someone else in Spanish if they should check on Mrs. Cole. "Better not man," the reply came. "You know how she is. Just hang loose, make the rounds." I wondered if they would discover Ryder's door blown open or hear Walters pounding on the door to the basement cell.

Broctor was holding his face and talking. "Why, did you know that Gandhi slept with virgin girls at regular intervals? Oh, platonically, of course—or so they say. The idea was to absorb their energy, the field which surrounds them, uncorrupted by *bharakati,* the incorrect sort of sex that has become so common in this age, or fourth Yuga. Now Gandhi was not what you would call a madman, would you say?"

"Yeah, you and Gandhi, Broctor." I was thinking about the two kids I had sent up to the servants' quarters to get the women. The place had to be guarded. Even if they did succeed in breaking them out, they would never get past the front gate. That had to be manned like Fort Knox. I could only hope that they were lying low and waiting for some kind of chance.

The idea of Walters down there bothered me too. I would like it better if he was where I could see him. I couldn't trust Maria to cover Broctor and Cole; she would either just shoot them or screw up trying. I wondered why Maria had never picked up a kitchen knife and put it through Rachel long ago if she hated her so much. Maybe it was because, like inmates in the death camps, a certain transference takes place, a kind of sick love that develops between captive and captor.

The Wild Turkey made me relax, but it didn't help me think.

"There's something else I think you should see," Maria said. "His laboratory, or study as *she* calls it."

"Why not? Lead the way."

I covered Cole and Broctor as we went back down the stairs. The candles were still burning. From behind the cloth where Broctor had emerged, Maria showed me a plain wooden door. Behind it was a room that looked like a high school biology lab. Aquarium tanks flanked one wall. Huge carp waddled or slept in dirty water. A long table held beakers, Bunsen burners, crucibles or whatever they were called. The place smelled so strongly of formaldehyde that I forgot I had been inhaling sulfur fumes for two weeks. Jars of gray-green organs and viscera with taped labels were arranged in rows on shelves. There was a writing desk piled with manuscripts, drawings, texts and notebooks. A full-scale, plastic skeleton hanging on a frame grinned from the shadows in a far corner of the room.

"You see, Mr. York, science comingles with the ineffable." Broctor sounded as if his cheeks were full of cotton. His jaw was swollen nicely. "Meditation, evocation, arcane rites, communion and idle philosophy, this must be how you see me whiling away my time. As you now perceive, I pursue other disciplines. Here is where I shall wrestle the Chimera, Death itself, onto the proverbial mat." His voice lowered to a whisper. "I am so very close. You can't imagine."

I was having enough trouble with my imagination. A rack of surgical implements including cleavers and saws hung from beneath one of the tables. One item seemed to be a pruning shears for a landscaper. I was trying to feature exactly what it was he used it for.

Maria ran to the jars of stuff I couldn't make out and didn't want to. "One of these may be my sister! Her heart, her eyes, her . . . insides. People. All of them people!"

"You are pointing to a pituitary gland and its surrounding tissue. An unremarkable and useless specimen," Broctor informed her dully.

The radio at my waist had been droning on and off metallically. I had been half listening for anything of interest and the words ". . . Blue Hunter. Walters, *aqui*" made me reach for the thing and turn it up.

In Spanish, Walters ordered men into the house. He called Yellow Hunter and Green Hunter in the mountains and told them to get some men down as quickly as possible. The boys making the rounds had sprung him. He had the radio, and if he didn't already, he would soon have guns from Ryder's apartment.

Muted gunfire stitched the air outside. It might have been Juan signaling.

What happened next happened very fast.

Maria picked up a cleaver and threw it at Broctor. It lodged in his left breast. It must have been very sharp and very heavy because it fell out again almost immediately exposing a wide area of bone and muscle that didn't bleed much. He fell against the lab table, upsetting glasses and beakers of solution. Rachel rushed to his side.

Maria was on her with a ten-inch knife. She drove it into her back and Rachel shrieked, staggering to her feet. I grabbed the weapon from Maria as Rachel fell onto the table and knocked the live Bunsen burner onto the floor. Something in one of the spilled containers started to burn like gasoline.

From the radio I heard Walters order White Hunter to come in and land near the tennis courts.

More gunfire.

Silently I urged Juan to get out of that tower. I needed him.

The room was burning. Maria looked stunned at what she had done. It didn't seem as though either Rachel Cole or Ian Broctor were going to get up. I felt for a pulse on Rachel's neck. There was a faint one. I tried dragging her to the door. Her caftan was burning. The room was full of smoke and I couldn't breathe anymore.

I let go of Rachel and I saw her crawl back to Broctor, her clothes and hair going up in flames. I took hold of Maria's arm and went through the door. We took the stairs together. Behind us, the silk wall hangings had begun to smolder. The one over the laboratory door was crawling with tall flames that licked at the great wooden beams on the ceiling.

I held onto Maria, and we came out into the library, smoke trailing from the top of the door behind us.

In the corridor, I hugged the walls, pressing Maria next to me. I pointed the Colt ahead and sprinted for the front door. Maria kept pace. I had to get Walters before he got to the tennis courts.

On the veranda Mariposa stood with his shotgun, waving at someone down the driveway. Maria jumped onto his back and bit into his neck. They fell down the stairs together. I grabbed his shotgun and pulled Maria off him. I hit him with the blunt stock and he went down into the gravel.

Juan was firing from the bell tower, pinning down two or three men who returned fire from behind the low, stone wall around the cul-de-sac.

Behind us, the living room filled with smoke.

"Juan," I shouted up at him. "Come down, the place is on fire!" He must not have heard me. His M16 kept cricking and ticking, the rounds pinging off the stone wall or biting into gravel.

The white and blue chopper came in low. I could make out the wolf's head insignia on its side. It made a pass over the house and then wheeled down the mountain toward the tennis courts. The radio was filled with static and babbling, everyone trying to talk at once. I threw it into a potted dragon palm.

If Juan was going to buy me some time, I would take it and hope he got out all right. "C'mon." I grabbed Maria and ran across the driveway past the dry fountain. I fired two shots in the direction of the stone wall. A few rounds went wild over our heads and we were into the relative cover of the stunted trees and scrambling downhill.

"Let's get on the driveway." We lost a few minutes edging awkwardly to the left. "I can't let Walters get out of here."

The chopper was down. Maybe a hundred yards away on the slope. It sat in the middle of the tennis courts, its blades idly swatting at the late afternoon air. I looked behind me, waiting for Walters to make a break for the helicopter. I was looking in the wrong direction. He was ahead of us and below us. He was crouched and running, firing short bursts from Ryder's Ingram. He was going to get into the thing before I got close enough.

The Colt bucked in my hand. I knelt, steadied my wrist with my left hand and tried again. I missed.

I told Maria to stay down and I took off after him.

Thirty yards from the chopper I was forced to hit the dirt as Walters let fly with a burst of twenty or thirty rounds. Most of them went over my head, some bit up the dirt behind me.

When I got to my feet, I could see that he was being helped into the machine by a white-jacketed sleeve. Before the door closed, I stopped, fired and hit something metallic from the sound of it. I fired again and my bullet broke through the safety glass bubble, turning it opaque in the sunlight. I pulled the trigger again and the thing just clicked. I stood there while the chopper blades gained speed. I kept pulling the trigger on an empty gun.

It rose slowly, cleared the trees and sheered off to the west as it gained altitude. After a minute it disappeared into the lowering sun.

Walking back I felt my knees buckle. I told myself, *You fucked up, York. Right from the beginning.* Maria ran toward me and put her arms around me. "Look!" She pointed up the road.

The estate was burning. The dying sunlight was further obscured by clouds of smoke that billowed from the first- and second-story windows of Rachel Cole's estate. Maria looked very happy.

"We've got to get out of the road," I said. My voice sounded hollow. "There's gonna be some traffic, I think."

We found the ruins of an old well and climbed inside, disturbing some field mice. I looked at my empty gun until I couldn't anymore. I closed my eyes, listening to the sound of gunfire trailing off.

From down the long driveway I heard the sounds of a small vehicle approaching. That would be the guys in the golf carts, the guards at the gate, wanting to know what was going on. Men with guns rushed downhill. One of them was Hector/Conan and the kid, Mariposa, was with him. Somewhere below us they must have conferred with the guards from the gate and decided to split. This was a very sensitive little soiree and this much unscheduled activity—Mexicans with guns and the estate burning down the way it was—must have constituted an unplanned-for contingency. I wondered if anyone knew that Rachel was dead or where Walters was; if they were deserting him or following his orders. I wondered how far they thought they'd go in golf carts.

People appeared from the woods, shadows in the twilight lit strangely by the now towering flames competing with the sunset. Some of them were men, some women. I recognized the kid who had been wounded by Eddy in the tower earlier. He seemed to be in charge of a small group of people. I crawled out of my ruined well and waved him over.

"Get them down the road," I said. "Past the gate, I don't think anyone will stop you now." His face was blanched in the weird light.

"Yes," he said. "Then what?"

"Then good luck."

"Buena suerte."

"Right. What happened to your friend, with the rifle?"

"We waited. There were too many guards. Then they were all called away and we got the women. He's coming down. I think he wants to kill some gringos first."

"If you see him, tell him the party is over."

"Okay. Goodbye . . . thank you."

"Yeah. Yeah, go on."

Smoke wound its way through the trees and the windless night. People staggered and coughed, making their way to the gate below. Some of them wandered the wrong way and I tried to herd them in the right direction. Sharp cracking and popping sounds echoed off the hills. It might have been burning wood or gunfire.

If Juan had been caught in the bell tower, even if he hadn't been hit, he would be dead from smoke inhalation by now.

There had to be another route off the estate because I saw only a few of the four-wheel drives full of rapidly sobering businessmen high-tailing it back to Rancho Santa Palma, La Jolla, Bel Air, LAX or wherever they'd come from. The fire was winning its battle for prominence with the sunset that was now just a smudge of pink on the horizon.

Any idea I had about witnesses seemed to lose its meaning somehow in the chaotic shadows of the inferno behind us. I trudged down the road with Maria, falling in and out of step with refugees from both sides of the border.

Another four-wheel drive came lumbering down the road behind us. It was silhouetted against the firelight, and people clung to the hood, the sides and back so that I couldn't see at first that it was Ryder's Renegade. The sharpshooter kid was behind the wheel. Next to him was Juan, his clothes soaking wet.

I waved them down and Juan leapt from the Jeep to slap both my arms. "You're okay," he said, smiling.

"How did you get out of there?" I looked up at the illuminated bell tower that poured clouds of smoke like an industrial chimney.

"Same way that other guy did, but I didn't wait to get shot. I dropped to the roof, rolled and jumped into that stinking swimming pool with the ugly fish and the dead guy." It was hard to think of him as the kid who had been hugging rocks and weeping a few hours ago. He had stayed in that tower above a burning house and covered my attempt to stop Walters, then jumped nearly a hundred feet into what must have looked like a glass of water. "Man, it was disgusting." He smelled his shirtsleeve.

Turning to the driver, I asked him what had happened up there. He told me pretty much the same thing as his wounded partner had. The servants' quarters were too heavily guarded, they waited for a chance and got one when Walters called everyone in to charge the estate. Fortunately for me, it took the troops a little too long to regroup and launch a concerted siege on the place. The resistance we had met on the way out was desultory and confused. We had gotten out before they could organize. He told me his name was Julio and shook my hand. "You gonna let me take this car?" He looked at me half challenging, half asking.

"I wouldn't try to stop you. I may be stupid, but I'm not crazy." He grinned and threw it into gear. "Wait a minute, you'd better leave that rifle. That's a bad bust if they stop you."

"No way." He shook his head. "I'm not taking another breath in this country without a loaded gun. You gonna stop me now?"

"No." What could I say? "Good luck."

"You too."

Juan climbed back into the overcrowded Jeep.

"You'd better hurry," I told them. *"La Migra* will be here soon."

They waved and took off through the gathering darkness. As it turned out, there was no hurry at all.

It was probably nine o'clock before the fire trucks arrived. There wasn't much left for them to work on except the surrounding woods. The columns of people who had poured down the road had long since dispersed on foot or in vans, Jeeps or golf carts. Maria and I stood across Route 18 and watched the flames on the hill subside.

"Why are we sitting here? What are you waiting for?" she asked sleepily. Her head rested on my shoulder while I sat on the dirt off the highway pavement.

"I want to see if somebody is going to show up."

"Can't you take me out of here? Someone will arrest me and take me back to Mexico if we stay here."

"Go then."

"No, I'll wait with you."

The turquoise Border Patrol car arrived some fifteen minutes later. Maria was asleep. Ybarra stepped out of the car and walked over to me, his headlights full on us. He was alone.

"Gato?" he asked.

"My name is York. Nathaniel York."

"I figure you were right," he said.

"You figure I was right," I echoed. I didn't know what he meant.

"I started calling around for authorization to move in here and it got very funny. Assholes tightened up all over the place when they figured the location and got the woman's name, Rachel Cole."

"You telling me she owned the fuckin' Border Patrol, the Bureau of Immigration and fuckin' Naturalization?" I seemed to be speaking from the depths of some dream. I'm still not sure I ever really talked to Ybarra that night at all.

"No, that's not what I'm saying. I'm saying we can't move in on private property without a lot of red tape. The red tape seemed to get pretty thick over this. If I thought the patrol's hands weren't tied on a higher level, I'd feel like . . ." He trailed off and started again. "I couldn't do my job anymore if I thought I was really working for somebody up here and didn't know it."

"Yeah, that's why I called you. I was right to call you. You showed up. It just didn't work out, that's all."

"What happened?"

"Drive me back to the city and maybe I can tell you about it."

"Okay."

"Her too. She's illegal probably. Then again maybe all her papers are up there." I gestured up at the dwindling flames on the mountainside.

"I figure they probably are. Where to?"

A good question. I gave him Dick Holster's address.

Maria woke up long enough to realize she was in a Border Patrol car. She said, "To hell with you both," and went back to sleep on my shoulder.

On the drive back I told Ybarra as much as I thought he would buy. I was tired and I told him more than made sense and left out a lot. He didn't say anything about any of it. Nothing at all except, "Jesus Christ."

22

By THE END of September, low clouds had moved into San Diego for a month-long visit like a brood of damp, gray tourists from Seattle. I sat on the deck at Anthony's at the Embarcadero eating oysters and drinking Beck's. In two hours I would have to be at work behind the bar at the Whaler in Mission Valley, but that was two hours I could stare at the water or the sky, listen to the plaintive screeching of gulls and empty my thoughts into the bay.

Maria and I had stayed with Dick for two weeks until I found a job and a cheap apartment downtown. She moved in with me for a few days and then I drove her up to Santa Barbara—her original destination before being sidetracked for a year by Rachel Cole—where she had family. Dick had listened to what I told him, which wasn't everything, with his usual stoic wariness. He didn't press me for details or anymore than I wanted to go over. He had quit the Low Down and was getting ready for a six-month survival trip in the Sonora Desert. When he left, I'd take over his place.

Ybarra called me once to let me know that from what he could gather there was some kind of low-key investigation going on up at the estate. The FBI and the INS were crawling over the place and being very quiet about what they found. Nothing appeared in any newspaper except a brief account of the tragic fire and death of southern California businesswoman, socialite and community leader Rachel Cole. He added that there was a guy from the San Diego *Reader* who wanted to dig into it. "His name is McGraw. He knows there's something in it. I can't talk to him, it's hearsay to me. If you wanna try him . . . what the hell? Maybe he can get it out."

I told Ybarra no thanks, that I had a knack for getting people croaked and I was trying to break the habit.

The afternoon grew colder. I pulled up the collar on Dick's flak jacket that I wore over Dick's sweatshirt and ordered one last beer. There weren't many tourists walking up and down the dock and there wasn't much traffic on Harbor Drive. A white Lincoln limousine pulled up to the passenger zone in front of the restaurant. I looked at it, drank and looked back out at the whitecaps on the bay. A moment later a voice behind me said, "Nathaniel?"

The voice belonged to Juana Villez. I turned and wondered if I was losing my mind because what I saw was a blond woman with an expensive makeup job dripping brass and bone earrings onto the shoulders of a white fur coat. She stood shivering in the chill on silver high heels.

"I got in touch with Dick. He said you come down here in the afternoons sometimes. Remember when you first took me here and you would make up funny names for all the people that walked by?"

My lungs weren't working right. I felt as if something in the middle of my chest had fallen onto my lap.

"May I sit down?" She didn't wait for an answer, but took a director's chair across from me. "I know I look very different now, I sound different too, don't I?" She smiled tentatively. "I even have a different name. I'm Jane Villa now."

I sat across from her wondering what I was feeling. For a long time there had been no sensation at all when I thought of her, just a memory of something fading like the last guitar note in an old blues song I'd heard once. Now I listened with fascination to my own heartbeat in my ears.

"Have you seen my commercials?"

"No, I haven't. I don't watch television much."

"That's right," she nodded. "I remember. Well, I did some anyway . . . and two movies. The first one is coming out this Christmas. I'm in it with Nick Nolte and Sigourney Weaver. It's about gangsters."

"What do you want, Juana?"

"Jane."

I didn't say it.

She took a deep breath and looked out at the water. "We're finishing up the second movie here in San Diego. A comedy." When she turned to face me again, she had tears in her eyes, but she was smiling. "I've met Burt Reynolds. Remember how I loved him? You're better-looking than he is."

"Juana, what did you come here for? To tell me you made it big? Fine. Great. I've got to go to work now." I finished my beer and started to get up. She grabbed my hand. I stood there for a moment looking down at it. She let go.

Tears streaked her impeccable makeup job. "I had to see you and tell you something. You have a right to know that I lied to you. After all you did, you have a right to at least know . . . that's all."

I didn't sit back down. I didn't say anything. If she wanted me to make it easy for her, it was too bad. She looked up at me with her wet laquered eyes and said, "Herman was not my brother."

Gulls wheeled over us, cawed and dove for the water where a small child threw his fish and chips over the side.

"Herman was my husband."

The kid's mother told him to stop throwing his food.

"I thought if I told you the truth, you wouldn't help me. I knew you loved me. You wouldn't have looked for a husband. But a brother . . ."

There was a long silence. When it went on for a while, I said, "You were right, I loved you."

"I had to say he was my brother." Her voice rose a little.

"No," I said. "You didn't."

"That picture, it was our wedding." She was crying into a napkin.

"Uh-huh."

"Can you forgive me?" She was a decent actress after all.

"You don't need it. Have a good cry, Juana, but do it without an audience. You'll feel more righteous about it afterward." I turned from her and walked toward Broadway, where I had parked Dick's Pontiac.

From the Alibi Lounge on University, I called the Whaler and told them I wouldn't be in that night. I tried not to slur my words. My recollection of leaving there is hazy, but somehow I made it to the Hillcrest Club.

As usual, I ended up talking at Bananas, the world's greatest listener. He couldn't have made any sense out of the disjointed monologue I delivered, but kept interjecting, "God bless America!" at what seemed to be appropriate intervals.

At last call I found myself staring at my hands on the bar. As I was gathering my strength and concentration to lift another shot of Kessler without spilling it, I heard myself asking Bananas for advice again. "So what the hell would you do about it? The fucker is as free as a bird and bloody as a butcher. What would you do? Wait out in front of his house with a deer rifle one night? Huh?"

No one but me heard it and I could never prove that he really said, "Call the papers," as he jerked his thumb at the pay phone.

I squinted up and saw both of him. I looked over at the phone and then down at my hands.

Gordon the bartender announced for the second time, "This is the no-shit, honest-to-God last call!"

The phone seemed very far away and my hands seemed clumsy and stained in the bar room lighting. I looked at the phone again. My hands. The phone.